Acclaim

"A beautifully crafted story of beauty and whimsy. Bustamante's world is full of twists, turns and magic that make you feel as if you stepped into Alice's Wonderland. I love the concept of luck and misfortune being tied to a physical object and the delightful chaos that ensues. *Miss Fortune* is the perfect blend of dark secrets, colorful characters, and witty romance and is sure to captivate long after the last page is read."
—Sara Anderson, author of The Mindhunters Dulogy

"*Miss Fortune* is a dazzling blend of romance, whimsy, and wonder that completely swept me off my feet! Bustamante conjures a world so rich with magic and mystery that it feels like stepping into a dream. Nia and Entian's sweet love story and adorable banter had me grinning, blushing, and hugging my pillow in pure romantasy bliss. In a tale where luck holds power and love is the ultimate risk, every page shimmers with enchantment."
—H.C.Lane, author of the Heir of the Haloed Sun series

"Whimsical and filled with wonder, *Miss Fortune* takes beloved elements from *Beauty and the Beast* and *Alice in Wonderland* and twists them into something attractively haunting. With immensely creative creatures, hilarious puns and a swoony romance, Ashley Bustamente's new novel checked all the right boxes for a binge-worthy read for any day of the week!"

—V. Romas Burton, author of The Legacy Chapters

"In every pretty turn of phrase and with endlessly lush description, Ashley Bustamante's beautiful prose shines on every delightful page of Miss Fortune. Every detail is gorgeous in this sweet romance set amidst an ever-thickening snare of magic that becomes more unsettling and beautiful as it unfolds. I was captivated beginning to the perfect end!"

—Brittany Eden, author of the Heartbooks series

MISS FORTUNE

Quill & Flame
EmberLight

Ashley Bustamante

Miss Fortune

Copyright ©2026 by Ashley Bustamante

Published by Quill & Flame Publishing House, an imprint of Book Bash Media, LLC.

www.quillandflame.com

All rights reserved.

No part of this publication may be reproduced, digitally stored, or transmitted in any form without written permission from the publisher, except as permitted by U.S. copyright law.

This is a work of fiction. Names, characters, and incidents are products of the author's imagination or are used fictitiously. Any similarity to actual people, living or dead, organizations, business establishments, and/or events is purely coincidental.

NO AI TRAINING: Without any limitation on the author or Quill & Flame's exclusive copyright rights, any use of this publication to train generative artificial intelligence is expressly prohibited.

Cover design by Ashley Bustamante

To Sara, Chantel, Hannah, and Elise. Friends like you make me feel truly lucky!

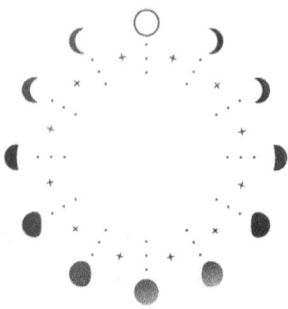

Prologue

Nia was desperate for air, but her garbled efforts rewarded her with nothing but water. Liquid pulled into her lungs. Each futile attempt to breathe struck like a blazing knife in her chest.

Inhale. Water. Knife. Inhale. Water. Knife.

A hand grasped her wrist with a sharp tug.

When Nia's head broke the surface, water still choked her airways, even as she slammed into a rough and splintered object. Her stomach heaved. She coughed. At last the fluid she inhaled burst free and allowed her a few precious gulps of oxygen.

"Don't let go!"

It took a moment to register the voice and remember the fingers gripping her like a tiny vice. Her vision and mind sharpened and details became clear. A boy with dark skin, perhaps a few seasons older than her seven years, held her wrist while she lay slung over a broken chair. The flimsy furniture teetered, threatening to break free from where one of its legs was wedged in the mud of the bank.

Rushing flood waters eroded the shore at a fierce pace. The boy slipped in the slick glop and nearly tumbled into the water. He wouldn't be able to pull her to solid ground without the risk of falling into the surge himself. Nia didn't want to die, but at least she would be with her parents. She couldn't rob this boy of his life.

Resigned, she slackened her grip, but the boy dug his fingers in so hard it hurt.

"Wait!" he pleaded. "Don't give up yet. I can help."

With his other hand, the boy pulled something from his pocket. Sunlight flashed over the charm on the bracelet he wore, catching Nia's eye. To free herself from the spiral of fear, she fixated on the charm—a copper dragonfly with tourmaline wings, a design common to their village. The eyes were made of a vivid rainbow stone she was unfamiliar with.

"Quick," the boy said, "what's your name?"

"What?"

"Hurry!"

"Nia," she managed to say, coughing once more and shuddering as the water whipped her small body and the fractured chair about.

"Don't forget what I'm gonna say. You might need it." He took a deep breath and released his words in a rush. "I, Enitan, do bestow this stone of fortune upon Nia that it may serve her all her days." He shoved a smooth, round object into her hands, and at that moment, the chair leg broke and the boy lost his grip on her wrist. As the torrent swept Nia away, she saw the briefest flash of terror in Enitan's warm brown eyes before the river claimed her.

Nia woke on a soggy bank in a fit of trembling coughs. Her lungs burned and her chest pounded as though she'd been hit with a hammer. A sound like tiny bells caught her attention, and she worked through the haze in her mind to find the source. A miniature humanoid creature with shimmering blue wings flitted in front of her face with excitement. A water sprite? Several more joined it and they danced about in the air, chittering like squirrels.

"You saved me." Nia's voice was a feeble croak, but the little creatures seemed to understand. They swirled around her before disappearing into the rushing waters as quickly as they had come.

Nia noticed the ache in her hand at last and relaxed her grip on the object within. The moment Enitan slipped the mysterious item into her fingers she'd held on like her life was tied to it. A stone. She examined it in her palm. It was no bigger than a pheasant's egg, its color a translucent, milky blue.

Why had he given it to her? She didn't believe the stone would help in any extraordinary sense, but she'd never owned anything so pretty. It might fetch a decent price at the market.

Guilt overtook her, almost as sharp as the pain in her chest and lungs. It was unlikely Enitan gave her something like that only to sell. Still, her parents were gone, taken by the flood. She was alone, and she'd have to find ways to survive and provide for herself. Surely the boy who saved her life wouldn't begrudge her that.

As she fought against the tears and waves of hopelessness, the stone in her hand grew warm. She could almost hear it soothing her and assuring her all would be well. A glint sparkled in the corner of her vision, providing a momentary distraction from her grief.

A gold coin?

That's lucky, Nia thought.

And that was only the beginning.

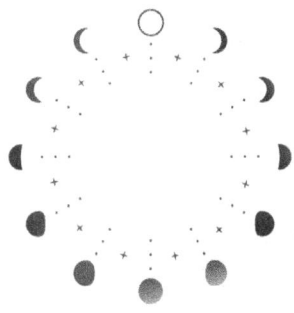

Chapter 1

Eleven years later

The night rang with a silence thicker than the forest's trees, and that was a problem. Silence meant the nightstripe might already be lying in wait, watching Nia and waiting to drag her to her grave in a tangle of fangs and claws. The other nocturnal creatures had a way of becoming deathly still when the nightstripe was near. Even the luna moths who normally flitted about in the evening breeze had landed on tree trunks and lay inert. She shivered, practically tasting the tang of danger in the air.

Nia needed to draw the creature's attention, without becoming its next meal, and lure it away from the patch of silverfern just outside of its den. The healing plant shimmered and swayed in the moonlight, innocently unaware of the risks required to procure it.

Silverfern could only be picked at night. If harvested during the day, it withered instantly.

Most people would deem it foolish to purposefully entice a nightstripe—and they would be right. But there was no other way to get the silverfern needed for her lungs. The dark moon was only three nights away, and it took time to brew the medicinal tea to full potency. Better to tango with the nightstripe while she had luck on her side than to be brutalized by maladies with luck's absence.

Where *was* the creature? It couldn't still be in its den at this hour, but the beast never ventured far from it.

At last, Nia spotted it. All silver and stripes and shadows, somewhere between canine and feline. Its turquoise eyes gleamed a few yards away in a knot of scrubby vegetation. Its tufted ears stood perked and fully alert.

Nia pulled the fortune stone from her pocket, but her hand stilled before the stone could reflect the moon's glow. She intended to use it to catch the nightstripe's eye, but perhaps it wasn't wise to bring it out in the open before wrestling a dangerous creature. She might drop it, and what then?

She would be done for. Vanquished at the tender age of eighteen.

Nia frowned and placed the stone securely in her pocket once more. She needed another reflective object. As she scanned the surrounding terrain, the stone grew warm in its resting place. It was already at work, helping her find what she needed.

There.

Her eyes caught sight of another pebble; black, but just as reflective as the fortune stone, if not more so. She stretched for it, but it remained barely out of reach. If she crawled to it, she was likely to make too much noise and send the nightstripe barreling toward her.

Just then, a little woodland vole poked its fuzzy head out of the ground beneath the pebble, throwing dirt every which way as it broke the surface of the forest floor. The disturbance moved the pebble close enough for Nia to grasp it. However, the scuttling of the tiny rodent might blow her cover.

No sooner had she thought it than the vole burrowed underground. More of the fortune stone's handiwork.

Nia stood, ready to set her plan in motion. The nightstripe immediately trained its keen eyes upon her, but it didn't run. Nia held up the pebble and rotated it back and forth, making sure it caught the gleam of moonlight in just the right way. The nightstripe cocked a curious head to the side.

Nia threw the tiny stone as far as she could, and just as she hoped, the nightstripe gave chase. She darted toward the silverfern patch, furiously yanking the plants free and stuffing them into the sack slung over her shoulder. She wouldn't have long before the creature caught on and changed course.

Once she had what she needed, Nia bolted for the trees, disregarding the burning in her lungs which bore permanent scarring from the river's attempt on her life. The *clomp* of heavy, padded footfalls reached her ears, and she changed direction. The nightstripe's heavy, frantic breathing remained close behind her. She stumbled over an uneven patch of ground, but the wind shifted at that moment, setting a willowy tree branch in her path that allowed her to regain her balance by grasping it. She pulled the same branch back and released it in time to hit the nightstripe in the face. The creature howled and started for her again, but the slick leaves caused it to slip and stumble.

Nia sprinted, knowing full well that *she* would not slip on the leaves.

Because as long as the moon was shining, she didn't need to be careful.

She just needed to be lucky.

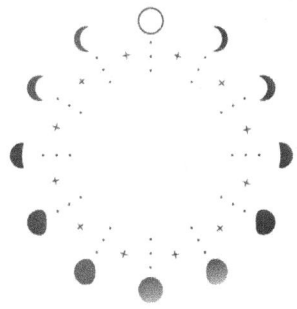

Chapter 2

One night before the Dark Moon

*O**h please, for the love of unicorns, don't let them notice me.*

Nia tugged the hood of her cloak forward to shroud her face as a group of rowdy teenagers passed on the opposite side of the cobblestone road through town. They wouldn't pay her any mind—not if she didn't want them to. The stone warmed in her pocket, feeling out her desires and determining how to work the situation in her favor. Nia waited, trusting it.

The lively gaggle didn't spare one glance in Nia's direction. They simply carried on as though the dark moon didn't loom a mere night away. And why shouldn't they? To most people, it was another night. A normal monthly occurrence. Nia exhaled and continued toward her destination. As the carefree laughter grew fainter against her ears, she had a fleeting vision of herself in the center of it, joining her merriment with theirs. She peered over her shoulder but whipped her gaze forward again just as quickly. Maybe another time.

A few days ago, you were tangling with the nightstripe, Nia chided herself. Where did that girl go? She already knew the answer—that girl disappeared every month when the moon did. Besides, even with the threat of fangs and claws, the nightstripe was predictable. People were risky.

It might have been Nia's imagination, but the town of Ravenskeep seemed more crowded than usual. Every storefront bustled with activity—dressmakers flourishing their latest styles in broad windows, the heavy clang of the blacksmith at work, horses with carts packed near to bursting. The air crackled with fires, wafting the savory aroma of roasted quail and spiced nuts in Nia's direction. She might have stopped to indulge, but the sun was already hanging lower in the sky than she would like. Hopefully Magala's stand wasn't too picked over. She would head there first, and then to the baker's to buy flour.

A scream of "Look out!" echoed from nearby.

Nia pivoted sharply to the left, pulled by instincts that were not entirely her own. The stray horse and cart careening down the road missed her by inches. Her heart *thud thud thudded* and as she coughed, Nia was grateful she merely breathed in the dust created by the disturbance instead of being trampled into it, even though it further irritated her damaged lungs.

"Wow! You got lucky," an onlooker exclaimed. "That was a close one."

"Yes. Very close," Nia managed a stilted reply, feeling her cheeks heat at the rasp in her voice.

Far too close. Nia's luck was already wearing thin. She quickened her pace and ignored the stares of the people surrounding her to avoid the embarrassment of further conversation. She pulled a flask from her bag and downed the last of her tea, which had long grown cold. It did little to quell the pain of breathing but would at least make speaking more manageable, which she would certainly need once she greeted the ever-talkative Magala.

Magala's produce cart was a rainbow of crisp carrots, plump berries, lush greens, and just about any fruit a person could desire. Everyone knew if you wanted to grace your table with something fresh and decadent, you visited Magala's.

Nia tapped her friend on the shoulder, distracting her from the wayward pears she rearranged. Even though Magala was around thrice Nia's age, she was the one person Nia felt at ease speaking with. It was easier than connecting with peers her own age, who had too many questions and not enough discretion, to say nothing of their excessive judgment of her condition.

"How's business, Mag?" Many of the carts in the square looked sparse, and Nia worried over her friend. A recent buzz of rumors claimed some of the eastern towns had refused to continue trading, but she didn't know if there was any truth to it.

"Ah, Nia." Magala laughed, her face as peachy as the fruits she sold. "Thriving as always." She winked at Nia and added, "Thanks to you."

Anyone who didn't know what they were looking for would miss the tiny glint of pale blue hanging from Magala's right earlobe.

Nia shook her head. "I still can't believe you keep it in the open like that."

"It's the best place for it. Nobody thinks twice about it when it's in plain sight. Be sneaky about it, and you've suddenly got everyone wondering what the story is."

The tiny shard of the fortune stone was a gift from Nia to Magala. When Nia first came to town, Magala's cart was a quarter of the size, and the produce looked like it was a breath away from spoiling. Still, she was always willing to spare an apple or some potatoes for Nia. The shard of stone was the least she could do to repay Magala's kindness. Since then, Magala kept Nia's secret, and customers preferred Magala's goods.

Magala tsked at Nia's appearance. "Take that hood off and stop skulking around, will you? You'll draw even more attention looking like a thief in broad daylight."

Nia's lips tightened, her hands pausing on the rough cloth of her hood for a moment before pulling it away. Magala was usually right about these things.

"What are you doing out so close to the dark moon, anyway? That's unlike you. No wonder you're on edge." Magala tucked a wisp of hair—all silver and sunshine—behind her ear, causing her stone earring to catch the light again. Such a risk.

"I lost track of time," Nia replied, prodding a fat red tomato to test its softness. "I'll be home before nightfall and tucked away safely until morning after next." She stuffed the tomato in her rucksack along with two others of equal perfection. "Want to join me for dinner the night after the dark moon? I'll make that risotto you like."

"I wish you were inviting a boy instead of an old woman, but I do like your risotto."

Nia shook her head and flashed a wry smile. "I don't do romance. Remember Alex?"

Nia had been charmed by Alex when she was sixteen, and it did not end well. At the time, she'd thought he looked like an angel, but now she would believe the devil himself had blond hair and blue eyes. Like everyone else, all he'd wanted was the stone and he'd set his companions on her like wolves when she refused to relinquish it. They wouldn't kill her because anyone who killed the holder of a fortune stone was cursed with eternal bad luck, but that didn't mean they couldn't hurt her. Two years later, the cuts and bruises were long faded, but the betrayal still stung.

Magala spat into the dirt. "Curse Alex. Not everyone's as bad as him."

As it so often did, Nia's mind flashed to a boy with warm brown eyes who gave up something precious to save her life. What sort of man had he grown into? He would be different from Alex, no doubt. Still, Nia didn't have the energy to explain she wasn't going to trust any romance that came about with the stone's influence, so instead she picked at her cloak until she sensed a change in the direction of the conversation.

Magala targeted Nia with a scrutinizing eye. "I could join you *tomorrow* night instead. Give you a distraction so you're not fretting away."

"I love your company, Mag, but I don't risk visitors during the dark moon. You know that."

With another tsk, Magala leaned on her cart. "The absence of the moon doesn't make you *un*lucky, you know. You'd be just like regular folk. Getting by on your own luck."

Magala had no idea just how bad Nia's regular luck could be, but if she tried to explain that to the high-spirited woman, who didn't care one whit about the dark moon, it would only open the door for more lectures she didn't have time for. Nia secured her rucksack shut and adjusted it on her shoulder, her jaw set. "I need to get to the baker before they close. I'll see you the day after tomorrow."

The "Closed" sign on the shop window took Nia by surprise. They must have concluded business early. Nia's expression fell. If her luck was in higher supply, she wouldn't have missed them. She should have gotten the flour first. If she had no flour, she couldn't prepare bread that night. She would have to go without until after the dark moon. Did she have enough provisions that didn't require cooking? There were the tomatoes she just bought, but they wouldn't provide much in the way of nourishment. And…that was it.

"Manes and tails," she muttered, though there was nobody nearby to hear her. The square was winding down. She adjusted her rucksack again and trudged down the street, trying to recall whether some forgotten morsel lingered in her cupboards at home.

She passed another shop, a place she had never entered but was always drawn to. It claimed to sell magical wares: potions, enchanted objects, spell books, crystals. Out of habit, she scanned the shelf of magical stones through the window, just to see. Of course, there was no fortune stone. There never was. As far as Nia knew, there were less than twenty stones in reported existence. There may have been more, but Nia suspected most of the owners would keep to themselves, like she did. If the shop ever did procure one, it would no doubt cost an exorbitant price and would be completely useless without the original owner, anyway. If the stone wasn't bestowed to someone new, the magic would not work.

Of course, there was always an abundance of dragonfly charms with long tails, some locally made and some traded. The dragonflies only appeared during seasons of plentiful harvest, so they were considered a sign of good fortune. Nia hadn't seen a real one in years, but the charms seemed to increase in circulation, perhaps as people clung to hope for better days. Some of the decorative insects were crafted from copper and tourmaline—resources her childhood town was known for. Nia fought a twinge of disappointment as she examined their gemstone eyes. She had never come across another dragonfly with rainbow eyes like those on the charm of the boy who saved her.

"Excuse me?"

Nia diverted her attention from the dragonflies to a young boy with his arms so full of bulging burlap bundles that he could scarcely peek over the top of them. What little Nia could see of his face was red and sweaty.

"Are you all right?" Nia asked.

"Yes, ma'am. Only…" He hesitated, his voice colored with a shade of embarrassment. "My mother sent me to buy flour. They were cheap, and I got carried away. I can't carry all of this home. Would you buy some?"

Nia smiled. Her luck was still looking out for her. "Yes, as a matter of fact, I would love to."

Nia pushed her legs to move faster as light deepened into warm dusk. In spite of Magala's advice about blending in, she pulled her hood on again, stuffing the springy coils of her hair inside. She was well out of town now, on her way to her cottage in a secluded area of the wood. Almost home.

Nia stopped short as a shadow glided over her. She lifted her gaze to the fading sun, and what she saw knocked the breath out of her.

Not a shadowscale. Not tonight.

Shadowscales were nasty creatures—a hybrid of dragon, bat, and nightmare. When they chose their victim, they would not rest until they were dead, but nobody could say why. They didn't eat them. Didn't seem to use the body for anything. All anyone knew was they became possessed with a wild, feverish desire to destroy the unlucky object of their attention.

Nia's luck might have been thin, but it wasn't the night of the dark moon yet. The shadowscale flew on. She didn't envy anyone out and about right now who might catch its eye.

Hurry, hurry.

Once safely back in her one-room cottage, Nia breathed a sigh weighted with relief. She set the heavy latch on the arched wooden door before slinging her cloak off her shoulders and hanging it on a splintered coat rack with care. She set her rucksack on a round hickory table, almost as worn as the coat rack. After ensuring no flammable objects were near, she lit a simple lantern and placed it at the center of the table. With the fortune stone's help, Nia could easily have lived in extravagance, but the attention it would draw was not worth the price.

She reached into the front pocket of her baggy tunic and withdrew a small pouch crafted of purple velvet. Even though she could feel the weight of the stone inside, she opened it to check every night before locking it away.

Still there.

She rolled back the stiff rug in front of the stove and pulled a small wooden box from a dug-out spot in the dirt floor. The box had a simple lock, and the key to it was always around Nia's neck. Nia opened the box and tucked the stone away inside, feeling an instant hollow ache as it left her person. She was so attuned to the object that putting it away was akin to losing a part of herself, but she didn't dare risk anything happening to it while she slept.

After Nia locked the box, she checked it three times to be certain it was truly secure, then nestled the box in the floor and put the rug back in place. Now her nerves could relax, but only a little.

Tomorrow, Nia would not be charmed with the good fortune she usually had. It meant she would be susceptible to ordinary accidents and maladies, as anyone else would. In consideration of this, Nia began her typical pre-dark moon ritual. She made certain she had more than enough water to last until the day after tomorrow. She swept and tidied the cottage to minimize any chance of stumbling over a mess. She drank an herbal tonic to boost her immune system in case there was any chance of catching an illness. She prepared all her food for the next day—including a fresh batch of tea—so she wouldn't have to worry about cutting or burning herself when her luck was gone. She verified that the windows and door were secure and in good repair.

Satisfied all was in order, Nia changed into her nightclothes, washed her face, blew out the candle, and settled into bed for the night.

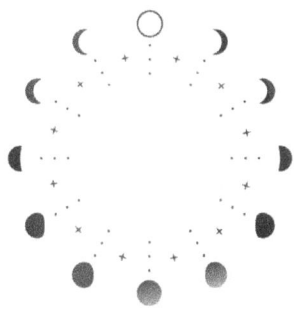

Chapter 3

The Dark Moon

The next morning, sunlight winked innocently into the cottage, dancing through the mottled shadows of leaves. There was no reason to hurry out of bed. Nia closed her eyes and attempted to drift back to sleep, but as usual on the day of the dark moon, her nerves would not settle enough to allow rest. She pulled her covers back with care and sat up—slowly, so as not to jostle anything by accident. Her feet hit the floor, and she shivered. On any other day, she would light a fire to warm her space, but not now. Today she would make do with changing into a warmer dress and wearing her cloak indoors.

The hours passed slowly, and Nia spent most of them engrossed in a book. There wasn't much she could do to hurt herself unless she swooned too hard over the gallant hero in the fairy tale she perused. The day outside was lovely, if a bit chilly. She was tempted to crack open a window to enjoy the breeze and bird songs, but doing so might invite insects or vermin, or who knew what else.

By the time the shadows outside grew long, Nia's body was languid and stiff. How strange that doing nothing all day could make one feel so tired. But she was satisfied with her progress toward survival of another dark moon. She would eat dinner and go to bed early, and in the morning her luck would trickle back into her life.

As Nia stood to stretch, the hem of her cloak caught on the handle of her water bucket and sent it tumbling. Nia hissed through her teeth as she watched the precious water turn her dirt floor to mud. She could go without water until the next day. It might get uncomfortable, but she would survive. The only alternative was a walk to the river. On an ordinary evening, this was not a problem. But on the night of the dark moon? Not a chance.

But then the ballad of "what if" played through her mind: What if something caught fire and she had nothing to douse it with? What if she injured herself and needed to clean the wound? What if she became ill and urgently needed hydration? On a luckless night, she may require water after all.

Nia still had a little time before sundown. She grasped the handle of the bucket, stepped outside, and hurried to the river that flowed just down the hill from her.

As usual, the rushing sound of the water wound her chest so tight it was difficult to breathe. She steadied each inhale and exhale, wondering if she would ever take a trip to the river without anxiety tagging along. She reached the water's edge and fought to keep her hands steady as she looked for a secure place on the bank. Nothing too muddy. Nothing that looked like it might collapse. At that moment, a blue sparkle lit the surface of the water, followed by another. And another. Nia smiled as a group of water sprites broke the surface, droplets glistening in the air around them.

"Hello, friends." She held up her bucket. "Here to help me again?"

Nia didn't know if it was the stone's usual influence or if the creatures were simply kind, but Nia rarely had to dip the bucket herself, and for this she was grateful. The further she could stay from the ever-moving current, the better.

The water sprites swirled in formation and dipped down toward the water, an azure cyclone. A pillar of water spun through the air and into Nia's bucket. She stumbled under the sudden weight of the water but regained her balance.

"Thank you so much. I have to get back before dark, but I hope I see you soon."

The sprites responded with several happy tinkling sounds and disappeared again beneath the water. Nia traversed the hill as briskly as she dared while still monitoring her footing, then secured herself in the cottage once more. This time she made sure the bucket was well out of her way.

Nia wouldn't risk preparing a hot meal on the night of the dark moon. For all she knew, she would have a mishap with the wood burning stove or cut herself while preparing the ingredients.

That night was a safe fare of the bread she'd prepared the night before and cold medicinal tea. The brew was bitter, but she gulped it down all the same, as it made her condition more bearable. She would never understand why it was the one thing the stone didn't seem capable of helping her with.

Nia chewed at a steady, careful pace, forming her battle plan for the evening. Once she finished eating, she would read a little more—she was certain the hero was about to find his love—and then turn in early. No sense being up and about. No need to keep the lanterns burning late.

As her thoughts turned to the lanterns, so did her eyes. Was the flame flickering more than usual? She swallowed the bread, her throat dry.

The table vibrated, low and steady. Soon the silverware danced and clattered against her plate. Nia gasped as the lantern tipped, and she quickly secured it by the handle. The vibrations intensified, and Nia's ears throbbed with a low pulse. It couldn't be an earthquake.

The world exploded around her. Shards of wood pelted her skin as the roof of her home splintered and flew in every direction. She threw her arms up over her head in protection. At once, she both felt and heard the whoosh of gargantuan wings as a dark form attempted to overtake her.

Shadowscale.

Nia dove under her table, already knowing it was a useless effort. The table soared above her and turned to mere scraps as it crashed into what remained of the wall. The lantern lay shattered on the floor, the crackle of flames growing louder. Nia ran to the rug and flung it away, the rough fibers scraping her fingertips. She fumbled in a desperate attempt to get the key off of her neck and into the lock of the wooden box. If she survived this mess, she was going to need all the luck she could get in the morning.

She managed to unlock the box and grasp the stone, even as her hands shook. The stone was cold in her palm. Nia often felt as though it had a mind of its own. She could sense what it wanted at times and feel it puzzling out the world for ways to solve her problems. But not now.

"Wake up," Nia begged, even knowing it was in vain. The stone never did anything when the moon was dark. "Can't you do something? Just this once?"

Nothing.

Nia's feet left the dirt, her breath constricted by the cold talons of the shadowscale around her middle. Knowing she had precious few seconds to remain close to the ground, Nia twisted herself around and bit into the scales of the creature's foot with all the strength her teeth had to offer. She clamped down until she feared her jaw would pop if she continued. The shadowscale didn't even flinch. Nia saw the blur of a burning chair as they lifted, and she grappled for the object with her free hand, uncaring as it seared her flesh. Better burned than dead.

She thrust the fiery piece of furniture into the shadowscale's curled foot, the flames slicing across her own skin as she did so. The beast unearthed a roar that split the heavens, and Nia spun as it reflexively loosened its grip. She braced herself for the fall as best as she could, clutching the stone, but the *crack* of her arm as she hit the ground sent her reeling.

Adrenaline temporarily numbed the pain of her shattered humerus and scorched hand as she scrambled to her feet. She needed an exit. Now. It wouldn't be long before the shadowscale recovered and attacked again. She needed her hands free in order to fight, so she stuffed the stone into the left pocket of her dress and buttoned it closed. She'd sewn pockets in every piece of clothing she owned so she always had a secure place for the stone on her person.

Nia retreated through the ruined debris of what was once a cottage wall and into the moonless night. As she tore through the trees and stumbled down the hill, she could hear the roar of the nightmare and the rush of its wings. It wouldn't take but a moment for it to rage down on her again. She doubted she would be lucky enough to be carried away in its claws this time. No—if it caught her again, it would be immediate death.

The river. It was the only thing that could whisk her away, almost as swift as the shadowscale's wings. And in the dark, the beast would be unlikely to see her in the current. Even if the river made the most sense, Nia scoured her brain for some other idea.

"Little sprites!" Nia's words came out a breathless, shrill cry from her weakened lungs. She wasn't sure what she wanted the sprites to do, but there had to be some other way. Anything but the river. *Please, somebody help me.*

The violent crunch of trees changed Nia's motivation. Her instinct to avoid the river gave way to something more primal, and she sprang into the water and let the current rip her downstream.

The torrent dragged her under without mercy, and Nia released a garbled scream that flooded her airways as the unyielding flow whipped her broken arm about. She wasn't sure if this was preferable to the shadowscale. At least death by the shadowscale would have been quick. She was going to drown and meet the same terrible fate as her parents. Maybe this was the way life always should have ended for her.

Nia crunched into a tangled net of branches and reeds at the shoreline. She clawed at them with her good arm as she coughed and gulped in air, grasping for anything that would keep her from sweeping down the river again. The bark of the sticks ground into her raw palms and she clenched her jaw through the pain as she pulled herself upward; first to a knot of roots jutting out from the side of the bank and then to the bank itself. She drug herself through the muddy shore and wheezed, pain stabbing throughout her body. There was one good thing—the forest she'd wriggled into was thicker, and there was no sign of the shadowscale. The river had done the trick of sweeping her away from the monster's menacing gaze.

But what in the world was she supposed to do now?

She slumped in the cold, slimy mud, whimpering as she cradled her ruined arm.

"Manes and tails...that hurts," she gasped to herself.

She assessed her condition, groaning again at the raw flesh where she burned her hand. Chilled. Soaked. Scratched to bits. Burned. Breathless. Broken.

Utterly out of luck.

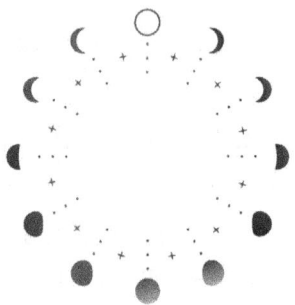

Chapter 4

Nia may have been wallowing in mud, but she wasn't going to wallow in her misery. It would be easy to find a new place to live with fortune as her chaperone and her belongings were too few to grieve. The stone would take care of her as soon as the moon lit the sky. She could possibly make it to Magala's house in the meantime, if she could only manage to stand.

Shaking, she labored to her feet, her arm and lungs torturing her with every movement. Maybe she needed a doctor before anything else. How far had the river carried her? Where was the closest village? How would she find her way without the moonlight guiding her?

Nia took careful steps away from the riverbank, treading lightly until the earth was less mushy. She used her good arm to feel the way ahead so she wouldn't run into any brambles or trees. Shivering, she hunted for a patch of sky through the thick woods to orient herself.

At last, she detected Orion's belt. Her village would be south of here, and she knew of a small outcropping of farms on the way. Someone there was sure to help. She inhaled, cursing the pain throughout her body and the raw burning in her lungs. She would not cry.

She trudged forward, grasping for pleasant distractions. Perhaps she would finally meet a unicorn. Didn't they come to maidens in distress? Few situations were more distressing than her predicament. But she supposed there were things to be grateful for. For example, she hadn't taken off her boots at home after fetching the water, so while they were soggy and covered in mud, at least they kept her feet protected. She had one good arm. She had her wits about her, more or less. She had the stone, even if it was temporarily useless. She had…

Well, she'd think of more things eventually.

Nia stopped and rubbed her eyes with one fist. She blinked and rubbed them again. An unmistakable twinkle of light moved toward her. Fast. She held her ground, doubting she could run even if she tried. She'd had more than her share of bad luck for the night—surely the odds tilted in favor of something good.

Nia relaxed when she made out the features behind the glow. It was only a pixie. This particular pixie had mint-green hair and lace-like patterns of the same color dappled across its wings. A wind type, by the looks of it. They occasionally granted fanciful gifts of flight to humans, when the mood suited them. Nia was no stranger to pixies—they seemed to favor her, with influence from the fortune stone, no doubt. The wind pixies loved to play their games with Nia, and she generally indulged. But the thought of spontaneous flight in her battered condition wound her stomach in knots, especially because she'd been dropped a time or two by less experienced pixies. There was no telling what this one would do.

"Please, not now," Nia begged. Her feet lifted, and even that small jostle sent pain through her. "I said NO!" Nia's cry was harsher than intended, a product of affliction and urgency.

The creature squeaked, indignant, and zipped into the trees, leaving Nia with a nagging twinge of remorse. She shouldn't have snapped at it. It wasn't the pixie's fault she was in such a poor state. Hopefully she would get a chance to meet it again so she could apologize and explain herself.

Nia continued onward, checking the stars on occasion to ensure she was still going in the right direction. She halted as the faint crunching of leaves and stirring gravel met her ears, followed by the slow whine of a struggling wheel. A cart? She fumbled toward the sound, ready to trust anyone.

Pick up the pace, she urged herself, following the creaking wheels and rattling wood. A faint glow came from a wobbling lantern hitched to the cart.

"Help," she croaked. "Please help." Her shout died in the trees, her voice weak. She'd have to work harder to catch up. She shouldn't have been cross with that pixie. Maybe flying wouldn't have been a bad alternative, even with the risk of a drop.

She tried shouting again but could not muster enough force behind her words to be heard over the racket the cart made. She bent down and fumbled in the dark for a rock. Thankfully, her uninjured arm was her dominant one, and she'd always had good aim. Nia put whatever strength she had left into her throw, wincing in pain at the motion. The rock found its mark on the side of the cart, and the horse whinnied, prancing back a few steps. The driver steadied his horse, bringing the cart to a full stop before holding up a lantern. His wide eyes caught the flickering light as he scanned the darkness. This was her chance. Nia moved as fast as she could to catch his attention.

"Sir," she panted, "Please."

He jumped and held out a fist when he saw her, no doubt prepared for something more sinister than the harried young woman who staggered towards him from the trees. The dim light danced across his white-knuckled grip on the lantern. His skin was withered and baked, definitely a man who spent most of his time in the sun. A farmer, perhaps?

His shoulders released their tension at last and his voice was steady when he asked, "What happened to you, miss?"

He wasn't going to turn her away. Nia could have cried, but instead she stated, "I fell in the river." Fell...jumped...nobody needed to know the difference. She didn't have the energy to tell the tale of the shadowscale tonight, especially if fear of the creature's wrath would extinguish the chance of his help.

"Arm's hurt?" he asked, nodding toward the arm Nia now cradled carefully. His voice cracked and his face drooped with exhaustion. He had probably been on his way home after working in his fields all day.

"I could pay you," Nia said in a rush. "I don't have money on me, but once we get back to my village, I can get some." Whether there was anything salvageable at her cottage remained to be seen, but she kept a stash of coins with Magala in case she ever found herself in trouble.

Hello, trouble. Meet Nia.

The farmer shook his head. "Naw. The wife would have my head if I took payment from someone in need. I know a doctor in Ravenskeep."

Nia sighed, relief melting through her. "That's my village. Thank you so much."

He hopped out, helping Nia hoist herself into the back of his cart among worn tools and a few small crates of summer crops.

"First of the harvest?" she asked.

He frowned. "Most of the harvest, I'm afraid. Bad year."

"Oh. I'm sorry." His story wasn't unusual. Crops had been impacted by an increase of disasters in all the surrounding villages.

He shrugged. "It is what it is." He hobbled to the front of the cart and hoisted himself inside, grabbing the reins once again.

"Heeyaw!" he called, and the large horse started its trot once more.

Nia gritted her teeth with every rattle and bump, but she stuffed down any thought of complaining. The cart ride might have been painful, but it was much faster than walking. She would do something to help the farmer, too. Even without giving him a piece of the stone, Nia could always get what she wanted with the stone's assistance, including help for others.

She closed her eyes and sang songs in her head to distract herself from the pain; old songs her mother used to sing. Nia may not have remembered the sound of her mother's voice or the way she looked, but she was determined not to forget the words of her songs. She would hold on to that one piece if she had nothing else.

Golden leaves in trees
Piercing skies of blue
Darling, none of these

Are cherished more than you...

Nia sensed the cart turning. She popped open her eyes.

"Why have we turned around?" Nia called. Had she been wrong to trust the cart driver?

"Just a detour," he said, a strange edge to his voice. "Didn't like the look of the way ahead."

Nia tried to sit up to get a look, but with only one good arm and the rest of her body screaming in agony all she could manage was an awkward fumble.

"What in the—WOAAAAAAAOoooh..."

Nia gasped as the farmer flew over her head and off into the darkness, his voice growing distant as he went from her sight. She scrambled to get upright, discomfort momentarily forgotten. The horse whinnied loudly and reared, and only then did Nia notice the glowing shape as big as a bear moving rapidly toward them. She realized it wasn't one large shape, but several smaller ones. Wind pixies. Angry wind pixies. Nia knew she should have treated that pixie better. She only hoped they let the farmer down gently after they sent him flying.

The horse bolted, and once again Nia was headed the opposite direction of where she wanted to go.

"Whoa!" she shouted. "*Whoa!*"

The frantic creature powered forward, as though Nia's forceful command was a mere suggestion. The pixies easily kept pace and now they darted at Nia, pulling her hair and scratching their tiny nails across her face. The sound of angry, beating wings filled the air as they continued their assault. Nia shrieked and swatted them away like insects, but they would not relent.

One pixie flew directly at Nia's face and blew furious raspberries in her direction. Mint-green hair and lace-like wings. The same one she met earlier.

"I'm sorry, ok?" Nia pleaded. "I shouldn't have been so mean to you. What do you want?"

The pixie kicked Nia in the nose and buzzed off, now turning its attention to the horse.

The poor beast picked up speed, desperate to flee its tiny assailants. At this rate, the cart would turn over. Nia screamed as one of the pixies grabbed her eyelid and tugged.

"Get off, you horrid little thing!" She pried it away, all thoughts of remorse gone as the new slices of pain bit into her. "All of you, be gone, or I'll feed you to the shadowscale that hunts me!"

A sudden stillness. A torrent of wind as the creatures departed. Had the threat about the shadowscale worked?

No. Nia shivered, unable to control it. There was something else in the darkness. Something more sinister than feral beasts. She could feel it in her core, and evidently, the horse could sense it too.

With the horse's frantic bucking, the cart at last turned over. The axle broke, and the steed rushed to freedom. Nia tumbled to the rough ground, and the impact on her battered body pushed her past the threshold of bearable pain. The edges of the world blurred. An even heavier darkness descended, deeper than the already bleak night. Nia could do nothing as the shadows dragged her away and consciousness failed her.

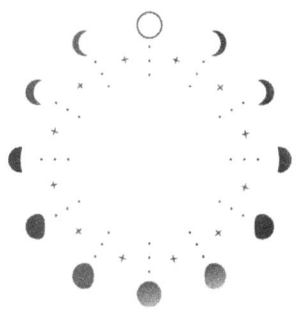

Chapter 5

Nia's mind tugged at her from the darkness behind her eyelids, beckoning her to wake. She resisted and tried to sink back in the blackness, unwilling to open her eyes to reality yet. Warmth cocooned her as she lay snuggled deep in something soft and luxurious. The material was a brush of heaven against her skin.

Heaven... Was that it? Was she dead?

The notion only intensified with the suspicious absence of pain. Her broken bones no longer seared beneath her muscle and the lacerations that covered her skin left no sting. Physically, she was fine. Better than fine.

If this was the afterlife, it was off to a pretty good start. What else might await her? Would her parents be standing by to greet her?

On the count of three, Nia thought, *I'll open my eyes.*

One.

Two.

Three.

She opened them slowly, carefully sliding into a more upright position. She stretched to work the stiffness out of her body and drew her arms out in front of her, only then remembering one of them was supposed to be ruined. She flexed her fingers. She rolled her shoulders. She brought the arm to her side and rotated it in a wide circle. Again, no pain.

Her skin was flawless. Not a trace remained of the injuries that had covered her flesh like cracks on porcelain, and it wasn't only the new injuries that had vanished. The scar on her right thumb where she sliced it cutting vegetables with Magala was nowhere to be seen. She kicked off the blankets and examined her ankle, expecting a line of uneven skin where an irate pixie had seared her as a child. The spot was now smooth and perfect.

"It's not possible," she said to the empty room. Then an even more tantalizing thought hit her. Her breathing.

She drew in a large breath and did her best not to let the disappointment stifle her when the usual sharp pain hit. The ever-present tightness from her near drowning remained.

Something even more urgent pressed on her, however. Where was she?

Nia took in the extravagance around her. The bed she currently occupied was piled with pillows, embroidered in soft shades of green and blue. Each elegantly carved piece of furniture was fashioned in ivory-finished wood, gold flaked detail accenting every bevel and curve. The light stone walls were adorned in tapestries of green hills and, oh–unicorns! Whoever lived here couldn't be all bad if they had unicorns on their walls.

The smell of citrus and lavender brushed her nose, and she scanned for its source. On the round glass table beside her bed was a crystal decanter stuffed full of purple flowers with slices of lemon floating in the water.

She pushed the plush, cream-colored comforter away and took a careful step out of the bed onto a rug patterned in green-and-blue florals. The fibers felt wonderfully soft against her feet. Only then did she notice the silky, indigo robe wrapped around her body, which was just a bit too revealing for her liking. Who had changed her? Her insides turned icy. The robe was one thing, but the thought of a complete stranger undressing her while she was unconscious was even worse.

Surely whoever left her here didn't expect her to stay in this scrap of a robe. Where were her clothes?

Her clothes.

The stone.

Nia's breathing grew tight and shallow. Where was it? She sprang to the chest of drawers but both it and the wardrobe stood empty.

As Nia released her breath, she mentally reached for the stone, trying to sense where it could be. The stone's energy tugged her toward the massive bed. Nia got on her hands and knees and grappled in the dark space beneath it. She exhaled when her fingers closed around the smooth object. Its warmth brought a familiar sense of comfort to this unknown place.

How did it end up on the floor without her clothes? If enough time had passed, it must have been luck working in her favor once more. That was the only explanation Nia had for how the pocket of her clothing could have come unbuttoned and let the stone drop without anyone's notice.

How long had she slept? The question propelled her to action. There was nowhere to conceal the stone in the silky robe, so Nia resumed her search for something more respectable to wear. She tested the handle to a wooden door that led to a washroom.

Yes, she definitely needed that.

The washroom alone was nearly as big as Nia's cottage, with all the necessities. It was bright and white, but she couldn't find a window or a light source anywhere.

After relieving herself, Nia stared at a polished, pastel-green basin atop a stone pedestal, along with a matching tub that must have been big enough to accommodate two or three people. She might freshen up if she had water to fill them. To the side of the small basin rested a silver dish with a pretty little soap in the shape of a rose. She couldn't resist leaning forward to smell it. Sage and something sweet.

A gurgling sound met Nia's ears, and she took a quick step backward as the basin filled with water. Where was it coming from? There were no cracks or holes in it. Curious, she dipped her fingers in the water and sighed. It was warm and wonderful. She set the stone down for only a moment as she washed her hands and enjoyed the soft perfume of the soap.

Another bubbling sound echoed through the room as the tub set to work filling itself. While the thought of a warm bath tantalized her, she drew back. Washing her hands in a basin was one thing, but she wasn't ready to submerge in a tub. This could only be magic, and until something led her to believe otherwise, everything in this place was suspicious, even if it was beautiful.

She paced for a moment across the cold tile floor, warring with her thoughts. On the one hand, if the occupant—or occupants—of this place wanted to harm Nia, they certainly could have done so. On the other hand, the fact that they hadn't probably meant they wanted something from her.

"Isn't that always the way it is?" Nia whispered to herself.

Nia had just about resolved to bathe regardless of her reservations when she heard the creak of a door and the soft shuffle of someone entering the room. She froze and clutched the stone tighter.

"Oh my! Young miss?" The female voice was soft but full of both surprise and worry.

Nia couldn't hide forever, so she might as well face things head on and find out what was going on.

"I'm in the washroom." Nia's voice came out slightly hoarse, likely from lack of use, which further fueled her fear that she had been out of it for some time.

A tall woman in a cobalt dress and servant's apron entered, her milky-white skin extra pale against the length of dark hair running down her back.

"Taking a moment to freshen up? Wonderful. I'm so glad to see you awake."

"Is this your home?" Nia asked as they both stepped back into the bedroom. She did her best to keep the stone out of sight behind her back.

The woman laughed. It was a pleasant, gentle sound. "Well, it's not *mine*, but I do live in the castle. I'm Antonia. The master has tasked me with your wellbeing."

A castle? And the master? "And who might that be?"

"Master Neilos. He asked me to send for you the moment you woke, so we'd best get you changed."

Nia pretended to straighten one of the pillows on the bed and discreetly tucked the stone underneath it. "Forgive me," said Nia, "but I know nothing about where I am or who this Neilos is." She didn't like the idea of waltzing in to meet this person completely unprepared, although what was her alternative?

"He means you no harm. I'll be right back with your gown." Antonia moved for the door. "I would have had it here already if I'd realized you'd be awake. I'll only be a moment."

Gown? The word had such a lavish sound. Nia had nothing against fancy clothing—she simply didn't feel it suited her solitary life. Who would she dress up for? She had plenty of practical, modest dresses, of course. But nothing she would describe as a *gown*.

"If it's all right," Nia began, interrupting Antonia's exit, "I'd prefer to wear my own clothes."

"Oh." Antonia paused in the doorway and bowed her head slightly. "I'm so sorry, miss, but they were too badly stained and damaged from your injuries. The master had me dispose of them."

Nia pursed her lips. It wasn't presumptuous to assume something in this magic castle could have fixed her clothes. After all, her broken body was good as new, which must have been more complicated than fabrics. The "master" must have thought the garments weren't worth the trouble. The notion needled at her as Antonia hurried out of the room.

Part of her wanted to press the matter, but Nia made a decision—one that had served her well in terms of survival over the years. Until she knew more about the castle and the people in it, she would be timid. Docile. It was better to be underestimated in an unfamiliar situation than to show her full hand. For her own sake, she would become a little mouse... At least while others were watching.

She pushed any inkling of irritation aside by the time the door opened again, announcing Antonia's return.

Nia had certainly never had a dress like the one Antonia flourished. The velvet gown reminded her of the reflection of storm clouds on water—not quite blue, not quite silver. The bodice was fitted and flowed into a gentle A-line skirt, falling to the floor in a cascade of soft, supple folds. When Nia slipped into it, the look was finished with a satin ribbon around her waist that tied in the back, leaving the ribbon's ends trailing to the floor. Nia felt like she had slipped into a pool of melted silver and come back with an enchanted outfit.

Next, Antonia used a golden oil to tame Nia's curls and pinned a few of her locks back with a white floral pick. "There now," she said. "Shall we go?"

Nia nodded, though it took her feet a moment to catch up with her acquiescence. She forced herself not to glance at the pillow as they exited the room.

She followed Antonia down the corridors in silence. The whole castle was made of the same cream-colored stone as Nia's room and had a soft shimmer to it. Rather than the blue-and-green color scheme of Nia's space, the hallways and common areas favored vibrant shades of coral and orange.

She paused at a row of sconces with lit candlesticks. She couldn't place it, but something rang peculiar about the flames and the light in the hallway. A soft sound escaped her lips as it struck her: the shadows from the flickering flames were in the wrong place for the direction of the light.

Magic, again.

There were little whispers of enchantment everywhere: well-lit areas even when there were no light sources present. Decorative pottery that changed colors before Nia's eyes. Doors that opened on their own. She was sure tickles of haunting melodies caught her ears, but they seemed to vanish as soon as she tried to home in on the source.

Perhaps she'd hit her head while the river tossed her about. The book she'd been reading had enchanted castles– maybe she was dreaming. Was the master of the castle anything like the hero in her story? The thought tickled her stomach.

Just as Nia started to think this level of the castle went on forever, they reached the end of the corridor. Antonia approached a large, hollow sphere made of slender wrought iron bars. It reminded Nia of a cage. This thought was only enhanced when Antonia opened a door on the sphere, which elicited a loud metallic creak.

Nia clutched her arms and took a few steps backward. "What is that?"

"Nothing to worry about, miss. Just a faster way of getting around." She motioned for Nia to enter.

Antonia seemed too kind to do Nia any harm, so Nia stepped into the contraption. A crackling noise filled the air almost the instant Antonia closed them inside. Nia's heart sped as she stared at the barred door, feeling more like a caged animal than she anticipated. She gripped her skirts in her hands and tried not to scream as they were swallowed up by a ball of green lightning. A sharp jolt shot from her head to her toes, and next thing she knew, Antonia was guiding her by the arm out of an identical sphere.

"Are you all right, miss?" Antonia rested a gentle hand on Nia's shoulder.

Nia took several quick breaths, waiting for her heart to slow. She couldn't answer.

Antonia gave her a sympathetic smile. "I should have warned you. The transphere does take some getting used to. Let's keep walking. I find it helps me recover faster."

Once Nia felt steady again, she caught a glimpse of the grounds out of one of the many windows in the halls. She'd never seen a courtyard with so much vegetation. Probably enchanted, too, like so many other things here. Nia had basically trusted her whole life to magic, so it shouldn't have set her on edge now. Maybe it was because she knew nothing about the man who possessed it.

They approached a towering, blood-red door that made the surrounding walls seem insignificant in comparison. The faint, metallic smell of rust from the handle and hinges only added to Nia's mental images of bloodshed. Why did anyone need a door that big? This man wasn't a giant, was he? She couldn't stop her wild imaginings of being served up on a platter and it was all she could do not to bolt in the opposite direction.

Antonia knocked twice and the door heaved open. Nia expected a footman to appear, but the door opened of its own accord. As massive as the door was, it made no sound whatsoever as it swung to give them passage. Something about it was deeply unsettling. Even so, she followed Antonia inside.

The door's size was an indicator of the expanse of the room beyond it. The ceiling stretched impossibly high, even past the height of the towering door. Just how tall was the castle? The entirety of the chamber was overgrown with flowering vines, which made it difficult to gauge exactly how far back the space stretched.

"Master Neilos," Antonia spoke loudly. "The lady is awake."

The vines shifted, parting down the center, pulling, slithering. They twisted into several tall pillars, revealing a long gold carpet flanked with soldiers on either side. At the end of the carpet sat a great throne.

"Ah, how wonderful. Do come closer." The voice was resonant and laced with silk, yet his words carried more than a mere request.

Nia squeaked as her feet lifted off the ground, and she flew toward the front of the room. Whatever this strange magic was, it gave her no choice in her target and before she knew it, she was right before the throne.

"There," the voice, she assumed belonged to Neilos, stated. "Now I can get a better look at you. You may go, Antonia."

"As you wish, master." Antonia bowed, and Nia's stomach twisted at the thought of staying behind without Antonia's soothing presence. She swallowed and dared a glance upward to see who the master of the castle truly was.

Nia's breath caught at the otherworldly quality of the man before her. He lounged on the throne in elegant jade robes, resting his cheek thoughtfully on his hand. His skin was pale and smooth, his eyes a piercing amber. And his hair! Nia had never seen anything like it. Wild, spiked tufts in the front with long strands by each ear and tied into a shorter tuft at the back. And it was as red as a poppy. Handsome wasn't the right word—he was beautiful. Even in her fairytales she'd never imagined a being like this.

Nia's focus shifted to the guard on Neilos's right, standing at attention in an emerald-green and gold uniform. While not striking in the same ethereal way as his master, his broad shoulders and sculpted features made him attractive in a more conventional way. As her eyes followed the details of the uniform's embroidery, they froze on the pin near his collar. A dragonfly with tourmaline wings? She would definitely talk to him later, if the opportunity presented.

"You're looking well," Neilos said, startling Nia out of her observations. He regarded her, his eyes keen and assessing. "That's good to see. What's your name, dear lady?"

"Nia." Nia's voice croaked in stark contrast to Neilos's dreamlike timbre, and she flinched at the difference. Neilos showed no indication that he noticed.

"Nia." He said her name as though those two syllables held the beauty of a poem. "Such simple elegance."

She couldn't believe the man living in such a magnificent castle would find anything about her elegant, but she responded, "Thank you."

"You must be wondering how you came to be here?"

Nia clenched her jaw. She'd been about to ask just that. Was he a mind-reader too? Unable to coax her words free, Nia only nodded.

Neilos gave a soft smile that quickened Nia's heartbeat for reasons she couldn't quite put into words. Something about it made her feel like a rabbit in view of a fox.

"My men came across you in the forest. They couldn't simply leave you in the shape you were in, so they brought you here."

Nia asked the question that pressed against her mind since she woke up. "Who healed me?"

His smile broadened. "I did."

She detected a hint of smugness in his voice. Even though the answer was already apparent, Nia asked, "With magic?"

"Naturally. Who could save you otherwise? You were delirious with fever from infection and broken all over. It was no trouble for *me* to patch you up, but in the hands of an ordinary doctor you would not have been so fortunate."

Well, he certainly had no trouble with confidence.

"I confess, your lungs were a bit more complicated," Neilos mused. "I couldn't heal them in one swoop, but I administered an elixir that will heal them fully in a month's time."

A flicker of hope stirred in Nia's chest. "You mean after a month my lungs will be healed? Completely?"

"Completely. However," His voice trailed off, and Nia sensed an impending caveat.

"Yes?" She prompted, though she feared his response.

"You must stay here in proximity to my magic in order for healing to reach completion."

Nia swallowed. "For the whole month?"

"For the remainder of it, yes."

The remainder...

The air in Nia's lungs suddenly felt restricted. "How long was I asleep?"

"A mere two days."

Neilos said it as though it was a good thing, but that meant if she wanted to be healed, she had nearly a whole month left in this strange place. A month of unknown magic, trapped under the unrelenting gaze of the castle's enigmatic master. If she had her way, Nia would return home the instant this meeting ended.

The flicker of hope wavered.

The vines along the interior walls slithered and Nia felt as though the magic in the castle worked its way over her, tangling into her hair and tickling up and down her spine. The strange cast of the shadows and the overall sense of *not right* threatened to crush her. It was worse than waiting for the nightstripe to pounce.

She forced as much strength into her voice as she could when she said, "I'm grateful for everything you've done. If I change my mind, can I go home before the month is up?" Healing or none, it wouldn't be worth it if he held her against her will.

Neilos flourished a hand. "By all means, go. But," he added, "You must inform me before you leave so I can allow you to pass through the castle's security measures. Nobody enters or exits the grounds without my permission."

Nia's heart thudded. She should have known it wouldn't be that simple. "Why?" She reached for the stone in her pocket before remembering it was back in her room and these weren't her clothes. Manes and tails...she could have used some luck at that moment.

The castle's master drew a lazy line down the arm of his chair with his fingertips. "Regrettably, we have a traitor crawling somewhere in the castle halls, passing knowledge to outsiders. I have enemies who would use any bit of information against me. For the safety of myself and all within these walls, the protective enchantment remains until I decide otherwise."

Was he truly doing it only for safety reasons? The guards and servants—at least those Nia had seen—did all look well. None of them appeared ill, abused, or underfed. And if he was holding his enchantment to protect his court, then he must not be a cruel man. Still, he himself admitted to having enemies. What sort of enemies, and why?

Neilos broke into her thoughts. "I can see you're having doubts. But consider it. You'll live like a queen during your stay. Whatever you wish for within the castle will be yours. Anything you could want, and at the end of it all you'll have the thing you most desire."

What could this man possibly know of her desires? But he wasn't wrong. She'd sought a cure for most of her life and all her efforts had been fruitless. Could she really let this chance slip through her fingers?

The castle's master seemed to take her silence as acceptance. "I promise this will be the most comfortable stay you have ever had." He regarded her more intensely and added, "You may even choose to extend it."

Nia doubted it but couldn't look away from those eyes.

Neilos nodded lazily toward the man on his right. The young guard was so stoic that Nia kept forgetting he was there. "Enitan, please show Nia around the castle and the grounds."

"Yes, my master."

Enitan.

The memories flooded Nia as fiercely as the waters that took her parents from her that day. Could it really be him? If he was indeed from her childhood village, it was a small community and the name wasn't common. Plus that dragonfly pin... Nia regarded him in more detail.

He stood stick straight, and his expression was so serious that Nia wavered in her desire to speak with him. The boy from her memories was kind and selfless, and she had always imagined him growing up in the same way. This steadfast soldier didn't fit that image. If he was the same boy, what if he wasn't everything she had imagined over the years?

Or what if he was?

Fine. Nia would stay and allow her lungs to heal. And in the meantime, she would get to know all she could about the master of the castle and the soldier who may have saved her life.

Neilos tilted his head, as though Nia was the most interesting thing in the castle, once more giving her that unsettling feeling that he was trying to pry into her thoughts. "Oh, one more thing," he said. "Please join me for dinner when the clock strikes five. Antonia will show you the dining hall."

Could she refuse? It didn't sound like a request. "Thank you," she said, though she struggled to summon true gratitude.

The soldier called Enitan strode to Nia's side and gave her a curt nod that sent her hopes plummeting. They turned and walked together toward the imposing red door, and Nia was sure she felt Neilos's eyes on her back. She didn't dare glance over her shoulder to confirm it, even when she heard the vines slithering back into place as they passed.

The instant the door closed behind them, Enitan let out a long sigh. He rolled his shoulders and immediately adopted a more relaxed posture, transforming completely from the tin soldier he had been moments before.

"Man, I thought he'd never stop talking." He glanced at Nia, then cleared his throat and straightened up again. "Sorry, uh, ma'am. Oh, you probably don't like being called ma'am. Miss? I'm not leaving a good impression, am I?"

Nia laughed in spite of herself, her walls slipping just the slightest. "It's all right. Really." The cracks in his stoney facade were a pleasant surprise. She preferred this version of Enitan to the statuesque figure he presented in front of his master. It was nearer to the Enitan she'd always imagined. "Nia is fine."

Her eyes met his. They were warm brown with a deeper ring around the irises, and so familiar. The same eyes that had burned into her memories for years. She waited for some kind of realization to dawn on him. A glimmer or an inkling to confirm her suspicions were correct.

"Nia," he murmured.

Her heart skipped.

He ran a hand over his hair—black, tied back in several tight braids that ran to his shoulders—and grinned. "Pretty name, but don't be shocked if you have to tell me again. I'm lousy with names as it is, and there's a ton to keep up with around here, you know?"

Nia swallowed her disappointment, but as they worked their way through the halls she got a better look at his dragonfly pin.

Rainbow eyes.

Her heart raced and her throat felt dry. She had to work to keep her voice steady when she asked, "I couldn't help but notice your pin. By chance are you from Swiftriver?" She rarely met others from her old home. Swiftriver was one of the bigger villages in the region, and well-capable of sustaining itself, so it was rare for people to wander from its bounty.

He paused, and Nia worried it was too familiar of a question.

"I am," Enitan said at last.

Nia's pulse quickened. The name, age, and appearance were all correct, and his hometown and the rainbow eyes sealed it. It was really him. The boy who saved her life. And he'd certainly grown up handsome. She opened her mouth to ask if he remembered her but stopped short.

The stone in her possession once belonged to Enitan. What had life been like for him in the years since he relinquished it? Did he ever regret his choice? Perhaps revealing herself wasn't the best idea while she was unfamiliar with his character. Instead, she asked, "Do you ever visit?"

"Haven't been in years. Things weren't the same after the flooding."

Sadness coated Nia's features, which Enitan immediately noticed. "Sorry. Did you lose someone in the floods?" he asked.

"My parents."

Nia held her breath waiting for this to spark something in him, but Enitan only whistled through his teeth. "Sorry."

"It's all right. It was a long time ago." Eleven years, in fact. She wondered if Enitan held the lost years like a millstone in his heart as she did.

"Still, losing your parents that young? Nothing comes easy."

Nia toyed with the ribbon on her dress. She probably had it easier than most, with the stone in her possession. Enitan's stone. She changed the subject. "How old were you when you left?"

His response was soft. "Ten. Pretty much right after the floods." Nia did the math. He was only about three years older than she was. He can't have been alone all that time.

"What about your parents?"

Enitan looked forward, a distant expression on his face. "Still there, I imagine. Hey, look, we're at the transphere."

Nia shifted, brushing a curl behind her ear and taking a hint at Enitan's deliberate diversion from the topic. He can't have meant he left his parents at age ten, could he? Everyone had their secrets, and she wondered if he would ever tell her his. Then again, she wouldn't be around long enough to get that familiar with him. Only a month. Less than that, if the stone could help her get out. The thought cast a shade over her.

Nia eyed the cage-like sphere, crossing her arms. "Are there stairs in this castle?"

"Not fond of the transphere?"

She wrinkled her nose. "No. I would rather walk a thousand flights of stairs than use it again."

He grinned, and Nia noticed a dimple for the first time on his left cheek. "You were so polite earlier; I'm surprised you're ok with *stairing*."

"W-what?" Nia stammered. Had she been staring? His smile *was* rather charming.

"It's a joke. Because, you know...staring with your eyes. Except with the steps kind of stairs."

Then Nia really was staring at him, unsure of how to respond to his terrible pun.

Enitan cleared his throat. "So, yeah. To the stairs it is." He paused and gave her a glance that seemed almost shy. "Unless you would rather look around a bit before returning to your room?"

Nia worried her bottom lip. Part of her wanted to return to the solitude of her chambers so she could process everything and get back to the stone. The other part was hesitant to leave Enitan's side. He'd lived in her mind all these years, and it somehow felt as though he would slip away again if she left him now. That fear won out.

"I'd love to look around."

"Do you have any requests?" He bowed and added in a dramatic voice, "What doth the lady wish to see?"

"*The lady* prefers to be called Nia," Nia said with a smile. She should have felt more uneasy given her circumstances, but something about Enitan made it a challenge to be anxious. "What's your favorite spot in the castle?"

"Hmm, let's see," He scratched his chin as he thought. "You know, I don't think you're ready for my actual favorite spot, but we'll work up to it."

"Now you have me curious."

Enitan gave a full grin, making that dimple even more prominent. "Gotta give you something to look forward to if you'll be here a month. For now, I've got another idea."

They exited the castle and entered a breezeway. The fresh air felt foreign on Nia's skin, and she reached on instinct for the cloak that wasn't there. She found herself searching for the stone's influence, even knowing it was tucked away in her room. The sunlight, while pleasantly warm, left her feeling exposed. The urge to melt into the shadows against the wall was close to unbearable, but she forced herself to keep pace at Enitan's side.

The breezeway stretched between two towers of dizzying height. The towers looked as though they housed a lookout point at the top, but Nia couldn't see any way of getting up. As they approached the base of the nearest tower, Nia nearly stumbled. Massive blossoms lay before her; stunning in vibrant shades of magenta and large enough for at least three people to stand in their sunset-orange centers.

Nia reached out to brush against one of the petals but stopped short. "Can I touch it?"

"You mean are you allowed to, or is it safe?" Enitan's grin stretched wide across his face.

"Both."

"Both," he echoed.

She tested the gargantuan blossom with her fingertips. The petal was smooth and soft, like any other flower, which shouldn't have been a surprise. Just because it was enchanted didn't mean it wasn't real.

Enitan strode past Nia, who still marveled at the flower's size, and stepped right onto the center of the blossom. Nia worried about crushing it, but the flower seemed undisturbed. Enitan extended a hand toward Nia. "Join me?"

Nia accepted his assistance with hesitation and stepped forward to meet him at the center of the giant bloom. Enitan leaned down, grabbed one of the petals, and gave it a sharp tug. At once, they were swallowed up. Nia screamed as all of the petals closed around them, shrouding them in pink-tinged shadows.

And then they were moving. Shooting up, up, up at rapid speed. Nia gripped Enitan's sleeve to steady herself, though he seemed completely at ease. Just as quickly as they'd started, they stopped with a jolt. The petals opened, letting the blaze of daylight enter at full force again. She stumbled out onto the stone surface of the tower's top, eager to be free of the flower as quickly as possible. Enitan followed after her with a lazy stride. Nia stared him down.

"What?" he asked, voice laced with feigned innocence.

"Maybe you could warn me next time?"

He laughed and gestured behind Nia. "I just thought you might enjoy the view."

Nia turned to take it in, and her breath was stolen by the vastness of the castle grounds before her. She couldn't even tell where the gardens ended, and the whole space was a maze of courtyards and archways. Her whole village would probably fit and then some. The area surrounding the castle was all rolling hills and towering mountains, currently bathed in yellow sunlight. They were in their own little universe.

"So?" asked Enitan. He seemed as eager as a child as he waited for Nia's response.

"It's wonderful." Wonderful, but still unsettling. It made home feel so far away. So foreign. So small. How little of the world had she seen? The endless sky stretched before her, and she was overcome with a dizzy wave.

Enitan cleared his throat, perhaps uncomfortable with Nia's silence. "So, you're here until the dark moon, huh? That's lunar-cy."

Nia furrowed her brows and gave a slight tilt of her head.

"You know...like, lunacy, but lunar. Because of the moon."

Was this person for real? She couldn't stop the smirk that curved her lips. "The word 'lunacy' already comes from the root 'luna.'"

Enitan's eyebrows shot up. "Pretty *and* smart. No wonder Neilos wants to keep you around for a while."

She might have stumbled over the fact that Enitan had just called her pretty, but the reminder that she was essentially trapped here until the dark moon at Neilos's whims sunk into her, turning her stomach to lead. Not only were the castle and its master complete mysteries to her, but she would have to conceal the stone, and her past, from Enitan the whole time. Her lungs burned, reminding her why it had to be this way.

Nia angled away from him, staring at her shoes. "Could we get back down now?" She wished she had her flask of tea to soften the grit in her voice.

"You okay? I didn't mean to make you uncomfortable."

"Oh, no. Nothing like that," Nia gave a hasty reply, inexplicably wanting to smooth the worry out of his brow. "Just feeling a little homesick, I think."

Enitan gestured toward the flower. "Well, if you're going to be here, might as well make the best of it, right?"

"Right." Nia took careful steps onto the unnaturally large blossom, bracing for the drop.

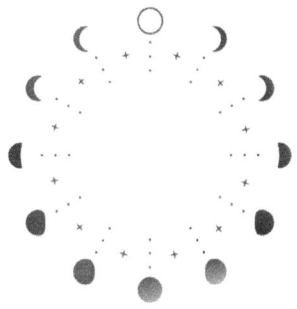

Chapter 6

Twenty-seven days until the Dark Moon

A month.

A month wasn't such a long time. Less than a month, even, since she had already been in the castle a couple of days before waking. However, Nia had seen entire villages fall in less than a day. Her own house had been destroyed in mere minutes. Anything could happen in a month.

Anything.

Enitan had escorted her back to her room so she could prepare for dinner with Neilos. Even with the flowers perfuming the air, her chambers felt smothering in comparison to the spacious halls and breezeways in the rest of the castle. She wished her room at least had a window. Every other space in the castle seemed to be full of them, so why didn't she have one? It was a poor way to convince her she wasn't a prisoner.

Nia retrieved the stone from under her pillow, relishing the warmth of luck rushing through her at last. She couldn't be separated from it again. She loosened the ribbon from her dress and grabbed a sachet she had seen in one of the dresser drawers earlier. She emptied the contents—lavender, from the smell of it—and hid them under the rug. She plopped the stone in the sachet and threaded the ribbon through the loops that drew the little bag closed. Then, she tied the ribbon around her waist beneath her petticoats. No one would be the wiser.

Antonia swept in moments later with yet another glorious gown, although Nia wasn't certain why the change was necessary when what she had on was already finer than anything she had ever owned. Nia played the game anyway, adorning herself in the deep-green velvet dress with gold trim. Thankfully, the skirt was full enough to conceal the stone. Antonia motioned for Nia to sit in a plush vanity chair and began fussing with her hair.

"We'll pull it back some so it won't fall in your face while you dine."

"Thank you." Even though Antonia was a stranger, the caring nature she exuded warmed Nia's chest. "Do you like it here, Antonia?" Nia asked, unable to stop the worrying echoes in the back of her mind.

Antonia strategically pinned back sections of Nia's hair, adding fancy baubles as she went. "It's a lovely place," she said. "My needs are met."

"That's not quite what I asked."

Nia perceived the stiffening in Antonia's hands for just a flicker before she answered, "I like it here, yes."

"Will you be eating with us, too?"

"Only if asked."

Nia sensed Antonia meant only if *Neilos* asked. The idea of dining alone with a man she just met, especially one with so much magic at his disposal, was about as appealing as slaying a unicorn.

"You may go, Antonia."

Nia worked to maintain her polite composure as Neilos dismissed Antonia. It would just be the two of them after all. Her stomach coiled in anxious knots.

She cast her eyes around the room for Enitan, but there was no sign of him. Even if he had been present, they wouldn't have been able to chat while he was on duty, so there was no reason to let disappointment weigh on her so heavily.

"Please be seated, dear lady. It would be uncouth of me to dine while leaving you standing in the corner."

The long dining table only had two chairs—one at each end. Like everything else, the table was ornate, carved with a leaf and vine pattern. Nia seated herself, smoothing the folds of her dress just to give her hands something to do. Neilos sat at the other end, and already Nia felt his piercing eyes upon her. Did humans have such eyes?

Only then did Nia notice the array of goblets before her —gold chalices filled with liquids in jewel tones.

"Please, try some of the wine. Each is exquisite."

No. Nia didn't trust anything set before her. She had never had an alcoholic drink in her life, and she wasn't going to start now. She wanted her wits about her at every moment.

When she didn't reach for a goblet, Neilos said, "Oh, do forgive me for assuming. Perhaps you find drinking disagreeable." He waved his hand in a graceful motion and the goblets disappeared, replaced with a single crystal goblet of clear liquid. "Water isn't without its charm. Simple. Refreshing. The essence of life."

Nia stared at the glass of supposed water, but did not make a move to touch it.

"I see." Neilos sighed. "It's the magic you dislike. Interesting, considering... Well, it does not matter." He clapped his hands twice, and a servant entered.

"A decanter of water for the lady, please. And two glasses."

Why two? Neilos still had his own array of goblets before him.

"Yes, master." The servant bowed her head and exited, leaving them in heavy silence. When the servant returned, she had two crystal glasses with a matching decanter. She set both glasses on the table and poured.

"Drink." Neilos nodded at the servant, who lifted a glass and drank its contents. Then, turning to Nia, Neilos asked, "Does that satisfy you? No tricks. No magic. It is only water."

With slight embarrassment at the fuss over a drink of water, Nia lifted the glass and tipped it to her lips. Surely the stone wouldn't allow her to drink if it was tainted. She inhaled as inconspicuously as possible before she allowed the liquid to reach her tongue. She didn't smell anything unusual, and she *was* thirsty. The water was cool and refreshing, like it came from the purest spring.

Neilos excused the servant and relaxed, leaning back with one arm resting on his chair. If only Nia could replicate the feeling. Her senses had been on high alert from the moment she woke up in the castle, like a flighty bird ready to retreat at the slightest rustle in the bush.

"Now," Neilos said, "what sort of life have you lived to be so suspicious of everything?"

Nia stared at him. How was she supposed to answer that sort of question?

He laughed. "I don't expect you to respond to that. But I do wish you would let your guard down. As this is your home for the next month, you should be able to feel at ease. Go on, ask me anything."

Anything?

"Are you a wizard?" Nia would not let the opportunity slip by without dousing some of the questions burning through her mind. Whether or not she believed his answers was another story, but she had to at least ask.

His perfect lips curved. "I suppose you might say that. But I came to the talent more naturally than some."

Slightly enigmatic. But she expected that. She pressed further. "What about the castle's enchantments?"

"All by my own design. Everything here is because I desired it."

"You must be very powerful." There was no point pretending she wasn't aware of that.

Neilos smiled. "Very observant. I'm sure you understand that level of power also means I have many enemies."

Nia set her glass down. "I think it's the way a person uses power that makes enemies rather than the power itself." She couldn't help herself. Nia mostly kept the stone's power to herself, and she didn't have enemies, at least, none she was aware of.

"And how do you suppose I use my power?" Neilos leaned forward, resting his elbows on the table, fingertips pressed together.

From what Nia could tell, he used his enchantments to make himself and those around him comfortable. He used it for his pleasure and entertainment. He kept himself secluded in a castle to protect those around him, and likely himself. She imagined that, like her and her fortune stone, many would try to take advantage of him. In that, Nia was empathetic.

"You just want to live and not be bothered," Nia conceded. Perhaps his enemies came from those who couldn't manipulate him to their wishes.

"Indeed. Certainly, I have used my power to my advantage. How could I not? But have you seen anything objectionable here?"

The castle was beautiful. The servants and soldiers looked well, and neither Enitan nor Antonia had spoken ill of their master. Nia had been treated with kindness. "No."

"Then let what you see put you at ease. Unwind."

Nia had learned throughout her life to examine more than what she could see. To look past the surface to where sinister things might wait. The hearts of others were full of greed. They only looked out for themselves. She couldn't envision a person with so much power at their disposal using it only for unselfish purposes. She just didn't know what his endgame was yet. But then again, maybe when a person had the world at their fingertips, they had no reason to prey on others. If she was staying in the castle anyway, perhaps she could unlock some of his mysteries.

More servants arrived, this time carrying trays of food: Roasted chicken, glistening with butter and fragrant herbs. Steamed vegetables with garlic. Fluffy rolls. Plump, colorful berries. Nia's mouth watered. When had she eaten last?

"Do I need to have someone taste the food for you, too?" Neilos asked, a hint of laughter in his question.

"No," Nia mumbled.

"Then please, go ahead."

Nia piled what seemed like a reasonable portion of each dish onto her plate, then picked up her fork and knife and sliced carefully into the chicken on her plate. The first bite made her pause.

She should have gotten larger servings.

Nia resisted the urge to glut the way she sometimes did at home. Magala might enjoy seeing her stuff her face, but she wasn't comfortable doing the same in front of Neilos. She kept her bites composed, even though everything she tasted left her tastebuds singing. If this was also the result of some kind of magic, then perhaps it wasn't all bad.

"Go on, have as much as you like," Neilos said, eyeing her empty plate. He had already finished, and now sat lazily swirling his goblet of wine.

"I'm stuffed, thank you." The lie did not taste nearly as good as the food. Nia could easily have had seconds. Or thirds.

"Nia," Neilos said again. The soft way her name glided off his tongue sent butterflies straight to Nia's stomach. "I won't press you with questions tonight, as I'm sure you have a lot to *digest*, in every sense." He laughed, but his pun didn't hit Nia quite like Enitan's had. Neilos leaned forward and watched her as if observing a work of art. "But I do want to know more about you during your stay here. Everything."

Nia's heart drummed faster, and she wasn't sure if it was due to flattery or fear. She had no intention of revealing more than necessary, but she would learn as much as she could about Neilos.

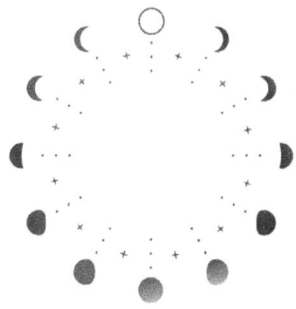

Chapter 7

Twenty-six days until the Dark Moon

The sensation of sunlight tickled Nia awake. No...not sunlight. She had no windows.

More enchantments.

Nia groaned and tucked her head under her blanket. With a full belly and a luxurious bed, she should have been primed for sleep the night before. Instead, her dreams had been full of objects that moved by themselves, goblets of potions, misplaced shadows, and glinting amber eyes—deep sleep finally greeting her in the early morning hours.

A soft knock tapped at her door, followed by the rattling of the knob and, "Miss?"

Nia sprang out of bed and dashed to let Antonia in, hoping she wouldn't take the locked door personally. Nia had secured it the instant the woman left the night before.

Nia observed the opulent gown in Antonia's arms. It looked just as enchanting as everything else in the castle, but she couldn't reconcile with the idea of dressing that way every waking moment. When she wore such unfamiliar clothing, it felt as though she were losing pieces of herself in the cracks and crevices of the castle, and she wanted to retain as much of herself as possible.

"Antonia, I'll wear that to dinner if you want, but do you have anything more simple?" Aside from the foreign aspect of the clothing, requiring assistance to get in and out of every grandiose outfit she wore for the next few weeks was about as appealing as another encounter with the shadowscale.

Antonia wordlessly laid the dress across the foot of the bed and moved to the wardrobe Nia had searched on her first day. It was still empty. With a swift motion, Antonia unfastened a tiny pouch secured to her waist, releasing its string. She grabbed a fistful of fine gold powder and tossed it into the wardrobe, closed its doors again, and waited. When she opened the wardrobe again, it revealed an array of clothing.

"Would any of these suit you better, miss?"

Nia rushed over to examine the new choices: several breezy cotton dresses of various lengths, tunics, blouses, pants. While more practical than the stately gowns, they boasted a simple beauty with their rich colors and lightly embroidered details. So many choices!

"If you could do this," Nia couldn't help but ask, "Why did you have to leave to get my clothes yesterday?"

Antonia glanced at the floor and smoothed the front of her apron. "The master wishes to personally select your attire for certain occasions. The wardrobe seeks to match your own preferences, but I believe he wants to show you what the castle has to offer."

So, Neilos really did think Nia's attire was inferior. And, she had to admit everything she owned was rather humble in comparison to what had been presented to her yesterday. But why was the castle's master so intent on keeping her there?

"Are the clothes not to your liking?" Antonia spoke too quickly, her tone slightly pitched. "I could fetch something different." She moved as though to close the wardrobe.

"These are perfect," Nia assured, staying Antonia's outstretched arm. The poor woman must have thought Nia's annoyance at Neilos was actually disapproval of the clothing. "Thank you, Antonia." Nia selected a royal blue tunic and black pants, making sure the tunic had pockets. She went to the washroom to change in private and when she returned Antonia was making up the bed.

The stone was still under her pillow.

"Oh, I can do that." Nia hurried to assist and managed to slip the stone into her fist before Antonia brushed her away.

"Please, let me. It gives me something to do."

"If you're sure." The idea of letting someone serve her in such a way was foreign, but if it was what Antonia wanted…

Nia pocketed the stone and waited, shifting from one foot to the other. Neilos insisted she was a guest, but she didn't feel at liberty to leave the room without an escort. How was one supposed to behave in a castle?

Antonia finished making the bed and turned to see Nia still standing there, like a school child waiting for instructions from her teacher.

"Are you hungry, miss?"

"Yes, a little." Her mouth watered of its own accord, recalling the phantom flavors of the delicious food she had eaten the night before. Would breakfast be equally tantalizing?

"Master Neilos usually takes breakfast in his bedroom, but said you are welcome to use the dining room if you would like. Otherwise, I can bring it here."

"Here is fine," Nia said quickly. Thank goodness she wouldn't be expected to share every meal with Neilos.

"Great galloping unicorns," Nia groaned. "I ate way too much."

Again.

She had excused Antonia, and with nobody present to hold her accountable, Nia had consumed her breakfast like a bear preparing for winter. While there were no other humans in the room, she could almost feel the furniture judging her gluttony. She patted the sage-green velvet chaise she lazily sprawled upon and laughed. "Well, this is an enchanted castle. Perhaps you *are* aware of me." The thought terrified her just as quickly as it amused her, and she shook out her shoulders in an attempt to brush the idea away.

"Now, what's my first move..." she mused to herself. *Just* herself, she assured, with another glance at the room's motionless trimmings. Neilos kept his secrets close to his heart, and she had been given a rare chance to pry some of them away while staying in the castle. If he proved untrustworthy, she would rather uncover that herself and escape as quickly as possible. Maybe she could even find another way to heal herself without Neilos's aid and leave sooner.

She plucked the stone out of her pocket and rolled it in her hands, drawing comfort from the familiarity of it. Luck was on her side, and as long as she kept her stone secret, she would always have the upper hand. Nobody could know.

Not even Enitan.

Her insides pinched with guilt. She owed him her life. Returning the stone to him was the right thing to do. But she didn't know enough to discern what type of person he was now. She wouldn't put the stone in the hands of anyone with devious intentions. Apart from that, if she had any hope of forming an honest relationship with him, the stone couldn't be involved. Alex's face flashed through her mind, speaking gentle words and sneaking up on her like a fox in a hen house. Would Enitan be the same if he knew?

Manes and tails...what was she even thinking? How could she entertain the thought of any kind of relationship with Enitan? She'd only just met him.

She stood with haste, heat prickling her cheeks. The windowless room seemed to close in on her regardless of its spacious size.

She shoved the stone in her pocket and slipped into the hallway, searching for signs of life. Nobody said she had to stay in her chambers, so why did she feel the need to keep her steps silent and her shadow close to the wall? The urge to slink around was instinctual after so many years spent maintaining a low profile. Nia stood straight, shoulders back, and walked like she knew what she was doing. The stone hidden away in her pocket further buoyed up her confidence.

The castle felt larger than it was before. Could enchanted castles grow? She should have asked Antonia or Enitan to explain a basic layout of the structure—she might have had some idea of where to go. The only thing she knew for certain was that she wasn't going to take the transphere again. She headed toward the stairs. The stone walls left her desperate for fresh air.

When she entered the breezeway on the first floor, she caught a glimpse of Enitan down the hallway. Her mood brightened. The moment felt a bit serendipitous; she *had* just been thinking of him after all, and her hand slipped subconsciously to her pocket.

Could it be more than a chance encounter?

"Enitan!" she called, throwing caution to the wind. She didn't want him to think of her as the moody girl she had been when they parted ways on the first day.

He stopped and turned, giving her a wave and a full smile that stirred something in her.

And then he kept walking.

Maybe not so serendipitous after all.

She huffed out a breath. He had work to do. That was fine. She couldn't detain him as her personal escort around the castle. Nia tossed her hair over her shoulder and convinced herself it didn't matter. It didn't.

She broke through the main doors into the sunlight, and any disappointment she felt a moment ago was snuffed out of existence. Nia was used to fairy gardens in the forest, which of course, had ample beauty and charm. But this was another sort of exotic. She couldn't possibly name all the flowers stretched before her.

It was a whole gradient of colors. She didn't even realize so many shades of pink and yellow and purple existed. How did Neilos do this? Was all of it magic, or did he just have the right resources to procure all the beauties of the natural world?

Nia started forward, eager to take in as much as possible. The air had the most heavenly smell, like a perfume shop with nothing but her favorite aromas. Each section she passed through brought another euphoric inhalation.

Neilos was proving to be an ever more complicated puzzle. He said he had enemies, but why? Was it due to the threat of his power? He seemed to use it for his own pleasure, mostly. And that of the servants, she supposed. That might be enough to warrant intense jealousy, but not enemies. There had to be something more lurking beneath the surface.

A flash of orange in one of the flower bushes a distance ahead caught her eye. She focused on it, recognizing the striking white spots and dark lines of monarch butterfly wings. There were so many! Delighted, she moved closer to get a better look at the beautiful, winged insects.

Nia let out a sharp breath and stumbled backward. They weren't butterflies—at least, not anymore. Shredded wings. Dislocated antennae. Mangled stick legs. What she believed to be a butterfly trove was in fact a spider's web filled with evidence of the futile struggles of its victims.

The air turned heavy and cloying, and Nia suddenly wasn't sure she wanted to be in the garden.

As she turned to retreat, Nia bumped into someone small. "Oh, I'm so sorry. I—" The words froze on her lips. A fragile boy stood before her, probably no more than ten years old, with his head shaved completely bald. He had a bandage tied at an angle over one eye and a mere stump where his left leg should be. He balanced with the help of a wooden cane.

Nia recomposed herself. "I didn't see you. I hope I didn't hurt you."

The boy flashed a wide grin that showed all his teeth and gestured to his covered eye. "I understand. I don't see much either."

"Oh! I really didn't mean—"

He roared with laughter. "It's ok. I'm used to people staring. It's not every day you come across one like me." He held out his tiny hand. "I'm Spencer."

Nia gave his hand a cautious shake. The boy looked so delicate. "Lovely to meet you, Spencer. I'm Nia." Judging by the gleam of mischief in his eyes, Nia had a feeling Spencer didn't have trouble finding his way around the castle. If anything, he probably got into more than he should. "How long have you been here, Spencer?"

"Just a few weeks now. One of the soldiers saw me and took pity." He made an exaggerated pout and slumped over, looking pathetic, then straightened and released a wry laugh. Perhaps the soldier's pity had been wasted.

"Can you suggest anything to see here?" Nia asked, although she doubted they shared the same taste in entertainment.

Spencer eyed her, his expression curious. "What are you looking for?"

"Just something to do." It would have been more honest to say she was looking for secrets, but she couldn't say that to this child.

"Well, I would say there's more to see in the gardens, but it looked like I caught you leaving. There's also the library." The child smirked and adapted a more casual lean on his cane. "But if *I* were you, I'd visit the seventh floor."

"What's on the seventh floor?"

With a widening grin, Spencer replied, "Go up there and find out."

In spite of his appearance, Nia sensed Spencer was one for mischief. If he said she should go to the seventh floor, she should probably do exactly the opposite. She was looking for information—not trouble. Even so, she tucked that bit of information away for later.

"I'll consider it," Nia replied. "In case I don't work my way up to the top today, is there anything else you recommend?"

Spencer huffed out a breath, as though disappointed. "If you're not willing to take any risks in this castle, then no. You'd better stick to the library. Fourth floor. Good luck."

Nia gaped as Spencer tapped his cane on the ground and floated up a few inches off the floor. "Neat trick, huh? Neilos knows his magic, I'll give him that. See you around, if you're *lucky*." With that, Spencer was whisked off deeper into the gardens, magic cane leading the way.

An irrational sense of irritation lingered after the encounter. Had she imagined his emphasis on the word "lucky?" Besides that, She was pretty sure she'd just been accused of being boring and unadventurous by a small child. Then again, thinking of Spencer's appearance, most people might seem boring by comparison. What stories could he tell?

Another whiff of too-sweet fragrance hit Nia, making her head spin. She rushed back inside the castle and to the stairwell she'd just come from.

Part of her wanted to ignore the fourth floor just to do the opposite of what that brazen child suggested. On the other hand, the library was a wiser choice for collecting information without drawing attention to herself at the outset.

She passed servants bustling about who gave her a quick glance before resuming their duties. She should learn their names. Memorize their faces. It must take a lot of work to run a place of this size, and they deserved some recognition for it.

Nia heard a rattling noise—the clang of metal on metal—and looked up to see several covered silver trays descending the stairs from the next level up and floating toward her. She yelped and hopped to the side as one nearly collided with her.

"Whoa! Sorry, didn't see ya there!" The lanky woman who orchestrated the parade of trays stopped, wide-eyed. She ran a hand through her crop of ginger hair and her large gold hoop earrings swayed. "Oh, you're the latest catch!"

"Latest catch?" How many "catches" did the castle take in?

"Forgive my bluntness. The master takes folks in now 'n again. Usually, the lost ones with nowhere else to go." Not pausing for Nia's response, the woman extended her hand. "I'm Uma. You?"

Nia grasped Uma's hand, which bore the look and feel of leather. Working hands. "I'm Nia. It's nice to meet you." Eyeing the trays, Nia asked, "Do you work with the chef?" She wanted a chance to send her compliments.

Uma grinned, her whole face crinkling. "I *am* the chef. Don't normally run the food myself, but the usual lad is unavailable. And if you'll excuse me, I'm runnin' behind."

Before Nia could compliment Uma's cooking or ask how she controlled the floating trays, the chef disappeared down the stairs with her parade of culinary decadence. Nia resolved to find the kitchens later and talk to Uma again.

The fourth floor took Nia by surprise. It seemed to be reserved for the library exclusively, with only one grand door and no other accents or artwork. The entrance was framed in a rustic stone archway and even with the door closed she was sure she caught the scent of old paper and aging tales. Well, what was wrong with spending the day with books? Nothing. She loved books. Fairytales and history could be just as exciting as...whatever was on the seventh floor. She paused with one foot in the library's archway as Spencer's look of disappointment shadowed her mind once more.

No. She wasn't going to be coerced into something that was probably a very bad idea by a little rabble rouser. She had gotten through most of life by leading people to believe she was uninteresting, and she wasn't about to jeopardize that now just to prove a point. The stone warmed in her pocket as though agreeing.

She reached for the brass knob of the door and opened it to reveal the largest library she had ever seen. It spanned the space of Ravenskeep's entire town square, and then some. A person could get lost for days. Book spines in every color from bold jewel tones to soft pastels beckoned to her from the expanse of shelves. The smell of parchment and ink hit her stronger, bringing with it a calm sense of nostalgia. Perhaps this was just what she needed.

She crossed under the archway onto the densely carpeted, emerald-green floor. It was the exact shade of Enitan's uniform.

There was plenty of green in the castle. Why was Enitan's uniform the thing that came to her mind first? *Stop thinking about him*, she chided. She forced her thoughts back to the present and marched deeper into the library.

A young lady with a frizzy braid and a few uncontained curls dozed off behind an executive desk. She had a stack of hardbacks beside her along with a quill and what looked to be a thick record book.

Nia hated to disturb her when she looked so peaceful, but not knowing what else to do, she softly said, "Excuse me?"

The desk's occupant didn't stir, so Nia gave a gentle shake to her bony shoulder.

The young lady's bespectacled eyes flew open. "Oh, goodness! I'm sorry!" She threw her hand to her chest. "Hardly anyone comes here besides the master, and he usually visits in the evenings. How can I help you?"

"Are you the librarian?"

"Yes indeed." She stood and tucked a few straying hairs back into her braid. "I'm Perla. I'd be happy to help you find what you're looking for."

What *was* Nia looking for? In a castle overflowing with mystery, it was hard to know where to begin. "I actually didn't have anything in mind. Do you have any suggestions?"

Something in Perla seemed to stutter, but it passed so quickly Nia brushed it off. The young librarian gave a wide smile. "Perhaps you would simply like to browse? Master Neilos said you could read anything you like."

So, he'd given the librarian instructions regarding her as well. It seemed everyone in the castle had heard of her. The idea was unsettling, but Nia thanked Perla all the same and set off to explore the pages in this great maze of books.

Nia surmised that her entire village didn't have even a fraction of the number of books housed here. Some of them appeared ancient, with weathered leather covers and faded titles. Others looked as though she might be the first to crack them open. She wandered through the rows in a sort of haze. Could one have too many books? They were so numerous she wasn't sure where to begin in choosing one.

At once, Nia was forced to a hard stop as her body smacked into an invisible wall. A shimmer of energy trickled in a wave before her.

"Those are the enchanted books," the librarian said. "Master Neilos prefers them behind a ward for safekeeping—they get a bit temperamental at times. But if you're interested in reading one, I can get whatever you like. What subject are you looking for?"

"Nothing in particular." Nia was simultaneously afraid and curious. She felt an enticing pull towards the books and their softly shimmering covers. She'd tried many things to heal herself, but she'd never had access to a magic library. Could one of these volumes hold a cure? "It's really ok for me to look at these?"

Perla knitted her brows together, and once more it seemed she had to consider her words carefully. "Well, they are only books, and Neilos did say *anything*. I don't see why not. I guess we'll know for sure in a minute."

What did she mean by that?

The young librarian produced a glass orb about the size of an apple from behind her desk. The inside of the object crackled with blue lightning. Perla threw it towards the enchanted books and the sound of broken glass filled the room.

"Well, I guess it's ok for you to look, then."

Nia raised an inquisitive brow at her, but Perla didn't elaborate further.

The orb floated back into Perla's hands. Nia peered at it, paying close attention to where Perla stashed it away once more. Could an orb like that break through other enchantments? She tucked the thought away in a pocket of her mind to revisit later.

Perla gestured toward the books. "You can go in now. I'll wait here."

Nia took a step forward then stopped. "It won't close me in, will it?"

"The ward stays inactive for a few minutes. If it does reactivate, I'll just open it again. Nothing to worry about. Take your time."

Something about Perla's reassurances made Nia worry even more. Nevertheless, she stepped through. The scent in this area was different, like freshly fallen snow. Even the air had a sharpness to it, but she didn't feel cold. She could practically taste the magic as she examined the shelves before her, determining where to start.

Some of the titles were no more than symbols, or in languages she couldn't decipher. Those would be of no use to her. She reached for one indigo volume but pulled her hand back quickly when she saw the words, "Dark Curses." No, thank you.

She whirled when she detected movement out of the corner of her eye, but all she saw was more books. A pretty teal cover caught her attention and when she reached out it fluttered, pages stirring like leaves in the wind.

"What—" before she could draw back again the book flew into Nia's hand. She looked at the title: *How to Curse Ancient Objects*. What was it with Neilos and curses? She made an effort to stuff the book back onto the shelf, but it remained fixed in her hand as though it was its own agent. Another book, this time in shimmering gold, jumped into her other hand.

"No," Nia said, trying to shake the book from her hand. The enchanted curiosity that lit inside her moments before had been snuffed out. "I think I'm done here."

Books flew off the shelves, oscillating around her until all she could hear was the wild rustling of pages, a flurry of wind across her skin as they piled around her. Her breath left her lungs in a panic. Was the stone still working? This wasn't the sort of thing that usually happened to her.

"Oh dear!" She heard Perla's fearful cry. "I haven't seen this before. Master Neilos!"

The sound of Perla's running steps fading away barely registered through the chaotic flapping around her. She would have to wait for Neilos to come to her rescue. Again. Nia let out a frustrated groan and thrashed at the books. Her efforts were rewarded with dozens of paper cuts across her arm. It was useless. She crouched and covered her head.

Her breathing slowed as she waited, and her mind cleared. The books that cocooned her weren't pummeling her. Why? The buzz of their energy tingled across her skin, and she sensed the tone of their magic. They weren't angry. They were just...excited? Nia's fear dissipated.

A cold wind swirled around Nia, and she squeezed her eyes shut. When the wind settled, she opened her eyes. Neilos had his arms outstretched, the books answering his unspoken command as they resumed their places on the shelves. The castle's master wore an expression of intrigue.

"I apologize for my temperamental books."

Nia stood and shook her head. "I don't think they wanted to hurt me."

"No," Neilos mused. "They seem to find you compelling."

"I can't imagine why." Nia could think of no explanation for the books' excitement in her presence, unless they were responding to the stone. Without the stone, there was nothing noteworthy about her at all.

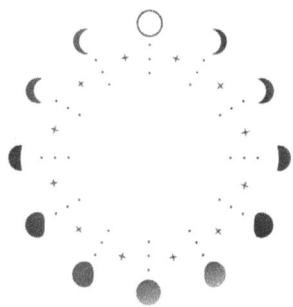

Chapter 8

Twenty-five days until the Dark Moon

Nia planned to return to the library the following afternoon, but when she saw Enitan in the courtyard from the fourth-floor windows, she resolved not to let him slip away. She rushed toward the stairs but stopped short. If she wanted to catch him in time she would have to toughen up and take the transphere. She turned around and ran into someone.

Again.

"You have an atrocious sense of your surroundings, don't you?"

The child did not speak like a child. But perhaps he had been forced to grow up quickly when...whatever happened to him happened.

"Spencer," Nia said flatly. "I'm sorry."

He raised the eyebrow over his un-patched eye. "You don't sound sorry."

She crossed her arms, unsure why the boy got under her skin so easily. "I'm in a hurry."

His eye twinkled. "Going to do something dull again? Or following my advice to see the seventh floor, perhaps?"

"No. And for your information the library is a splendid destination. Even the books love me."

She stalked off towards the transphere before he could make another snarky comment, but that didn't spare her from the sound of him snickering behind her.

When Nia wobbled off the transphere, Enitan was still in the courtyard, leaning against one of the stone walls. His posture was slack, and he didn't bother to stifle a wide yawn. He was clearly oblivious to his surroundings, and Nia saw a fun opportunity.

Mischief curled her lips as she snuck up alongside him, and she bit back a laugh so she wouldn't give herself away.

She stood on her tiptoes and leaned into his ear. "Careful, or I'll tell Neilos you're sleeping on the job."

He startled, which was exactly the reaction she'd hoped for. She giggled and he shot her a mock glare, but his ears were red.

"I wasn't sleeping on the job. I was only *thinking* about sleeping on the job." His expression changed and his dimple flashed. Warmth flooded through Nia that had nothing to do with the stone.

Now that she thought of it, she couldn't feel the stone at all. She ran her hand over her pocket and furrowed her brow. It was there. But why couldn't she sense it?

Conscious of Enitan's eyes on her, she leaned against the wall at his side, hoping she looked as relaxed as he did. She directed her gaze towards the gardens and pushed the stone from her mind. "What are you doing now? Looking for prowlers in the petunias?"

He glanced down at her. "I finished my guard shift in—" he stopped, seeming to have caught himself saying something he shouldn't have. "I finished my morning guard shift. Now I float around the castle wherever I want, looking for anything out of the ordinary."

Nia wrinkled her nose. "There was a suspicious little boy near the library."

Enitan's eyebrows pinched together. "Little boy? Oh, do you mean Spencer? He's harmless."

"But annoying."

"So annoying," Enitan agreed with a grin. They shared a laugh and Nia found that even when the sound of her laughter stopped, the evidence of it lingered in the smile on her face. She pushed off from the wall and crouched down to pluck up a stray twig from the cobblestones. She twirled it between her fingers and glanced up at Enitan. "So, you can go wherever you want right now?"

"More or less."

She brushed one finger back and forth over the twig, unable to maintain eye contact. "Are you allowed to have company?"

She didn't want to irritate him by inviting herself to be his shadow, but she ached to know more about him. Something about him blanketed her overactive nerves in security. It was entirely different than being around Neilos, who made her so flighty.

Enitan bent down beside her and inexplicably, her breath caught. He took the twig—which she had been absently shredding—and cast it aside.

She gave him a wry smile to conceal her fluttering emotions. "How dare you? That was a special twig."

"I just couldn't stand to see you fidgeting like that. If you want some company, you only have to say so."

His words were sincere, free of any teasing or malice. For a moment their eyes locked and Nia's heart beat a little faster. She needed to be careful. If she formed any ties to this place, she was likely to become hopelessly knotted and tangled in them. Even if Enitan felt safe, she knew close to nothing about him. How much remained of the boy who saved her life and sacrificed the fortune stone?

Nia sprang to her feet and brushed off her clothes, determined to be more cunning in learning about him without lowering her guard. "Where do you want to go? Can I see your favorite place yet?"

Before he could answer, a loud roar split the air.

"What was that?" Nia scanned the area for the source of the feral sound. She didn't see any creatures, and certainly none big enough to make a noise of that caliber. Her pulse quickened and she whipped her gaze to the skies, fearing the shadowscale had caught up to her at last. But there was nothing there but blue and clouds.

Enitan didn't seem frightened, but he grimaced. "I think I know where we have to go next. Follow me."

He secured Nia's hand in his. While the touch was gentle, it sent a current through her. How could he be so casual about something that left her emotions spinning? Her mind raced back to years ago when that same hand brought her up out of the dreaded river. Part of her had a desperate desire to ask if he remembered, but she bit back the words.

Enitan led her through the gardens. The grand trellises, trees and flowers went much further back than Nia expected. At last, they arrived outside a set of wrought-iron gates. They were tall, and so overgrown with vines that Nia couldn't see anything inside.

Enitan released her hand, and the absence of his touch immediately weighed on her.

"This is the menagerie." Enitan's voice was weary, as though someone had taken his words and bogged them down with mud.

"Don't you like animals?" Nia asked.

He released a short laugh. "I don't like *magical* animals. I'll put it that way."

Magical animals...

"Does Neilos have unicorns?" Nia couldn't help herself. She felt childish for asking, but if the end result was getting to see a unicorn, she hardly cared.

"Unicorns aren't real."

Nia gave Enitan a look that would wither a flower. "Don't you dare say that."

He held his hands up in playful surrender. "Whoa. Ok. They are totally, completely real."

"Of course they are."

The gates creaked as Enitan pulled them open and a breeze blew the scent of rust and dirt in Nia's direction. Enitan paused. "You don't have to go in if you don't want to. Most of the animals are probably just *lion* around anyway."

Nia strode past him, pretending his pun didn't exist. "I like animals."

As she walked through the gate, Enitan shouted, "Wait!"

An unfamiliar, gruff voice shouted an obscenity.

A massive blur of silver rushed straight towards her.

In an instant Nia was knocked to the ground. She processed the flash of stripes as she prepared to be mangled by the nightstripe's fangs and claws. But the pain didn't come. Instead, her face was battered around by the creature's great tongue.

"Get off, you brute!" The gruff voice sounded nearby and the nightstripe stopped licking Nia's face so it could turn towards the voice's owner with a snarl. A tall, burly man in leather armor stood in Nia's view. He threw glittering powder into the nightstripe's face, and the beast sneezed, blinked a few times, then collapsed to the ground, its breathing heavy.

"Put that sword away, boy." The man growled. "The girl was never in danger."

Only then did Nia notice Enitan with his sword drawn, looking shaken. "I hate those things. My cousin lost his hand to one."

"Your cousin was lucky not to lose more. But this one only wanted to play," the man said.

Nia wiped her face on her sleeve, shuddering at the slimy texture of the nightstripe's saliva. She would need a wash basin as soon as possible.

"How can you be so sure?" Nia asked. It would take a mountain of confidence for her to ever assume a nightstripe was only playing.

The man regarded her. "Its ears were up. They're only in an aggressive mood if the ears are pulled back."

Nia imagined the tufted ears of the nightstripe that guarded the patch of silverfern near her home. Had she ever seen them down? She had never once thought of the creature as playful.

The man extended a hand to Nia to help her to her feet. Enitan looked abashed for a moment, as though thinking he should have done that already.

"Name's Aldric. I'm the beast keeper of the castle. Sorry for the rough introduction to the menagerie." He shot Enitan a nasty look. "The nightstripe was out for exercise. Someone should have told me to expect visitors."

Nia cut in quickly to defend Enitan. "We heard a roar. Enitan was coming to make sure everything was ok, and I barged in on my own."

Aldric gave a mighty roll of his eyes. "Just that dragon being temperamental again. Can't blame it, I suppose."

Nia's eyes grew round. "You have a dragon here?"

"Neilos has just about everything here," Enitan replied, still eyeing the nightstripe with suspicion even though it was fast asleep.

Nia swallowed. "Does he have a unicorn?" She meant the question to sound casual, but it came out slightly breathless. Even though she'd asked Enitan earlier, she thought the gamekeeper might have a different answer since he was the one looking after the creatures.

Aldric's reply was curt. "No. That's one thing he'll likely never have."

Strangely, this didn't hit Nia with as much disappointment as she expected. As much as she wanted to see a unicorn, it would have felt wrong to cage one.

The dragon gave another terrible roar.

"C'mon." Aldric motioned for Enitan and Nia to follow him. "Let's see what has the big crybaby worked up."

Nia attempted to get a full view of the creatures in cages as they worked their way towards the dragon, but they were shy and elusive. She only caught flashes of rainbow feathers, pearly scales, and patches of wild fur.

They arrived at a large pit, covered by a metal grate. The odor of sulfur and smoke lingered in the air.

Aldric waved a hand. "Go on. Take a look."

Nia took a few tentative steps forward and peered down at the creature inside. It was big, but not as big as she had always imagined dragons. Its scales were rust red and its great wings lay folded across its spiked back. The dragon stared up at Nia and gave a little wiggle, and Nia sensed its excitement, just as she had with the books. It didn't appear to be injured or in any sort of distress. Why had it been roaring?

Nia jumped as Aldric clapped her on the shoulder. "You've seen a dragon now. Best to get you both out of the menagerie before the nightstripe wakes. He'll be on edge at first and they can be nasty when they're out of sorts."

Enitan shuddered. "Yeah, let's go."

As they stepped away, the dragon roared again.

Nia rushed back and it stared up at her once more. Curiosity sparked in its eyes. Its feelings seemed more settled when they were near.

"I think it's lonely," she stated.

"How can you tell?" Enitan's question was all curiosity with no hint of skepticism.

Nia had no explanation for him. "I just know."

Aldric released a guffaw. "It's not lonely. It's just hungry. Hold up a moment."

Aldric disappeared and returned a few moments later with a massive ham hock. He opened a flap in the grate and tossed it in. The dragon snapped the meat up without hesitation, seemingly mollified.

"See?" Aldric dusted off his hands, his face smug. "Now, get out of here."

Nia and Enitan left the menagerie and returned to the gardens, but nothing could stop Nia's heart from pinching when the dragon's bellowing began a few moments later.

Nia fished for something to say to the master of the castle. The heavy silence with the weight of uncertainty between them was both uncomfortable and unnerving. She couldn't stomach the thought of enduring it at every dinner for the rest of the month. Enitan stood guard at the door, once again wearing his stoney mask. He became a completely different person when Neilos was around. Every now and then Nia stole a glance at him, but he remained stoic. His presence somehow made conversation with Neilos even more awkward.

The stone rested cold, tucked once more in the pouch beneath her petticoats, which further diverted Nia's thoughts. Could the castle block its magic? She was certain it was working when she first awakened. She had sensed it then. She tried to recall if she had felt it at all today, but most of the time she wasn't actively thinking about it, so it was difficult to judge.

For his part, Neilos was polite and didn't seem to mind that Nia had nothing to say. Finally, he asked, "What did you amuse yourself with today? Is the castle to your liking?"

"It is," Nia replied, perhaps too quickly as she broke out of her musings about the stone. "I explored the gardens. I hope you don't mind." She couldn't bring herself to mention the menagerie and the woeful dragon inside. A weight settled on her heart when she thought about it. For a moment she worried Enitan might interject and reveal all that had transpired, but he did not.

Instead, Neilos continued, his voice light. "Oh, of course I don't mind. The gardens are there to be enjoyed. What did you think of them?"

"They are wonderful. Did it take a long time to grow and design them?"

He paused to take an indulgent gulp from one of his many goblets before replying. "Not as long as it would for most. I have a particular talent for manipulating plants. Over the years I have created new varieties."

"So, they aren't all natural?" Nia had suspected that.

"No, not anymore. When they first started to grow, I used only what I could find and expanded it. But I progressed to creating something entirely new with my abilities."

More silence.

"Do you have a favorite flower?" Neilos asked.

"The roses were lovely."

"No, not from my garden. What is *your* favorite flower?"

Nia's fork scraped against her plate as she entirely missed the roasted cauliflower she was aiming for. "Oh. I like daffodils."

"Daffodils," Neilos mused. "I'm surprised your tastes aren't rarer. But I suppose I see their appeal."

"I suspect you prefer the rarities?" She thought of the creatures in the menagerie. Of the lonely dragon.

"The rarest I can find. Or create."

What would Neilos do if he knew Nia had a fortune stone in her possession? Trinkets didn't come much rarer than that. Of course he would want it. And there, Nia realized the reason Neilos might have enemies. Maybe his enemies were those who sought to take what he had? After all, she had come across many people in her lifetime who wanted her stone. She hadn't considered them "enemies," exactly, but things might be different if what she had could be taken by force.

Nia shivered, and hoped Neilos didn't notice.

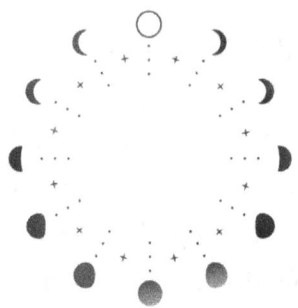

Chapter 9

Twenty-four days until the Dark Moon

Before she even opened her eyes, Nia sensed a change in her room. The air was somehow fresher and more fragrant. She lifted her lids and let herself adjust to the mysterious light source that mimicked the bright morning sun. She blinked. Then blinked again to be sure she was seeing properly. Was she dreaming?

The flower vases on either side of her bed were filled with daffodils of every variety, a happy medley of whites, peaches, yellows, and golds. More than the vases, however, Nia's entire room was adorned with various arrangements of her favorite flower. It almost put the blooming hills by her cottage in the springtime to shame. The comforting aroma whisked Nia back to her childhood days when she would gather the flowers and dance with the fairies in the first beams of dawn.

It must have been Neilos. It was no coincidence these flowers made their appearance the very morning after she revealed her flower of choice. Her view of the blooms shifted at once from delight to suspicion.

"Oh my! What an enchanting room you have this morning." Antonia swept in holding two colorful tunics. "Either of these appeal to you, miss?"

Nia glanced once more around her floral dreamland of a room. She tuned her emotions to the stone resting under her pillow and found its warm current of magic encouraging her. Regardless of where the flowers came from, the adornments made her feel more elegant and with the stone working again, her spirits lifted. "Actually, I think I might wear one of the dresses today."

Nia blessed the stone for her avoidance of Neilos that morning. Etiquette suggested she should thank him for the flowers, but something nagged inside of her, saying it would be a bad idea to encourage that kind of behavior from him. She needed to clear her head.

She found her way to the garden again, hoping the early morning air would do her some good. If possible, it was even more spectacular in the fresh morning sun. The bubbling of the fountains soothed her nerves, and the perfumed air further calmed her with its invitation to breathe deeper. The aroma didn't feel as stifling as it previously had. She walked, admiring the many flowers, and stopped short at a bush of lilac-colored roses. Oh, they were lovely!

"Those were tricky. It's surprisingly difficult to master that shade of purple."

Nia jumped and searched for the source of the voice. Neilos was just a few yards off, sitting on the edge of one of the courtyard's many fountains. His arm was extended, but not towards her. A sharp caw echoed from above and a large raven descended to perch on his sleeve. Nia ducked as two more soared over her head, one landing on Neilos's shoulder and the other at his feet.

Still there, stone?

It was. Her desire to avoid the master of the castle must not have been clear enough.

"You surprised me," Nia said at last.

"My apologies."

Nia had to admit, Neilos himself was quite a sight. His vibrant red hair and striking features made him just as exotic as the flora surrounding him. The golden-yellow robes he wore only added to the effect. He seemed less like a human and more like a creature out of a fairytale.

But beautiful things in fairy tales often turned out to have teeth and claws.

"That's a lovely dress." Neilos flicked his wrist and produced food for the ravens, seemingly out of nowhere. Their midnight wings flapped furiously as they dove for it. "That orchid shade suits you very well."

"Thank you," Nia said, feeling a touch warmer than the weather called for. She idly grasped one of the rose buds in her hands, examining it as though it was her life's work to study it.

"I wish you would relinquish your suspicions toward my magic and instead embrace what it has to offer you. There is something about you...the magic seeks you. It's very appealing."

The branch of the rose bush bounced as the bud slipped from Nia's fingertips. She quickly drew her hands to her sides. He found her appealing? Or rather, his magic did, whatever that was supposed to mean.

He gave a soft, silky laugh. The ravens cawed, as though joining in his amusement. "Has magic done you some ill? Or are you not yet ready to reveal that to me?"

Nia considered how to answer him. Contrary to his thoughts, magic had actually been quite kind to Nia for the most part. The fortune stone took care of her. Magical creatures, with the exception of petty pixies and the shadowscale, had been her friends. It wasn't the magic itself that she didn't trust—it was its wielder. Even at that moment, he was piercing her with those eyes, and Nia had no idea of his intentions.

"The magic is lovely," Nia answered at last. "If not a bit unpredictable."

"So, it's a matter of control?"

"Something like that." Nia shifted her gaze to one of the ravens as it eyed her with a curious tilt of its head. "I like a simple life. Magic is anything but."

"Neither are you, it seems."

Now it was Nia's turn to laugh. "I'm not so complicated."

"We'll see, won't we?"

He left her feeling completely disarmed. A change of subject was in order. "Thank you for the daffodils, by the way." Her voice sounded more like an accusation than genuine thanks, but she hoped he wouldn't notice.

Neilos gave a light scoff and then rested his chin on his hands, smiling. "I wish I could take full credit for that. Enitan suggested daffodils for your morning bouquet after overhearing our dinner conversation. I merely amplified the idea."

Enitan? Butterflies took flight in Nia's stomach, and the sensation caught her off guard. The stone warmed at last, as though saying, "you're welcome" for this new bit of information. There were no warring emotions this time and the blush on her cheeks was clearly one of delight. She checked herself and steadied her expression as she saw Neilos turn cold.

"Tell me," he asked, "Have you spent much time with him?"

"No." At least in this, Nia could tell the full truth, although she found herself wishing it was different. They had only spent a few hours of her time here in one another's company. "Should I not?"

Neilos pressed his fingertips together and closed his eyes in contemplation. "He is busy with his duties. While I'm certain he would welcome the distraction, it is better he avoid it."

"I see." Of course. The one person she thought might make the month more bearable, the one person she could relax around, was the one she wouldn't be allowed to see.

"However," Neilos said, "It's to your discretion. As I said, you are no prisoner here."

While the words seemed cordial, Nia could detect the darkening in his mood. Could this be jealousy? Nia's heart thumped at the thought of being a point of contention between two men. On the surface, she had to admit the idea was a little thrilling. But she was quite certain Neilos's jealousy was not something she wanted.

Neilos stood. "I sense you may like some time alone with your thoughts, so I'll leave you to them. I must say, you are a lovely sight in the garden."

He strode away, not waiting for a reply, which was fortunate because Nia couldn't begin to formulate one.

Manes and tails.

Nia wasn't going to be fooled by heart-stopping smiles and pretty words. Not from Enitan. Certainly not from Neilos. She fortified the fortress of her heart, at once fearful of how easily her defenses had started to crumble.

The ravens took sudden flight, making a racket as they went. Nia envied their wings, feeling even more trapped in defiance of Neilos's assurance that she wasn't. She had an unsettling notion that if she chose to spend time with Enitan, someone was going to pay for it. And spending more time with Neilos was a dangerous game. She couldn't allow herself to get too complacent here. Her chest suddenly felt too tight.

But she was resourceful when it came to survival. She had been on her own for over a decade. Perhaps she had lost some of that fire in the security of her solitude, but she could renew that willful girl inside of herself again and find a way out.

Her eyes wandered past the bench where Neilos had lounged, noticing the thick tangle of vines that adorned the courtyard walls like a woven carpet. They looked strong. She was certain they would support her weight. Maybe she didn't need wings to free herself from this place.

What time was it? Nia didn't dare try to find one of the many grand clocks she had seen on the walls. It was late. That would suffice. Under ordinary circumstances, she would appreciate how well-lit the hallways were, but in this case, she felt betrayed by the steady glow in every sconce, even with the stone in her pocket. She had picked the darkest tunic and leggings she could find in her wardrobe, but she couldn't blend into the shadows when there were practically none to blend into.

She only heard someone shuffling in the halls once, and with the help of the stone they quickly turned to investigate a noise in the other direction. She took the nearest door she could find to the courtyard.

The night air was heavy and warm, making her clothing stick uncomfortably to her sweaty skin. Nia was thankful for the full band of crickets—less chance of someone noticing if she made a sound. Unlike the castle halls, the courtyards were dark. Good.

Something about the expanse of vines looked more intimidating under the blanket of night. She had so easily imagined scaling them earlier in the morning, but it appeared less simple now.

She didn't intend to leave for good yet. The allure of a remedy for her condition was too strong. But she did want to ensure she could find her way out if necessary. She could be gone and back before anyone noticed.

Still, was this really a good idea? Was it wiser to keep a low profile and wait out her time? She caught a whiff of floral perfume in the humid air that sent her head spinning with the scent of daffodils. Nope. No second-guessing. She needed to at least have an escape route that didn't involve talking to Neilos before life got more confusing and she lost her motivation.

Nia grasped a vine and gave a hard tug. Nothing came crashing down, which was a good sign. She heaved herself upward, searching for a foothold on the stone walls. The vines gave enough covering that she could support herself without too much difficulty and a relieved sigh escaped her. This would be easier than she thought.

As Nia climbed upward, hands stinging slightly from the coarseness of the vines, a faint rustling whispered in the dark. She froze and listened. The same crickets she had been grateful for moments earlier were now an annoyance. Still, she couldn't detect any other sounds, so she continued.

The stone warmed in her pocket, but as she adjusted for her climb it slipped out and rolled to the ground, landing under one of the bushes. Nia sucked in a breath. Maybe it had been a bad idea to try this while her luck was so weak. If she had waited a few more days for a fuller moon, the stone likely wouldn't have fallen. Attempting to escape without the stone was out of the question, so she prepared to ease herself back down.

There. That was definitely a noise, like the rustle of leaves.

She held back a yelp as something brushed against her ankle. Probably just a moth or something. There had to be all sorts of critters in these vines, which wasn't comforting, but she could handle critters. As long as they were the ordinary kind.

Nia tried to slide herself further down but couldn't. Only then did she notice the squeezing pressure around her ankle. One of the vines was wrapped tightly around her boot, coiled like a serpent.

Nothing to worry about. She'd just gotten tangled. That was all. She began the awkward dance of trying to reach down to free her ankle while at the same time holding herself secure with her other hand. At once, she felt the sliding, slithering feeling of another vine, this time around her wrist.

No, no, no, no.

Nia struggled as the vines closed in on her, wrapping and twisting around her limbs. A tendril of pressure squeezed her stomach as another snaked around her middle.

"Help!" Nia hissed, no longer caring if they knew she was trying to escape. Being found out was better than being strangled or squeezed to death by enchanted vines.

The plants cocooned Nia, and she attempted one final scream before her mouth was overtaken.

What a stupid way to die.

Nia's breathing failed her, and she descended into darkness.

Nia gasped.

The pressure around her body released and she gulped in the muggy evening air. A pair of strong, cool hands pulled her to the ground. She tumbled on all fours. Sweat dripped down her brow and onto the gray cobblestone as she continued to gulp in precious oxygen.

"I must admit, I thought you would wait a day or two more before you did something like that."

Neilos. Nia couldn't answer him even if she wanted to. He waited in silence as she caught her breath, and she finally managed, "Will I be punished?"

She would not be toyed with. Best to get it over with. Perhaps he would lock her up for the remainder of her stay. Maybe she wouldn't be allowed to leave at all.

Neilos's laugh cut through the night, and for a moment the crickets stopped their chorus. "Did you not think the vines were punishment enough?"

Nia looked up at him in confusion. "You said anyone who wanted to leave needed your permission, and I tried anyway. That doesn't make you angry?"

"I would have been disappointed if you hadn't tried. It would mean I misjudged your spirit."

Nia grew more self-aware of her position and forced herself to her feet. She knew she was a mess—drenched in sweat, hair in shambles. But the least she could do was stand. She stifled the urge to glance over at the bush where the stone fell. She didn't want Neilos to catch on that she was looking for something and search for it himself. She kept her eyes squarely on him.

"Do you take me at my word now?" Neilos asked. "I said you would not leave this castle without me. I meant it."

"As you said, I had to try." She was all too aware of the rasp in her voice.

"Try again, if you like." Neilos gave a sly smile. "If you had somehow escaped the vines, you would have fallen into sinking sand on the other side of the wall, which would have pulled you right back into the courtyard. If you had managed to evade the sand, the sleeping spores would have put you into a deep slumber until I woke you up. Shall I go on?"

"No. Your point is made." Nia found the amusement in his voice unsettling. She might have preferred it if he yelled.

"Did I neglect to mention," Neilos said airily, "That if you leave before the end of the month, all effects of the elixir will be reversed? All the healing you've already benefited from will be lost. But perhaps the price is worth it to you."

Even as he said it, her lungs burned. If she left, she may be burdened with this pain for the rest of her days, and she may never again have the chance to learn more about this place, or the boy who saved her.

She would regret it.

Neilos brought his fingertips under Nia's chin and forced her to look at him. "But if you want to leave, all you have to do is say the word. Go on," he said, his eyes locking with hers.

Nia stepped back, away from his touch. "I'm not leaving. Goodnight."

Nia knew one thing in that moment. She was caught in a game. Neilos might believe he won by compelling her to stay, but she wasn't going anywhere until she'd at least figured out precisely what the game was.

As Nia strode past the bush with the stone, she feigned getting her leggings caught on the branches and swiftly scooped the stone up again before retreating from the gardens.

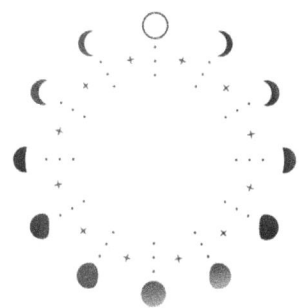

Chapter 10

Twenty-three days until the Dark Moon

"Morning, Nia!"

"Good morning, Enitan." As always, his smile was contagious—dangerously so—and it was almost enough to cut through the fog in Nia's brain after her reckless, sleepless night. Why did he have to look so good in that uniform?

As Enitan approached, Nia felt the stone grow cold, the luck whooshing out of her like air. She stiffened. Every time the stone had failed her in the castle, Enitan had been present. But how?

Nia kept her voice polite as she asked, "Finished your morning patrol?"

"Yep. Now I'm back to…my other duties."

Nia wondered if it was her imagination, but Enitan's eyes seemed to lose some of their sparkle. He had hesitated when speaking of his work the other day too. What was he hiding? Still, even with his secrets and the new development with the stone, Enitan felt safer than Neilos. If she became friendlier with him, perhaps she would uncover a way to escape.

"Can I keep you company?" Nia offered.

"You probably shouldn't."

Nia raised her eyebrows, her annoyance at Neilos pushing her to deny him in any way that she could. And Enitan hadn't exactly said no. Did that mean he wanted to get closer to her too? "You know, Neilos hasn't given me any restrictions." Other than not allowing her to leave without his blessing. "If he catches me shadowing you and doesn't like it, I'll simply apologize for my ignorance." She batted her eyes innocently.

He scratched his head and pulled his brows together. "I wish it were that easy. But I have to say no. You can't join me for this part of my duties."

"All right." Neilos *had* just warned her not to spend too much time with Enitan. Maybe it would be problematic for Enitan if Neilos spotted them together. Guilt needled at her at the thought of putting him in a bad position. She had to think of Enitan as well as herself, although this did nothing to end her curiosity about his work.

"If you're looking for something to do, though, I'm sure Uma would love some help in the kitchens." The way he said it puzzled Nia. He seemed almost guilty.

"I've been meaning to go there anyway," Nia said. "I still haven't told her how wonderful her food is."

"I'll walk you there."

The idea that he wanted to be with her a little longer brought a flutter of delight, but Neilos's warning blared in her thoughts again. It wouldn't look good for her to take Enitan's time immediately after being advised not to. Still, Neilos gave her a choice, and she was going to take it. This time, at least.

"Are you sure you don't have something better to do?" Nia kept her tone light as they ascended the stairs toward the kitchens on the sixth floor.

"I'll be passing right by on my way up."

If the kitchen was on the sixth floor, Enitan must have been going to the seventh. Spencer's sly grin flashed through her mind.

"Fine." Nia forced a smile as they climbed the stairs. What she really wanted was to ask him what was on the seventh floor. But instead, she said, "I heard you were responsible for the daffodils in my room yesterday." Her heart fluttered with that confounding feeling again, but she swallowed it down.

Enitan's face took on a subtle glow, his smile boyish. "I couldn't help overhearing your conversation with Neilos since I was his personal guard for dinner. It was no big deal."

Nia wondered how many conversations Enitan overheard. If he was always patrolling, there were probably many.

"Were you keeping watch on the grounds last night?" It was embarrassing enough being caught by Neilos in the vines. What if Enitan saw everything, too?

"Nah. There are night patrols and Neilos has extra enchantments in place at night. I gotta sleep sometime."

Well, that was a relief.

Nia paused when they reached the fifth floor. She hadn't explored it yet. There was a grand door just past the stairwell, ornately framed in dark wood carved in floral patterns.

"What's on this floor?" She was curious, but perhaps she just wanted to stall their parting a little longer.

Enitan gave a light smile. "This entire floor is reserved for the ballroom. We can check it out if you want."

She raised her eyebrows. "Neilos holds balls here?"

"Once a month, but only for the castle occupants. He doesn't invite outsiders." Something like hesitation flashed on his face and he quietly added, "He'll likely want you to attend this month's ball, if you're still around."

He pushed the door open, and Nia peered inside at the wooden floors, polished so sleek that the surface resembled glass. Something about the dark, empty room gave her goosebumps, so she stepped away from the door. "I'm sure it's lovely when it's full of people."

"It can be." Enitan sounded like he wasn't quite sure, but he said nothing further, and she followed him in silence to the next floor.

They arrived at the kitchens too soon for Nia's liking. She would rather carry on with Enitan, but evidently that wasn't an option. His whole demeanor had changed as soon as he mentioned the ball. It didn't feel right to leave him on a sour note.

"Do you want to have breakfast with me tomorrow?" What made her ask that all of a sudden? That was the complete opposite of not getting too comfortable, to say nothing of Neilos's warning. Nia swept a coil of hair out of her face. It did no good and the strand immediately found its place again at her cheek.

Enitan raised his hand as though he wanted to brush the strand away, but he stopped. Nia wished he had followed the urge. What would his touch feel like against her cheek?

Enitan cleared his throat. "I can't tomorrow. Or the day after."

"Oh." Nia quashed the disappointment.

"That's quite a face. Aren't you going to ask me why?"

Nia's fear was he simply didn't want to join her, but she covered the worry with humor and attempted to disguise her expression better this time. "Off to battle trolls?"

"No, that's not until next week." His flash of teeth sent a little tickle through Nia's stomach. "As it happens, I have early duties within the castle and can't stop to eat." He winked before adding, "No matter how desirable the company."

Based on the flames his words ignited in her cheeks, Nia was certain Enitan would notice her blush no matter how hard she schooled her features. "In two days, then?" Her voice came out at a higher pitch than she wanted, but if Enitan noticed he didn't show it.

"I would love to."

"Great!" Inviting a boy to breakfast? Magala would be shocked. And delighted. Tempting fate might be worth it if she could see Magala's face. "I'll see you then."

Nia slipped into the kitchens before she could do or say something embarrassing and wondered if her invitation was something she would later regret.

Or maybe he would be the one to regret it.

The instant the door closed behind her, the surge of warmth and good fortune enveloped her once again. Her stomach gave an uneasy turn. It could just be a coincidence. It had to be.

A cacophony of clangs and cursing met Nia's ears. She paused, unsure of whether Uma would appreciate the extra help or if coming here now would just be a further annoyance. Well, the least she could do was ask. Uma didn't seem the type who would accept the help unless she really wanted it. Nia took timid steps through the hall full of serving trays and silverware to the main kitchen, Uma's uproar growing louder by the second.

"Excuse me," Nia said. Not loud enough, however. Uma continued her tirade as she dumped a pot of something that probably wasn't supposed to look like charcoal into a large basin. Nia raised her voice and called, "Excuse me, Uma?"

Uma jumped and the large pot clattered into the wash basin with a metallic thunk. "What the blazes are you doin' here?"

"I'm sorry, I didn't mean to startle you. I came to see if I could help."

For a moment Uma looked as though she might brush Nia away like a pesky fly, but then her face softened. "Actually, that'd be nice. Mind scrubbing the pot so I can peel a fresh lot of potatoes?"

The pot would take some serious elbow grease, but the effect was cathartic. It felt good to do something useful. Good to use her hands and put effort into something. The stone's effects flowed freely, and the burned bits flaked away at the lightest touch. Nia gave a small chuckle—so much for hard work. If she had been in the kitchen a few moments before, the food would never have burnt to begin with. Poor Uma.

"Do you make everything by yourself?" Nia asked as she scrubbed. The sound of Uma's quick dicing at the counter behind the basin was soothing.

"Yep, just me," Uma huffed. "Wasn't always that way, but I lost my kitchen boy. Can you hand me that bowl?"

Nia passed a large metal bowl to Uma, and she slid the mound of chopped potatoes inside.

"It doesn't seem fair to expect you to feed an entire castle by yourself."

"It is what it is," Uma shrugged. "I'm not about to complain. Plus the magic helps me along. Pot's clean enough, let's get that water boiling."

In no time, the delicious aroma of potato soup filled the kitchen and Nia's mouth watered. Uma grabbed a pinch of something from a pouch at her waist and sprinkled it inside the pot, stirring vigorously.

"What's that?" Nia asked. She took another whiff of the air but couldn't detect any particular spice.

"Flavarrange. Something Neilos came up with to help the cooking."

Nia's eyes widened. "Magic?" Wasn't there anything natural in the castle?

Uma waved a dismissive hand. "Harmless stuff. All it does is alter the flavor palate to a person's liking." Nia must have looked confused, because Uma continued, "Say I'm making trout with lemon and capers—dinner tonight, by the way. If one person likes capers, that's the flavor that will come through more. If lemons are their thing, they'll get more of the lemon."

"So that's why everything tastes perfect," Nia mused.

"Make no mistake, missy," Uma tsked. "I'm still a fine chef. This flavarrange just spruces things up a bit."

Uma wiped her hands on her apron. "Well, that's that. And a moment to spare for a drink, even. Care to join me?"

"No, thank you," Nia said, noting the jewel-colored liquid in the bottle Uma produced.

"You sure? You've never had anything like this. Guaranteed."

Nia shook her head. Liquor was bad enough. Magic liquor was something else entirely.

"More for me," Uma said with a giddy laugh, tipping the bottle back. "Thanks for the help."

"Can I help you again tomorrow?" Nia asked. "I could use something to do."

"Sure, sure," Uma waved her away, already taking another swig.

Nia stepped from the kitchen into the hallway and bumped into Spencer, knocking him to the ground.

He scowled at her, an effect that managed to be scathing even with one eye covered. "Really? I'm beginning to think you simply like mowing down children."

"Manes and tails," Nia muttered. She extended a hand to help him to his feet. He refused her help, using his magic cane to pull himself up instead.

"Manes and tails?" Spencer asked, his voice appraising. "What does that even mean?"

Nia ignored his question, having no desire to explain her unicorn-inspired epithet to a child who was likely to make fun of her for it. "I'm sorry I knocked you over. Why were you standing outside of the kitchens?"

"It doesn't matter. It's probably far too exciting for a dull person like you."

Nia should have sent him to the floor again. Instead, the gears of her mind turned. Spencer might be an easy outlet for information about the castle and its master.

"Try me," she challenged. "Were you going to the seventh floor?"

Spencer adjusted his eyepatch. "No, but this may be equally informative."

So, he considered the seventh floor informative? Interesting. Perhaps it would be worth her time to investigate it after all. Especially because that's where Enitan was spending his time. She didn't know what Spencer actually had in mind, but whatever it was might say something about his judgment and intentions, which would help her decide whether or not the seventh floor was a wise decision.

Nia followed Spencer—magic cane and all—back down the stairs and to the courtyard to a neatly trimmed line of square-cut hedges. With a swift look around, he ducked into a gap in the foliage and motioned for Nia to follow. It was a tight fit and the branches clawed her skin. Nevertheless, once she was through, there was enough space between the hedges and the castle wall for Nia to walk comfortably.

Spencer reached a vine-laden section and Nia shied away.

"No thanks. I'm not messing with those again."

Spencer rolled his good eye. "I heard about that. But these vines aren't going to ensnare you."

A mortified heat rushed to her cheeks. If Spencer knew about the vines, did that mean people were gossiping about her?

Spencer prodded the vines with his cane, and they parted to reveal an intricate metal grate, its design almost as twisted as the vines themselves. He gripped it and pulled, loosening it from the stone wall and revealing an opening into a tunnel.

"Follow me," Spencer said, dropping to the ground.

Nia frowned. She might have been able to squeeze through the hedge, but those were pliable branches. The tunnel's opening was surrounded by stone, and much too small for her. Spencer was a wisp of a boy and it wasn't very roomy even for him.

"I'm not sure why I'm stating the obvious," Nia said, "But I won't fit in there."

"Not without my help. But today's your lucky day. Get down here."

Nia blew out an exasperated breath and humored the boy by crouching on the ground beside him. He reached into his pocket and produced what looked like a smooth, oval-shaped piece of chocolate with a spiral pattern.

Spencer held the chocolate out to Nia. "This will make you temporarily smaller. I use it myself sometimes, even though I don't really need it. Occasionally I just like it to be a little roomier in there."

Nia took the chocolate and examined it. "So, I just eat this?"

"Yes, and—"

Nia popped the chocolate into her mouth. It had a spicy bite to it, but otherwise tasted normal. Spencer's uncovered eye grew wide and then his face stretched into a grin. "Uh-oh. You ate the whole thing."

"Should I not have?" A pang of worry shot through Nia's chest. What had she been thinking? She'd been so careful about the magic around her till now. "What's going to happen to me?"

As she said it, she began to fall. No, she wasn't falling. She was shrinking. Her eyes became level with Spencer's own, only to lower further until he was taller than she was.

"How do I stop it?" Nia's words came in a rush.

Nia's body jerked forward and back, and the world stopped moving.

"Already done," Spencer said, waving his hand. "You weren't supposed to eat it all at once, you dolt. Little bites to adjust your height."

"Well, how was I to know that?"

He pulled another piece from his pocket and gave it to Nia. "Don't eat this right now."

Did he think she was a complete idiot? "Why would I? I'm already too small."

"It seems like you need people to state the obvious."

What a disrespectful little—

"You should always keep an extra piece with you in case you aren't out of the tunnels before you start to grow again. Don't want to get stuck in there."

Nia's irritation died on the spot. "Yes, good idea. Thanks."

Spencer dropped down in front of the tunnel and held his cane in front of him, letting it pull him inside. Nia would have no such luxury. She got on her hands and knees and heaved herself in. Even though she was smaller, the space made her feel claustrophobic. The inside was stuccoed and rough on her palms. She was grateful her long dress at least provided some cushion for her knees, though she didn't want to see what state the fabric would be in after this.

The tunnels were dark, and Spencer didn't say a word as they traveled. Goosebumps popped up along Nia's skin. Where was this boy taking her?

After a moment, the tunnels opened up somewhat. Nia still couldn't stand fully upright, but it was an improvement. Spencer stopped and Nia nearly ran into him. Light streamed in through a slatted area above them. The tunnel offered enough space for Nia to look upward toward the slits of light. She realized there were people walking above them. A gaggle of female servants, giving a rather good view of their petticoats.

Nia's face flushed but she kept her voice quiet. "Were you... Do you use this to look up ladies' skirts?" Why would he think Nia was interested in something like that?

The indignation on Spencer's face seemed genuine. "What? No. Everyone's got a backside. What's so intriguing about that?" He paused and inclined his head. "I'm not interested in what I can see. It's what I can hear that's fun."

They both waited in silence.

"Neilos is in a foul mood today," one of the servants grumbled.

"Can you blame him?" Another chimed in. "He paid a fortune to have that dragon trapped."

Nia became much more interested in the conversation. What had happened to the dragon?

A different voice piped up. "Aldric is lucky he's not losing his head. He should have taken better care of it."

The first servant scoffed. "That wasn't Aldric's fault. It's nearly impossible to keep a dragon alive in captivity. The master should have known better. The fact that it lived as long as it did is a testament to Aldric's animal husbandry."

"Sounds like you're more interested in Aldric."

As the ladies teased and giggled, Nia's heart caved in. The dragon had died? Her eyes watered unexpectedly. She knew the creature felt lonely, but it had looked healthy. Was there anything she could have done for it?

While Nia sorrowed, Spencer appeared rapt with attention. He did seem like a curious child, and she supposed she could understand why the morsels of gossip appealed to him. The castle's servants were a web of observers, privy to the hidden corners and whispered secrets of their employer. These tunnels might be her best chance of discovering Neilos's mysteries.

Nia wiped her eyes across her sleeve and took a deep breath. "I've heard enough," she whispered. "Let's go back."

For his part, Spencer didn't hesitate, and he didn't tease Nia about her red eyes and sniffling. Perhaps the child had some sense of decorum.

As they crawled back toward the gardens, she paused as her palm rested over something bumpy. She looked down and found a necklace made of a delicate black chain. She peered at it.

"Does someone else wander these tunnels besides you?" she asked.

Spencer was quiet behind her. The tunnels in this spot were too narrow for her to turn and see what kind of expression he held.

When he gave no answer, Nia said, "Well, perhaps I'll bring it out in case someone is looking for it. Maybe it fell through one of the vents." It would be easier to wear it out than to crawl through while holding it. Nia slipped the necklace over her head and when she did a shock ran through her. Her body seized up and she couldn't move an inch.

Spencer laughed loudly and she felt the crook of his cane slide under the necklace, removing it. As soon as it was off, she had power over her limbs again.

"Leave that thing here," Nia demanded. There was no way she was bringing some sort of cursed jewelry back with her.

"Are you really that short-sighted?" Spencer's voice was laden with irritation. "You don't suppose something like this might be useful in the future?" His cane slid over her shoulder, dangling the necklace in her reach.

Nia gritted her teeth, unsure why she should care one whit about this arrogant child's opinion. "Fine," she muttered, clutching the necklace in her fist. "Maybe I can use it on you someday."

The sunlight glared too brightly as they crawled out of the tunnels and back into the gardens. Nia blinked a few times to adjust. She felt disoriented, and realized the ground was moving further away. She was returning to her normal size. Thank goodness they left when they did.

"The tunnels go all throughout the castle," Spencer said, breaking his silence. "You're welcome."

Nia frowned at the boy. He seemed to think he had done her a big favor. "What makes you think I want secret access to the castle?"

Spencer merely shrugged. "If you don't now, you will." He reached into his pocket and pulled out a few more pieces of the shrinking chocolate. "Take these, in case you decide to come through again on your own."

Her first instinct was to decline, but as her mind returned to the dragon and the days she had remaining here, she thought better of it. If she could sneak around undetected, she might not have to stay for the month after all. Surely someone knew a way out. Or maybe she could gather some piece of information that would persuade Neilos to release her.

"Thank you," she said as she pocketed the chocolates, both hoping and fearing she would have the chance to use them again.

Each step Nia took through the castle halls felt heavier. As much as she hated the transphere, using it might be worth it to avoid dragging herself up the stairs to her room.

Nia jumped back when she saw a masculine figure seated on the floor in a shadowed corner of the main lounge. The shoulder of his uniform—and perhaps the shoulder itself, judging by the blood—was shredded. He cradled his face in his hands. Nia recognized the dark braids, even though they were more disheveled than she had ever seen them.

"Enitan?" she whispered, taking a tentative step closer.

He peered out from his fingers and showed recognition. "Oh, Nia."

He sounded so tired, and his words carried such sorrow behind them. As Nia drew closer, she could see it was more than his shoulder that had been injured. His face bore several lacerations, each gash a crimson tattoo of violence. His right side had a dark, wet stain that seemed to be slowly growing.

Nia knelt down in front of him. "What in the world happened to you?"

"The dragon," was all he said.

"You...you killed it?" How could Enitan be the one who killed the dragon? Why would he do it?

Enitan seemed just as confused as Nia. "Killed it? No. I was there when it died. Trying to comfort it. But it was too late. I—" he broke off and stared at his blood-stained hands, then dropped them uselessly to the ground.

Nia stood. "I'll get Neilos. He healed me when I got here. He'll know what to do."

"No!" Enitan's voice had found its strength again. "He doesn't know why I did it. You said it was lonely. He—"

It seemed like Enitan wanted to keep speaking, but his words failed him, coming out in a strangled groan instead.

"You're not making any sense. We need to heal you."

But before Nia could leave or Enitan could protest again, Neilos came to them instead.

"What has happened to my guard?" Neilos asked, his voice sharp.

Nia spoke so Enitan wouldn't have to. "He said it was a dragon."

"So, it's true, then." Neilos narrowed his eyes. "You did visit the creature in its death throes. I warned you. The dragon was already too far gone. A human could not possibly have brought it comfort at that stage."

You said it was lonely.

Enitan's words from moments before clicked into place. The dragon was already dying, and he went to be with it, getting himself hurt in the process. She turned wide, woeful eyes toward Enitan. "Did you do this for me?"

Enitan froze and Nia caught the glint in Neilos's eyes. She wished she had not spoken, for now she feared it was the wrong thing to ask.

Neilos's attention turned full force on Enitan now. "Tell her the truth, Enitan."

As soon as he commanded it, Enitan said, "Yes, I did it for her."

The seconds passed in silence, but they were filled with something heavy and dangerous that Nia could not understand. When she could bear it no more, she directed her gaze to Neilos. "Please," she begged, "Heal him like you did for me."

Something in Neilos shifted, as though he were a performer remembering he was still on stage. He gave Nia a light smile with his lips, but he could not deceive her with his eyes. "But of course. You may go, Nia. I will attend to Enitan."

Enitan would not look at her.

While it was almost certain that her silence would be the best shield in this situation, her heart would not let her leave without giving Enitan a whispered, "Thank you."

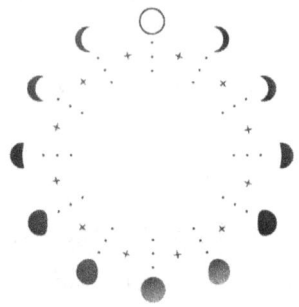

Chapter 11

Twenty-two days until the Dark Moon

"Manes and tails..." Nia heaved a sigh as she exited the kitchens and leaned against the door. She feared she might stink of dead sea creatures for the rest of her life. Washing dishes and cleaning up after the latest meal of seared fish proved a messier task than she anticipated. Uma must have prepared the food with only speed in mind, leaving the kitchen a maelstrom of scales and bones and slime. Nia shuddered. Still, she wasn't going to complain. Uma obviously needed the help, and it was the least Nia could do when Uma was cooking for the whole castle.

"Rough day?"

Nia started at the voice. "Enitan!"

Her eyes ran over him, seeking any trace of his injuries from the previous afternoon, but she found none, and he looked every bit the part of a guard in his fresh uniform. "I'm glad Neilos helped you."

He turned his eyes to the ground. "Yeah, well. How could he refuse if you asked?"

Yes, I did it for her.

Her insides heated at the recall of his declaration, and she grasped for words to keep the conversation moving. "You look good." She bit her lip. She had meant to say "better."

"So do you." His face lit up in a playful grin.

In an instant she turned from pleased to embarrassed. She pressed her back into the door as though she could melt into it. "I probably smell bad. Sorry. I was helping Uma clean up after lunch."

He sniffed, made a slight face, then said, "You're sure you're not just up to something *fishy*?"

"...Really?"

"You walked right into it," Enitan said, his palms facing her in surrender. His features softened. "Thank you for helping Uma. She's a good woman. And an amazing chef."

Nia could still taste the savory fish that practically melted on her tongue. "That's for sure. The fish in this castle is unlike anything I've ever tasted from our rivers."

Enitan's lips quirked into a smile. "That's because they don't come from the river."

"But there isn't an ocean anywhere near here. How would it travel without spoiling?" Nia paused. "Although, it *is* Neilos we're dealing with. He can probably fly there or something." Nia suddenly felt foolish for being surprised. Neilos probably had dozens of ways to get fish from the ocean.

Enitan's burst of laughter was far from eloquent, and Nia felt even more silly.

"What's so funny?" She demanded.

"Just—" Enitan tried to speak through his mirth. "Just imagining Neilos f-flying." He had tears in his eyes, and his laughter seemed to spread to Nia's chest until it was bursting from her own throat. Why was it so easy to laugh around him?

"Ok, fine," Nia said, once she had caught her breath. "How does he do it, then?"

"You'd never believe it without seeing it."

Nia gave an exaggerated sigh. "Then show me."

His eyes sparkled with delight, and he motioned for Nia to follow. "Come with me."

He led her through the breezy hallways on the first floor. All the windows were open today and Nia longed to go outside and feel the sun on her skin. As they approached a tall, curved door she wondered if she was about to get her wish.

"Ok, get ready. I think you're gonna love this." Enitan thrust the door open and didn't hesitate to pull Nia through with him.

Nia was hit with the damp chill of salty air. A roaring sound met her ears, and the wind whipped her hair into her face. Her eyes grew wide as she took in the clashing waves and tumultuous tide creeping ever closer to her feet. Her breath came in rapid, searing gasps and she was frozen on the spot.

The flooded river had claimed her parents' lives and nearly took Nia's. But this, the ocean, was the river's fierce older sister who had brought an end to thousands in her depths and laid waste to villages with her swells. The power in these waves made the river docile in comparison. Nia's lungs burned and she took in ragged gulps of air, remembering how it felt to open her mouth for oxygen only to be met with endless fluid.

"Nia? Nia!" Enitan stood in front of her, hands firm on her shoulders. She grounded herself in his worried face as his eyes searched hers. Eyes in warm shades of brown that made her think of autumn and the last hints of golden comfort before the onset of winter's chill.

"Just look at me, ok? You're safe. I've got you." He slid his hands from her shoulders to her arms. "Don't take your eyes off of me. Walk backwards. I'll guide you. One step at a time."

Nia fixated on his face, even as her chest still heaved and the world spun around her. But she took a step. And then another. The more she studied his face the more she realized what a rather handsome face it was. Soon she wasn't thinking about the ocean at all.

Before she knew it, they were back inside the door. She jumped at the clunk of the latch clicking into place and then she let out a slow, steady breath. She withdrew from Enitan and turned away.

"I'm so sorry. I'm embarrassed you saw that."

"Don't be." His voice was feather soft and made Nia feel as though she could snuggle into it. "I'm the one who's sorry. I never would have taken you there if I had known. I'm a total idiot."

"You're far from an idiot, Enitan." Nia leaned against the cool stone wall and hugged her arms around her middle. "My parents died in the flood. I almost did, too." Her lungs burned again at the memory. "I still can't breathe right sometimes." Though Neilos's elixir had dulled the pain, the sensation remained.

"Of course you wouldn't like the ocean." He ran his hand through his hair. "Aw man, I'm sorry. I thought you would be impressed. I blew it."

It was endearing that he wanted to impress her to begin with, and it was a safe bet that her reaction wasn't typical. "Enitan, it's ok, really. You couldn't have known." She eyed the door. "And it is really impressive, I have to admit. What exactly is it?" How did Neilos have a room with the ocean in his castle?

"It's literally the ocean," Enitan said with a shrug. "Neilos enchanted that doorway to transport him straight to the seaside, though he's never told me the specific location." He must have read Nia's expression, because he added, "Don't try to escape that way. Anyone who crosses the doorway automatically has a spell placed on them that won't allow them to travel more than a mile out. You'd waste a lot of effort just to end up right back here."

"Don't worry," Nia said with a shiver. "I won't go there." She could hardly stand being on the shoreline. Anyone who actually wanted her in the water would have to drag her there kicking and screaming. Not even a unicorn prancing through the surf would get her back there again.

Enitan placed a hand on her shoulder, but something about his touch was different this time. It sent a little buzz of lightning through Nia's skin. She ducked her head down, hoping the heat she felt in her cheeks wasn't too apparent on her face.

"Let's get you something warm to drink. Uma makes an outrageous spiced cider."

A few minutes later, with two steaming mugs of cider in his hands, Enitan led her to the sitting room around the corner from her bedroom. The space had a cozy feel, adorned in thick, fuzzy rugs and plush furniture. They settled onto a velvet couch with luxuriously soft cushions.

"Ignite," Enitan said. A fire blazed to life in the room's stone fireplace and Nia was immediately grateful. Even after returning to the castle, she felt the chill from the ocean down to her bones.

Nia paused to inhale the comforting aroma of the cider before taking her first sip. The scent of apple, cinnamon, and clove wafted up to greet her. Enitan was already halfway through his own drink.

"How can you do that without burning yourself?" Nia asked, taking another careful sip. Her voice was still a bit wheezy, but she hoped the hot drink might help.

Enitan merely shrugged in response and took another hearty swig. He didn't say anything for a while, as though he intuitively knew she just needed a pause to collect herself. Nia didn't feel the need to ramble to fill the silence with Enitan as she might normally do with others. His presence made her feel like it was ok to simply be. There were no pretenses, no social formalities to follow.

He set his empty cup aside on the little wooden table in front of the couch. Then, he reached into his pocket and pulled out a small, lumpy cylinder of wood and a whittling knife.

"You carve?" Nia asked, intrigued as she watched his hands make swift, sweeping motions, sending little curls of wood spiraling down.

"A little," he said. "Just as a hobby. It relaxes me."

Did that mean he was nervous?

She leaned in closer to observe his work. It was a figure of a little man, and though it fit in the palm of his hand, the carving was detailed, with folds in the clothes and wisps of curls in the hair. It didn't have a face yet, and Nia wondered what sort of expression Enitan might carve.

Enitan paused. He gave Nia a heart-stopping grin with a hint of youthful shyness. And that dimple again. Manes and tails...

Still smiling, he asked, "Would you mind not staring at me like that?"

She hastily turned her attention to the cup in her hands, adjusting herself away from him.

He gave a slight laugh. "I should explain. I hate people judging what I'm working on before it's finished. Self-consciousness, I guess."

"Oh!" She meant her laugh to sound lighthearted, but it came out nervous. "That makes sense."

She tried not to gawk and focused instead on the soothing scrape of his knife on the wood. "You will show me when it's done though, right?" she prodded.

"Of course."

She attempted to respond, but a rough croak came out. She cleared her throat and tried again. "Great. Sorry."

"Sorry for what?" His eyes and hands remained focused on his work.

Did he really not notice? "For my voice. It comes and goes."

"You mean that little husky sound?" He didn't look at her, but she observed his playful grin. "I thought you were just being sultry."

"W-what?" She stammered.

His answering chuckle brushed across her ears in a pleasing way. "But seriously, don't worry about it. I like your voice, no matter how it sounds."

Warmth spread through her from head to toe, centering in her chest. All she could manage in reply was a whispered, "Thank you."

She'd been teased by her peers about her voice for most of her life. Nobody had ever complimented it before.

Several minutes passed and Nia let the crackle of the fire soothe her. She started to nod off when she heard Enitan say, "Just a few last touches."

She peeked at him and noted the front of the carving was turned towards him. He must have been working on the face now.

"Done!" he exclaimed proudly. "*Wood* you like to see it?"

"Was that a wood pun?"

"Of course it was." He handed the carving off to Nia, ignoring her eye roll. "What do you think?"

Nia ran her thumb over the piece, examining it. The work was very fine, but...

"Excuse me, dear lady, did you just snort?"

Nia covered her mouth in embarrassment and tried to stifle her giggle. "I'm so sorry. It's just..." The carving had the ugliest face she had ever seen. Uneven eyes that went in different directions. A bulbous, misshapen nose. The eyebrows were ragged, and the lips seemed to grimace. The poor wooden man looked as though he had stepped in something unpleasant.

To his credit, Enitan joined in Nia's amusement. "Ok, you know my secret. I'm lousy at faces."

Nia scrunched her nose. "You could just make them without faces. The rest of it is admirable."

A shudder rippled through Enitan's body. "Now *that* would be creepy. They'd be a bunch of nameless, mindless nobodies. I don't wanna do that. These guys may be ugly but at least they're somebody."

"Well, the world needs unique characters too, I suppose." She grinned and turned the carving over in her hands. "Do you mind if... Could I keep it?"

His eyebrows reached for the ceiling. "Really? You want to?"

"I do. He's already growing on me."

Enitan's sunshine of a smile radiated through again. "Then he's all yours. Be nice to him. He's got a good heart."

Enitan had a good heart, too, but Nia couldn't bring herself to say the words out loud to him. Instead, she shyly tucked the figure into the ribbon at the waist of her dress, somehow feeling lighter with its weight there.

"We're still on for breakfast tomorrow, right?" Nia asked. She hoped her extreme reaction today wouldn't put him off the visit. She also wasn't sure if Neilos would still allow it, given his reaction to the incident with the dragon.

But her fears were evidently unwarranted as Enitan beamed at her and replied, "I wouldn't miss it."

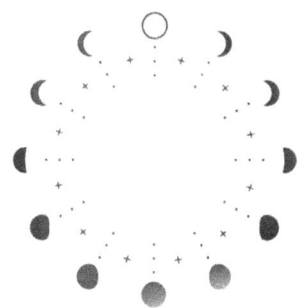

Chapter 12

Twenty-one and a half days until the Dark Moon

Nia's eyes popped open, her senses on instant alert. She could have sworn she felt her bed shaking. She scanned the room, even though she knew it was useless in the all-consuming darkness of night. Her heart thrummed in her chest, and she held herself in perfect stillness. Listening. Waiting.

There it was again. A low rumbling through the castle. The vase rattled on her nightstand as she felt the vibrations beneath her. Was it an earthquake? An attack? She thought of the door on the first floor with a gulp. Could it somehow be the ocean?

Whatever the case, Nia wasn't going to be a victim in her bed. She threw the covers off, grabbed the stone, and fumbled through the dark to the door. Her fingers found the latch and loosed it. The corridor was mercifully well-lit. Nia pattered down the hall, following the growing sound of commotion. Upstairs. The ballroom?

She expected to see more servants as she made her way, but the halls were empty. She couldn't have been the only one awakened by the noise. Why wasn't anyone else out of their beds? Nia shivered, wondering if maybe they all knew something she didn't. She quickened her pace as she ascended the stairs to the ballroom floor.

She spotted the back of Enitan's emerald uniform blocking the ballroom doorway. Flashes of multi-colored light cast strange shadows on the wall. Nia tasted a metallic tang in the air and heard crackles, sizzles, and bangs. It was nearly enough to distract her from the sensation of her luck disappearing again.

"Enitan?" Nia whispered in concern, though with the racket she wondered why she bothered keeping her voice down.

Enitan whirled and grew wide-eyed. "Why are you here? Go back to your room!"

The voice was harsher than she was used to hearing from Enitan, but she held her ground. "Tell me what's going on." If he didn't want her here, he could just try and make her go. She crossed her arms and steeled her gaze.

Enitan looked for a moment as if he would double down, but instead he sighed and ran his hand over his braids. "A speculo. Neilos is fighting it."

"What's a speculo?"

"Trouble. They conceal truth and deal in secrets. They have dark, powerful magic."

The last thing the castle needed was a creature that could further conceal its secrets. Its residents already did a fine job of that. Still, Nia couldn't resist watching. She peered over Enitan's shoulder, despite his attempts to block her way with another frustrated sigh. She glimpsed a tall figure in a heavy cloak as it came at Neilos with a wooden staff. Neilos blasted the creature back with a flash of red, shaking the castle walls. The speculo rushed him and he sped out of its way, his body enveloped in a blue glow. It was such a change to see him this way, looking feral and ferocious instead of lounging about in the gardens. His amber eyes gleamed, his teeth pulled back in a snarl. He hit the creature with another red blast and the staff fell to the ground.

"The staff, Enitan. I want it." Neilos's voice echoed off the stone walls.

Enitan surged forward, seemingly forgetting his desire to shield Nia. She wasn't concerned about him exposing her so much as puzzled he could rush in so readily for the sake of procuring an object. Is that what soldiers did? Dive right into danger the instant it's asked of them? Nia gasped as the creature shot a silvery light from its hands in Enitan's direction. Enitan lifted his shield as Neilos sent another burst of magic to envelop it. The shield illuminated with vibrant red light and the speculo's spell bounced harmlessly off. Nia breathed again.

Enitan grabbed the staff as the creature rose. The world seemed to grow silent and a smoky, pitch-black dust rose around the speculo. Enitan raised his sword as the dark substance enveloped him, but the smokey spell shied away from his still-illuminated shield.

"Run, Nia!" Enitan shouted, but it was too late. The dark clouds had already snaked around her. Nia was instantly paralyzed. She was floating out of herself, being pulled in every direction. Her head spun and the darkness whirled and engulfed her entire being, body and mind.

At once she heard the ear-splitting roar of rushing waters. Her little body was slapped about as she gripped a branch with all the strength her numb hands could offer. She saw her mother's body whisked away. Saw her head thrown against the rock. Her father's futile attempt to save her as he, too, was taken by the flood waters. Then the branch broke.

Nia wailed, and just as suddenly as the torrent of fierce waters, she was cast out on the street. Shivering, her stomach aching with the stab of starvation. She looked at her skeletal hands and fell to the dust, wishing for her demise over this hunger. This cold. The stench of death and decay filled her nose as she passed a dank corner where orphans less fortunate than her had earlier succumbed. Was it a foreshadowing of her own fate?

Now she was slammed to the ground of a cobblestone street, moonlight reflecting in the cold eyes of her former boyfriend Alex as his friends beat her in the darkness. Only hours before he'd claimed to love her but turned rabid when she refused to use the stone for his benefit.

Then, another low rumble. She was back in her cottage, her roof being blown to bits by the shadowscale. She saw the gleam of its eyes as it swooped in to grab her. To steal her away once again from the security she had built.

"Nia."

The voice came as an echo. Nia could hear it, but unpleasant moments continued to flash before her eyes. A burst of heat racked her body, and the voice became clearer.

"Nia, are you all right?"

She opened her eyes and found herself in Neilos's arms. She quickly pulled herself upright, forcing down the dizziness that threatened to send her to the ground. "What happened?"

"The speculo sent out a shadow that forces everyone it touches to relive their most unpleasant truths. You were one of its victims, I'm afraid. But you have nothing to fear from it now. I have incapacitated the creature and reversed the effects of the magic."

"Where's Enitan?"

"Taking the beast to its prison. He is fine."

"I see. Good." Nia closed her eyes, trying to dim the newly felt memories.

"Would you like to forget?"

Nia popped her eyes open again. "What?"

"Antonia is skilled in preparing magical remedies. She could prepare an elixir for you. It could erase the unpleasantness entirely, so it never troubles you again."

Nia could never. While the memories might be unpleasant to relive, they were still part of her. They helped shape her. Neilos had already taken her scars. She couldn't relinquish her memories too.

"They're my memories," she said. "I'll decide what to do with them." She didn't want to lose any part of herself in Neilos's castle.

"Suit yourself," Neilos said with a shrug, his wild hair falling across his shoulders. "At least let me see you back to your chambers."

He got to his feet, pulling Nia up with him. The touch felt foreign, and she let her hand linger in his for just a moment, seeking out any sort of comfort. Then she recalled his face from moments before as he fought the speculo, and she let her hand drop.

"I'm sorry you had to see that," Neilos said as they made the long walk to Nia's room. Perhaps he sensed her increased unease. Seeing him enchant flowers was one thing. Watching him fight with such ferocity was another. As she suspected all along, he was not someone to be trifled with.

"Why was it in the castle?" Nia asked. "How did it get in?"

"A rare oversight on my part. Not long before your arrival, it concealed itself as a crippled child. It has been residing in this castle for nearly a month now under that guise."

Nia's eyes grew wide. "Spencer?" That cheeky little boy had been the speculo all that time? No wonder he had always seemed so much older than his appearance. She began replaying their conversations, wondering what she might have inadvertently revealed to the creature.

"Yes. You've met him, I see." Neilos waved a dismissive hand. "The mistake wasn't entirely unexpected, given the creature's talents. The speculo gets what it wants by trading information. Concealing lies. Revealing truths," he chuckled, "Or sometimes doing the precise opposite. The secrets of this castle are likely valuable."

"What secrets?" Nia found herself asking the question before she could stop herself.

"Nothing of concern. The extent of my power. The quiet solitude of the castle. There are many who would like to see this place uprooted and transparent."

There was more to it than he was letting on, but she was smart enough to know not to press it. She changed the subject. "What does its staff do?"

Neilos gave a sly smile. "As far as I know, nothing. Just for ornamentation and defense, I believe. But the staff of a speculo is a nice memento from the moment I captured it."

A trophy. He ordered Enitan into the line of fire for a mere trophy. Nia took a steady breath and clenched her fists, fighting to restrain her anger. Thank goodness they had arrived at her room.

"Are you sure you're all right?" Neilos asked, opening the door for her. "I could stay for a while if it would calm you."

"No, I'm really fine," Nia insisted, unable to abide the thought of Neilos in her quarters. "The danger is gone."

"Very well. I will send Antonia up with some tea. Whatever you say, I know how the nerves get worked up after an unexpected event." He must have seen the look of uncertainty on her face, because he emphasized, "Just ordinary herbs. I promise. I know you prefer your beverages magic free."

"Thank you." Nia wasn't sure she would even trust the tea Antonia brought. Not after talk of her preparing a memory-erasing elixir.

"Please indulge me for a moment, Nia."

Nia looked up and tensed in spite of herself. What was he going to bring up now?

"Many times now, I have come to your rescue—healing your injuries, rescuing you from the tangled garden, the magic books, and now from the speculo."

His words implied she owed him a great debt, and she didn't like that. "For my wounds, I thank you. But I should remind you that the vines, books, and the speculo only happened to me because I'm here."

Neilos gave a light chuckle. "Fair enough. But I went to your aid nonetheless. Why, then, do you still act as though I'm a serpent who might strike you at any instant? If I wanted to see you come to harm, I've had many chances."

"I'm tired," Nia said. "Could we please have this discussion another time?" Or never. But certainly not now, when Nia herself wasn't sure of the answer to his question. She didn't know what to call it other than a gut intuition.

"Of course. My apologies. Goodnight, Nia."

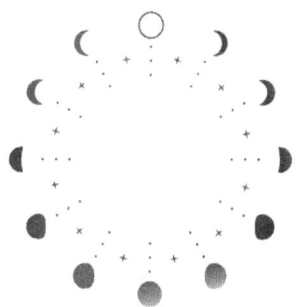

Chapter 13

Twenty-one days until the Dark Moon

Sleep evaded Nia as thoughts of the speculo and her haunted memories intruded every time her eyelids dropped. At least she had the morning with Enitan to look forward to. Enitan, who, unlike "Spencer," was exactly who he appeared to be. She hoped.

When the strange sunlight enchantment finally flooded her room, Nia was already debating over an array of garments strewn out before her. What was appropriate for breakfast with Enitan? Was a tunic too casual? A gown too formal? She decided on a simple sky-blue dress— unadorned, but still flattering.

When Antonia entered a moment later, Nia frowned at the single breakfast tray she carried.

"I'm sorry, miss," Antonia said, placing the tray on the table before Nia. "Uma said Enitan took his breakfast already."

"Oh. That's all right." Had he forgotten? It had been a strange night, so she couldn't blame him. Or was it more than that? Did something happen to him when he took that speculo creature to the dungeons? No, Uma said he had breakfast. He was probably fine.

Antonia left Nia to her meal. She picked at a pastry with some yellow fruit that was probably delicious, but the taste was lost to her. She shoved the tray away. She paced her room. Maybe he had been injured and had breakfast in his bed. Maybe Uma was mistaken.

Or maybe he just changed his mind.

That was fine. He had a right. But why wouldn't he at least say so? Nia sighed and flung the door to the hallway open. Better to get a straight answer than to stew about it in her room all morning.

Nia's emotions swelled and ebbed in a discordant mixture of relief and irritation when she at last saw Enitan. She met him at the entrance to the courtyard, bright beams of sun streaming in behind him. "So, you *are* ok."

Enitan furrowed his brow at her statement. "Why wouldn't I be?"

Nia shrugged and gave a wry smile. "That creature was very powerful, and you didn't show up for breakfast."

"Neilos had it incapacitated. Moving it to a cell was no big deal after that."

"...and breakfast?" Nia pushed again. Really, why did it even matter? She would be gone in a few weeks. Sooner, if she could find another way.

Enitan shifted his stance, looking uncomfortable. "I wanted to go, Nia. Really. But I have work to do."

"Was it Neilos?"

Another long pause, and Nia got the sense he wanted to say more than he could. "Last night reminded me what I need to focus on. I'm sorry."

"I see." Why was she angry about it? Really, it was better. She didn't need to form attachments or put herself in situations that lowered her guard. She quickly diverted the conversation and hoped Enitan would dismiss her irritation.

"Can a cell even hold that creature?"

Enitan smirked. "*This* cell can."

Ah. Of course. The cell must be enchanted, like most everything else here.

"Well, good. I'll let you return to your important work."

"Thanks for understanding," Enitan said, though his eyes looked somber.

She watched him go—probably back to the seventh floor—and stomped down a loose cobblestone, pretending she was being useful. She kicked about the gardens, though they didn't feel as charming as they had before. The bees were too loud. The sun was too bright.

Nia stomped over to a stone bench, but as she carelessly swung her legs up onto it, she failed to notice the ornate pottery vase to the side of it.

Crash.

"Oh no!" Nia jumped off of the bench and sifted through the shattered pieces with frantic fingers. It was useless. Even if she could miraculously piece every chip back together, the vase would never be the same.

The pile of ruined pottery glowed with green light. Nia jumped away from it as it lifted into the air and swirled, a cyclone of fine dust and larger shards. She watched in awe as the shape of the vase formed once more, and when it rested again gently on the ground, it was whole.

She whirled around to see Neilos there, looking as though he hadn't just done something amazing. Although for him, it probably wasn't.

"I'm sorry for breaking it," Nia muttered. "It was an accident."

"As you can see, it is not an issue. Feel free to break something else if it would help your mood."

Nia flushed and stared at the ground. Why did he have to keep finding her in vulnerable states? Still, she couldn't help but wonder what he would do if she took him up on the offer. She glanced up at him, her mouth pursed. She strolled a few steps forward to a large sphere that appeared to be some kind of ceramic. She kicked it full force, but it didn't give way at all. Nia let out a yelp, falling to the ground and clutching her foot.

Neilos chuckled, kneeling down beside her. "When I said you should break something, I didn't mean yourself. May I?" He gently took her throbbing foot in his hands, and Nia flinched both at the pain and at his touch.

It felt as though her foot was being drenched in warm water, then in an instant the sensation vanished, along with the pain.

"Thank you." She had intended to convey gratitude, but her voice came out annoyed, which only made Neilos laugh at her again. Nia scoffed and got to her feet.

"Nia," Neilos said softly, standing with her. "Will you walk with me? I have something I would like to show you. Things I would like to discuss."

Her knee-jerk reaction was to decline, but she stopped herself and let her thoughts clear of emotion. Why shouldn't she go with him? What else was she going to do right now? She wasn't going to get such attention from Enitan... Manes and tails. She didn't want to focus on Enitan right now.

"Ok, let's go."

He guided her through the gardens to a door she hadn't paid any attention to before. There was nothing remarkable about it—just an arched wooden door like she'd seen on practically every cottage. Neilos opened the door to reveal wide stone steps, descending into... who knew.

Neilos swept his hands apart, and the tunnel lit, revealing that the stairs went quite deep. The stone walls were covered in vines adorned with tiny white flowers. How did the flowers grow without sunlight? Neilos took the first step and motioned Nia to follow.

"Is that the dungeons?" Nia asked, unsure of what else he could be keeping so far down.

Neilos laughed. "Taking you to the dungeons would make me a very poor host indeed. I feel you'll like this better. Come."

She followed him carefully down the twisted staircase, her chest never quite losing the tight pinch of unease that accompanied her every time she was with Neilos. She took a few deep breaths to try and relax herself. It wouldn't be hard for him to hurt her, if that's what he wanted. He could probably do it without anyone in the castle even knowing, so that must not be his intention. And if he wanted her dead he could have just left her to the vines in the courtyard or the speculo. Normally, her instinct steered her true, but in this case, she really might be worrying for no reason.

"How is your breathing?" Neilos asked suddenly.

Nia paused. Now that he brought it to her attention, she wasn't struggling as much as she normally would when climbing a multitude of stairs. There was still a rawness in her lungs, but it wasn't what it was. "It's starting to feel better," she admitted.

"Wonderful. Imagine how much better you'll feel at the month's end, and forever after that."

She kept silent, recognizing his attempt to reinforce her staying. She was here on her own terms—not because Neilos willed it.

The stairs ended and the walls changed, stone bricks turning into cave walls and ground. The air felt cool and moist against Nia's skin, and she wished she had dressed warmer. As if reading her thoughts, a ball of fire at once appeared before them.

"It gets a bit cold down here. Keep close to this if you're uncomfortable."

Nia inched closer and couldn't deny the soothing warmth of the fire. The walls took on shades of deep emerald and blue. She occasionally caught a flash of something sparkling. The *drip drip drip* of water running down cave formations echoed in her ear. As they moved deeper, more colors appeared. Purple, magenta, rich golden yellow. Rainbows painted every surface of the room, and it was easy to imagine a unicorn living there.

She stopped and gasped at the room that opened up before them. At its center rested a pond that resembled aquamarine crystal. The water glistened and reflected like the surface of a diamond. It wasn't like the river, which was full of trauma and terror. The water before her beckoned with beauty and light and intrigue. When was the last time she had wanted so badly to touch something?

"Is it safe?" Nia asked.

"Perfectly."

Nia dipped her fingers in the water, surprised to find it warm. It soothed her and she swirled the water gently. The pond's surface came alive, and several creatures burst from it, showering Nia with droplets. Nia blinked the water from her eyes and refocused her vision.

"Pixies?"

"Yes. What do you think of them?"

Nia watched the tiny creatures as they glided about the room, giving off pastel glows of light in different colors. They had a transcendent beauty, and yet, there was something not quite right about them. The aura they gave off felt wrong. Nia sensed their essence—they were out of their element.

"I think they're sad."

"Sad?" Neilos raised his eyebrows. "They have a splendid home here. Everything they could want. They do not seem sad to me."

Nia held her hand out, and Neilos's face showed surprise when one of the pixies came to her in an instant and rested in her palm. A tiny thing, glowing in gentle lilac.

"Fascinating," he mused. "Even they are drawn to you. I have never seen them approach anyone."

"I've seen many pixies in my life. These seem hollow. I don't know how to explain it. They belong outdoors, not in a cave. Even if it's a beautiful cave." She thought of the times they frolicked with her in the shade of the forest, danced on the swirls of the wind or glided along the surface of streams. She had never seen them confined like this.

Neilos frowned, staring out at the shimmering wisps around the room. He lifted his hand, and Nia felt a deep, rumbling vibration. Sunlight burst into the room as a hole appeared above them, cutting through the many layers of rock straight to the surface. On cue, the pixies shot upward towards the opening, not wasting a moment to claim their freedom. The tiny lilac pixie gave a happy tingling sound and took flight from Nia's hand. The room was empty of them in seconds.

"So, it seems you were right." Neilos stared at the hole in the ceiling, aghast. Had it really never occurred to him that the pixies didn't like being trapped? And yet, he let them go without hesitation when Nia said they should be free. She didn't know what to make of that.

"You let them go? Just like that?"

"I told you I'm not in the business of keeping prisoners. I doubt the pixies are any danger to myself or the people here once free." He gazed at Nia once more. "I hate to see *you* feeling so trapped here instead of enjoying yourself."

Nia sighed and seated herself on a sizable boulder. She listened to the dripping water and stared at the patterns of the pond's surface reflected on the walls and ceiling of the cave. She wasn't sure what she was seeking there.

"Do you think everyone in the castle is unhappy here?" Neilos finally asked.

"They seem fine."

Neilos seated himself beside her, setting Nia's senses on overdrive again. "What sort of people do you think I employ here?"

Nia gave a light shrug. "Anyone who needed a job?" She didn't know how people usually went about filling their castles.

"Everyone who came here was in need of help. The wandering soul. The destitute. The hunted. I gave them all a home. A purpose. Safety." His voice softened. "I could do the same for you, if you would allow it."

"What makes you think I'm in need of help? I just want to heal and go home."

"A person doesn't carry the constant air of suspicion you do without some kind of trouble behind them. Wouldn't it be nicer to live a life where you're not always looking over your shoulder? When you leave these walls, what will you return to?"

What indeed? A decimated cottage, and trouble. There was the matter of the shadowscale, who would still be seeking her out. She counted on the stone to help her out of that predicament, if it could. These were problems she wasn't eager to face. Maybe there was some appeal to what Neilos offered.

She wrung her hands in her lap. "And what would be my purpose here if I stayed?"

"I'm sure we could find something you would enjoy. But before anything else, you have to allow yourself to feel comfortable here. Allow yourself to be comfortable with me."

Was there anyone who was truly comfortable around this man? He seemed so beyond anything in this world.

Nia faced him, determined not to let her gaze falter from his. "I have made it this far in life by trusting my instincts. I can't just force myself to feel—or not feel—something other than what's inside me."

He looked on with fascination. "Or perhaps you've always lived your life on edge and simply know nothing different?"

"Maybe."

Neilos stood and offered a hand, indicating that Nia should do the same. "I can't force your feelings. But I would like to extend an invitation."

Nia ignored his outstretched hand and got to her feet, waiting for him to continue.

"Our monthly ball will happen on the night of the full moon. I suggest you attend. This will give you a chance to experience something lighthearted and get to know the castle's inhabitants in a casual setting, if you'll allow it. I would like you to consider the possibility of staying here seriously."

Nia thought about the beauty and wonders of the castle. Of the kindness she had received from basically everyone she had interacted with.

Of Enitan.

Besides that, Neilos had so much power at his disposal already that he wasn't likely to pester Nia about the fortune stone if he learned she possessed it. Was she being ungrateful? Was she blind?

She let out a long sigh. "I will try. This is all out of my element, but I will try."

"Good," Neilos answered with a smile. "That's all I ask."

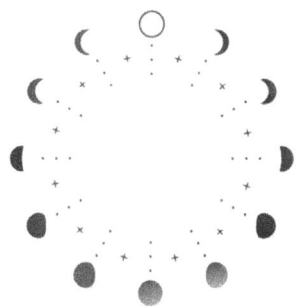

Chapter 14

Sixteen days until the Dark Moon

"I don't have anything for you, so you can stop looking at me like that." Nia cast a wry smile at the ravens on the garden wall as they peered at her with their dark, beady eyes. If she brought food, would they flock to her the way they did with Neilos? Instead, seeming to understand they wouldn't get any handouts from Nia, they took to the skies.

Nia chuckled and sat on the cool stone bench, closing her eyes to take in the comforting warmth of the sun. These last few days had wrought a change in her. She tried—really tried—to do what Neilos had suggested. She worked to break down her walls and instead let herself be enchanted by the castle. She allowed herself to stroll through the gardens without searching for the source of every rustling leaf. She indulged in warm bubble baths in her magically filling tub. She gazed at the crystal pool in the cave with her thoughts. She'd even had lunch with Neilos yesterday, and the conversation wasn't painful. When she wasn't on constant alert for reasons to be suspicious or afraid, she found the castle was actually quite lovely. It was peaceful. She wasn't yet sure if she wanted to extend her stay, but she was at least warming to the idea of lingering for a few weeks more.

Nia's luck rushed out of her, and she popped her eyes open, even though she already knew who she would find there. She had grown used to the unsettling phenomenon that happened every time the castle's young guard drew near.

Enitan smiled as though he wasn't the most interesting thing in the garden. "You look like you're enjoying yourself."

He was the one person Nia made a point of avoiding the past few days. She still wasn't ready to come to terms with her feelings after he didn't show up for their breakfast together.

"Yes, I was." It was hard to restrain the cold note in her voice. At her core, she didn't want to harbor a grudge against him, but getting her emotions to play along proved more challenging.

Enitan sat beside her and Nia assumed a more rigid stance, her hands folded tightly in her lap.

"Listen, Nia," Enitan released his breath in a long sigh. "I feel lousy about the other day. I can't stop thinking about it."

Really? Over the last few days, a thread tugged at her heart, entreating her to cast her pride aside and follow it back to him. Was it too much to hope that he spent the last few days feeling the same way?

She steadied herself to appear uncaring. "It's ok. Like you said, your work is important."

"I promised to meet you. I should have kept that promise. I'm sorry."

Nia stole a glance and saw the apology all over his face. Her heart softened. "I forgive you." She could feel the thread pull tight between them.

Enitan grinned, ensuring any coolness Nia might still have felt stood no chance. "Today just so happens to be my day off."

Nia raised her eyebrows. "You get those?"

"Of course I do. Neilos doesn't work us into the ground, you know."

"Hm." Yet another unfair assumption she had made.

"Anyway," Enitan peered at her, looking like a shy child. "Let me make it up to you."

"Breakfast was hours ago," Nia said with a smirk. Perhaps she still held a tiny grudge over his previous slight.

Enitan rolled his eyes. "Better than breakfast."

"Better than Antonia's strawberry crepes? I think you're lying."

"I'll admit that's hard to beat. But I was thinking it's time to show you my favorite spot in the castle."

Nia instantly perked up. "Can we go right now?"

Enitan's dimple appeared as he grinned. "As you wish, good lady."

They walked deep down into the chambers of the castle. Not as deep as the crystal pools, but deep enough. Nia expected it to get darker, but the tunnels were well lit with whatever enchantments Neilos had in place.

"Are we close?" Nia asked.

"A little further."

"Aren't you going to ask me to close my eyes or something?"

Enitan laughed. "If you want, but I'm not catching you if you trip."

"Oh, what a gentleman. I suppose I'll keep them open."

"I lied," Enitan quickly amended. "I will catch you."

His voice was so warm. So sincere. Falling might not be so bad if she ended up in his arms. Nia pretended to examine the cave wall so Enitan would not see her absurd thoughts written on her face.

At last, the tunnels opened up into a spacious cavern. The air was warm and heavy, and a musky smell caught Nia's nose. She was certain there were no pixies here.

"Stand in the center," Enitan commanded.

Nia walked across the chamber, marveling at the many tiny glittering jewels inlaid in the stone tiles that covered the ground. At the center of the chamber a large swirl carving decorated the rocky floor. She stood and waited, her heart fluttering. The lights snuffed out, and for a moment the world was darkness.

Nia gave a nervous laugh. "Is this the part where you kill me?"

Silence.

"Enitan?"

Enitan offered a nervous laugh of his own. "Remember, you asked for this. Don't hate me." Enitan clapped three times, the sound echoing through the chamber. The walls glowed a strange, deep neon blue. Nia heard the sound of something—several somethings—sliding across the floor, scraping along the dirt and stone. She looked down and gave a gasp.

"Snakes?"

Enitan grinned, his teeth glowing in the darkness. "You're not screaming."

"Disappointed?"

"A little bit."

Aside from the shadowscale, creatures didn't bother Nia. She had always had an affinity for animals of any kind. She suspected the fortune stone might have had something to do with their easy-going nature around her, but the stone wasn't active at that moment.

"These aren't poisonous, right?" Nia asked, feeling less sure of herself around them.

"No, Neilos doesn't keep poisonous ones. These are just here to entertain."

Nia watched the strange glow of the snakes' patterns. Stripes, diamonds, splotchy spots. They were fascinating to watch. Beautiful, even. She could see why they might appeal to someone with virtually everything at his disposal. Something like this—this ethereal experience—was more than a mere possession.

"Are you the only one besides Neilos who gets to see them?" Nia asked, watching one thickly striped creature weave underneath a rock.

"I take care of them, though they don't require much. Just access to rodents, mostly. You could say they don't mind being *ratted* out."

Nia groaned. "And here I was thinking you hadn't graced me with a bad pun in a while."

It was no wonder this was Enitan's favorite place. It gave him an escape. Something to do other than stand at attention before his master or patrol the castle. With his carefree nature, Nia thought it a terrible waste. Enitan was the type who should be out roaming the countryside and making friends. Going to fairs. Wooing ladies.

Nia shook herself out of her thoughts, feeling her cheeks heat.

"Neilos wouldn't mind you bringing me here?"

"I don't think so. But who cares if he does?"

A small thrill went through Nia knowing Enitan would want her here whether Neilos did or not. At the same time, she hated to think what might happen to Enitan if he was caught in defiance. Still, she hadn't yet heard of Neilos being cruel to a servant, and he hadn't forbidden her from any place in the castle. She wasn't being fair.

She recalled Neilos's words about the inhabitants of the castle: The destitute. The hunted. The lost. Who was Enitan?

"Enitan," Nia began, her voice echoing off the walls. "What brought you to this castle?"

At first, Nia thought he wasn't going to answer. The only sound was the slither of scale on rock.

Nia was about to tell him not to worry about it, but then he spoke in a quiet voice. "A great debt was owed. He offered a way to pay it."

"That was...kind of him." Neilos truly had a habit of collecting desperate people.

"Yes."

Nia focused hard on the swirl of serpents before her, fixating on their gentle glow under the strange lights. Why did she have to feel this way? Even as she became more at ease with the castle itself, she couldn't fully extend that comfort to Neilos. The servants spoke well of him. Enitan seemed appreciative. Nia had passed half a month in the castle walls without any harm done to her outside of the consequences of her own rash behavior. So why couldn't she shake these suspicions? Magala always said Nia was too paranoid, but Nia argued that was because her intuition was usually right. Maybe this time she was wrong.

"Are you going to the ball?" Nia traced the grooves of the stone wall beside her. It was an innocent enough question to ask.

Enitan gave a lopsided smile. "Of course. I'll be on guard."

"Oh." Nia tried not to sound too disappointed. "No dancing, then?"

He gave a loud laugh, the sound bouncing around the room.

"What's so funny?"

"Just your face right then. If I didn't know better, I would say that disappointed you."

"Well, maybe it did. So?"

He inched closer to Nia, and her heart *thump thump thumped*.

"I was kidding," he said softly, nearly a whisper. "Well, mostly. I will be on guard, but we go in shifts. Everyone gets dancing time."

"Isn't that dangerous?" Nia asked, though she couldn't conceal her delight. "Not having everyone on post?"

Enitan shrugged. "I don't think someone as powerful as Neilos needs guards at all. I think he wants people to feel useful, or maybe take a little of the load off his shoulders. We're safe here."

"Yes, it seems you are."

Nia hadn't realized how close they were. She was staring at him and couldn't seem to stop. For a moment, his eyes traveled to her lips and the longing she saw there sent sparks through her. If she just tipped forward a few inches...

"Anyway," Enitan said, drawing suddenly away. "I'll be there with friends. Come find me for a dance, all right?"

Nia quashed her disappointment. "All right."

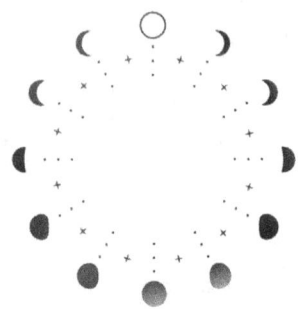

Chapter 15

Fifteen days until the Dark Moon

Nia caught a rippling glimpse of herself in the pool in the courtyard and scowled at her reflection. Ever since she left Enitan the day before her mood had been sullen.

She pretended the person in the water staring back at her was a stranger and she scrutinized her, doing her best to be objective. Nia had never obsessed over her appearance, but she knew she was attractive. At the very least, she was sure she wasn't *un*attractive. She didn't think she and Enitan had a personality clash—they always seemed to enjoy themselves and get along. While Nia would be the first to admit she wasn't well-practiced in social affairs, she didn't think she'd committed any serious faux pas. So, what was the problem? Why wouldn't Enitan kiss her? She was sure he had wanted to. Maybe he thought her boring.

Maybe there was someone else he wanted to kiss more.

Nia splashed the water, as though she could shoo her reflection away.

She couldn't keep her feelings at bay any longer. What she felt for Enitan was more than friendship. She had romantic feelings for the castle guard, the young man who was her personal dark moon. Nothing good could come from attempting to stay at his side.

Her lungs strained, but this time it had nothing to do with her injury. She took in several breaths, overcome. She had to get out now. The ball was that evening, and going there would only tighten her bonds to this place.

Neilos may have locked the castle down with enchantments, but she was no ordinary person. She was the owner of a fortune stone.

She recalled a long-ago conversation with Magala, as she attempted to teach Nia some responsibility with the magic relic.

Keep it close and let it be your friend. It will take care of you. I've heard it said that when its luck is strong, the stone can even help the holder pass through magical wards.

Would the stone be strong enough to help her out of the barrier now?

Show me what you've got, luck.

Nia wouldn't wait until dark. The stone had always looked after her before and would give her what she needed. The moon was full tonight, so her luck was strong. Therefore, it was no surprise when she didn't encounter a single guard or servant as she moved through the gardens.

"Where should I go?" she asked out loud. The stone's force whispered back, urging her towards the menagerie. She arrived just in time to see Aldric exiting the gate in a hurry, leaving it open just a smidge. He didn't notice her from her spot behind the hedges, and she smiled as she entered the gate.

No nightstripe pounced upon her this time. She followed the stone's pull but hesitated when it beckoned her towards the dragon's pit. She didn't want to be reminded of the lonely creature who had died too soon, and wasn't sure she could bear it if Neilos had trapped another. Still, the stone had never misled her before, so she continued.

The pit did in fact, have a new occupant, but this one wore feathers and fur instead of scales. The griffin peered at her with dark, curious eyes and the stone enticed Nia to continue. She cranked the lever on the winch that opened the top of its enclosure. The griffin made an immediate escape but instead of taking to the sky to seek its freedom, it landed in front of Nia and waited for her to make the next move.

She'd heard of people getting ripped to shreds when attempting to ride a griffin, and everything she'd read in books said not to approach unless invited. The griffin tilted its head, ruffling its neck feathers. This one seemed to be inviting her, and the hum of her luck still ran strong. She approached with more confidence and climbed on the creature's back.

"Let's get out of here," Nia whispered as she gripped the tufts of fur at the griffin's shoulders.

The marvelous beast took flight, seemingly as eager to escape as its rider. It soared up over the hedges. Over the trees. Over the massive wall surrounding the entirety of the castle.

Away from the boy who stole her luck and her heart.

The griffin stopped short and screeched, rearing its front legs.

"Keep going," Nia urged.

The creature continued beating its wings and kept them steadily airborne, but it did not progress further. Nia reached out and the sharp twinge of magic buzzed against her fingertips.

She pulled the stone from her pocket, finding it warm against her skin. Still alive with good fortune. Had she misremembered Magala's words about magical wards?

"Let me through," she pleaded.

The enchanted barrier remained firm.

Crestfallen, she patted the griffin on the side of its neck. "Sorry, friend. It looks like neither of us will be leaving today."

Once they returned to the ground, Nia hesitated. Should she take the creature back to its pen? She took in the griffin's glistening feathers and silken fur. Its powerful form. She couldn't bear to be the jailer of something so magnificent. She did not doubt Neilos would recapture the griffin again before long, but she could allow it a measure of freedom for as long as possible. She led it to some of the taller hedges.

"I'm going to leave you here. If you're clever, you might escape them for a while. But, don't hurt anyone, ok?"

The griffin made a soft trilling noise and moved into the shadows of deeper foliage.

Nia felt a little envious of the creature. She wouldn't get away with hiding in the gardens for the rest of her stay. She padded about the grounds, restless. The ball was that evening. Enitan had asked her to dance with him. That might have cheered her up if their circumstances weren't so complicated. Instead, being so close to him would only entangle her further.

She. Needed. Out.

Her gut told her it would be a mistake to ask Neilos for passage to leave. The stone warmed in agreement and warning. There had to be an alternative tucked away somewhere in the castle.

She took a breath, realization hitting, and set an immediate course for the transphere.

Before she had the chance to overthink it, Nia heard her voice whisper, "Seventh floor." Spencer would have been proud...if he had actually been Spencer and not the speculo locked away in a dungeon somewhere. She shivered at her thoughts of the dubious creature. If he had been pushing her there, then going would almost certainly be a bad idea. Yet, the stone warmed in her pocket, compelling her onward.

Nia lurched out of the transphere and took a moment to orient herself. The seventh floor appeared deserted, and the complete silence almost made her reconsider exploring it. There was an odd stillness in the air, and it was the sort of place you would whisper in if you were with company. The dim hallway carried an ancient musk—a smell that was more than simply dust or decay, but something that belonged to another time.

A glint at the far end of the corridor caught her eye, compelling her to investigate despite her reservations.

The glint was only a doorknob, but Nia had never come across a doorknob so mesmerizing. It looked as though someone had contained the sky at midnight and sent it into perpetual motion. Deep blues and purples swirling with silvery twinkles made up the surface. Did the knob really turn? Nia grasped the knob and found it warm to the touch. It was not like metal warmed in the sun, but more like a comforting handshake. The deep colors and glitter of the knob swirled and beckoned. She gave a twist, and it didn't budge, but Nia could sense that it *wanted* to. The stone warmed, matching the warmth in the doorknob.

"Would you let me in?" she asked, her voice low and gentle.

The pressure of resistance beneath her hand gave way and Nia took a surprised step back when the door opened; It didn't seem like the sort of door that should open so easily, but she had good fortune on her side.

The door contained...nothing. Perhaps this was Spencer's idea of a joke.

It was only a small empty room with deep purple carpeting and dark wooden panels covering the walls and ceiling. A closet, perhaps. But what was the point of an empty closet? Nia glanced toward a creak above her, followed by the hiss of something sliding across wood. A square of the ceiling folded down. A trap door? A smooth wooden ladder slid to the ground and then stood upright. Waiting.

"I'm not going up there. No way," Nia told herself. Anything at all could be up there. Beasts. Poisons. Neilos.

Unicorns?

She reached for the first rung of the ladder.

Nia climbed into the sky, or at least, that's how it appeared. The large room was a domed, circular shape and the ceiling was made entirely of glass; Yet, somehow even with the bright blue sky shining through, the rest of the room seemed dark. Nia could just make out several pedestals around the room's outer perimeter, each with objects of various shapes and sizes on top. Clearly no unicorns, but interesting all the same. She walked carefully through the dim space, approaching the pedestal furthest from her. The stone's warmth left her.

"I showed you my favorite spot in the castle and you repay me by sneaking to the one place you shouldn't be?"

Nia gasped and threw her hand to her chest as she whirled around. "Enitan! You scared me!" The stone should have been a warning, yet he still caught her off guard.

Enitan laughed, the sound distorting into odd echoes. The unnatural darkness combined with the way light came in through the room's opening made him look like a disembodied head. He hoisted himself all the way in, disappearing into the shadows. Nia stood still listening to his footsteps, and suddenly he was right in front of her. Up close, however, she could see the light in his eyes, the soft kindness in his face. Her overexcited nerves melted into something gentler.

"Am I in trouble?" Nia asked.

"Yep."

"For coming in here without permission?"

Enitan grinned. "No, because you didn't even say hello."

Nia rolled her eyes. "Hello."

"It's too late. Moment's gone."

"Oh, what a shame." Nia gave her best pout, surprising herself with her coquettish tone. Then she once again remembered his eyes lingering on her lips and she turned away.

Enitan shook his head at her, evidently oblivious. "Seriously, though. You shouldn't be here."

"What is this place?"

"This is where the master keeps his relics. Things he's collected over the years."

"Magic objects?"

"Some of them." Enitan scratched his head. "Or maybe all of them. I don't really know. But I guard the place. I take inventory three times a day."

Nia cocked her head. "Shouldn't a place this important be kept behind a locked door?" Of course, this wasn't really a fair barb since she had the stone's assistance.

Enitan's face fell. "It should have been locked. I'm usually very careful about that."

"So," Nia smirked, "It's really you who would be in trouble if your master learned I was here."

Enitan's face paled and Nia regretted the tease in an instant. Neilos must be serious about this room for Enitan to react that way.

"I'll let you off the hook," she said, "on one condition. Can I see some of these things?"

Enitan pondered her request with a brow knit in careful concentration, and then sighed and waved her forward. "Come here."

She followed him to the center of the room. He cleared his throat and said in a loud, clear voice, "Dagger."

To Nia's left, one of the pedestals flashed bright green. An ornate dagger rested on its surface. Something about it struck a chord of familiarity, but before she could contemplate it, Enitan spoke again.

"Amulet."

The light on the dagger faded and this time a deep blue flash filled the room, illuminating a pedestal ahead of Nia with a shining amulet.

"Mask." A flash of yellow, illuminating a plain white mask with a wide grin.

"What does that one do?" Nia asked, studying the somewhat unsettling expression.

Enitan gave an exaggerated shrug. "Don't *mask* me."

Nia groaned. "Not your best effort."

"Yeah, I'll admit that one was way off. In seriousness, though, supposedly if you wear that one you can pass through any area undetected. Never tried it, though. Neilos would kill me."

Nia gave a sly smile. "Not if he couldn't detect you."

Enitan laughed. "I like the way you think. But knowing Neilos, I'd still die."

An uninvited chill crept down her spine. Surely Enitan was being hyperbolic. She hated to imagine the castle's master would actually put Enitan to death for testing one of his trinkets.

Enitan called out several more objects for display, each with a flash of blue, yellow, or green.

"What do the colors mean?" Nia asked.

Enitan shrugged. "I don't think they mean anything. Just for the spectacle."

"Hm." Nia wasn't sure if Neilos was the type of person who would do something like that just for show, but she supposed she didn't know him the way Enitan did.

"Now," Enitan said in a commanding voice, "time for you to go."

Nia struggled with the idea of leaving, but she knew there wasn't a point in arguing—he didn't want her in this room to begin with. "Do you have to stay here?"

She was more hesitant to leave Enitan than to leave the relics. She felt lost in this place, and he was an anchor to security. Even if he didn't want to kiss her, she still wanted him as a friend. The inescapable weight of reality sank into her as she stared into Enitan's eyes: she wasn't going to leave. She would go to the ball and lose another piece of herself to the boy who gave her a second chance at life. She wished the stone was working so it could tell her if she was making the right choice.

"I'll be here for a while still," he said. "But I'll see you this evening. Just try not to wander into any more strange places, ok?"

"Does Neilos have a lot of secrets?" Nia asked, pausing to run her fingertips over a pedestal as she passed it. She wasn't usually so bold, but her security with Enitan prompted her to ask some of the questions burning on her lips.

Enitan seemed to be thinking over the question carefully as he removed Nia's hand from the pedestal. Gently. Was it her imagination, or did his hand linger on hers? Imagination or not, her skin prickled with heat.

After a heavy pause, Enitan answered. "No, not a lot of secrets. But he does have some dangerous things. It comes with the territory."

He escorted her back to the ladder and watched after her to make sure she made her way safely down.

He tilted his head. "See you tonight?"

"See you tonight."

It was hard to believe just that morning Nia felt trepidation over the ball. Now she tittered around in her room wondering how to make the right impression. Did she want to appear poised around Neilos? Dazzle Enitan? She hadn't worked out her goals, but she felt certain she wasn't elegant enough for anyone in the castle.

"Please stop fidgeting, miss, or I'll never get these flowers weaved."

Nia picked at a seam in her tunic as Antonia put an array of fair blossoms in her hair. Periwinkle, daisies, and lilacs cascaded through her curls. Nia wasn't even sure yet what she was going to wear, but she thought it might be easier to let Antonia do her magic first and dress around it.

"It's beautiful, Antonia!" Nia admired the perfect weave of springtime in her hair. Antonia gave a soft smile.

"Do you enjoy this type of work?" Nia appreciated Antonia's kindness, but she always wondered if she would choose to do something else given the option.

As always, Antonia held a careful pause before responding. "For you, I enjoy it. Come, let's get you dressed." She whisked her to the wardrobe before Nia could ask her to clarify the statement.

When Nia opened the wardrobe, she expected to be greeted with a magical assortment of garments as usual. Instead, there was only one dress inside. Nia's breath caught as she pulled it out to examine it. It was like holding moonlight in her hands. The dress was a pale shade of silvery fabric that cascaded over her fingertips. The sweetheart neckline was stitched with tiny flowers in pastel shades. The skirt was full and soft with... Oh! Unicorns! Embroidered unicorns. Nia was sure there had to be some sort of magic involved with the creation of this dress, but she had to put it on notwithstanding her reservations about enchantments. Of course, it fit her perfectly, flattering in all the right places. Nia felt like a forest fairy.

"Beautiful," Antonia said with a smile. "Now, go enjoy yourself."

Nia wanted to formulate an excuse to hang back and get the stone, but no words formed. The dress had no pockets and tying it around her waist beneath her magnificent gown seemed like too much of a hindrance to both the fashion and the dancing. Besides that, if she hoped to spend the evening with Enitan, there was no point in having it anyway. For once, she left the stone behind intentionally, and it didn't bring her as much anxiety as she expected.

Nia walked too carefully in the dress. Too stiffly. She was worried about damaging something so perfect. She had to remind herself it was made with exceedingly fine craftsmanship, and she would have to do a lot more than simply walking in it to damage it. She expected navigating the stairs to be a challenge in the gown, but the fabric felt light as air as she moved in it. It was a dress made for dancing.

Perhaps she shouldn't attend after all. Everyone in the castle was used to balls and dancing and would probably be full of elegance. Nia was likely to injure herself—or someone else. Still, she knew Neilos expected her, and the least she could do was thank him for the dress. Enitan was expecting her too. His gaze on her lips flashed through her mind, making her feel dizzy. Nia inhaled deeply and blew the breath out in a puff, pretending that the burst of air held all her anxiety. She opened the door.

Immediately the tinkling sounds of music met her ears. It was an oddly beautiful sound, unlike anything Nia had ever heard. She scanned the crowded ballroom for its source but couldn't see any obvious signs of an instrument or musician. She closed her eyes for a moment to listen more intently, and only then did she realize the sound was coming from above. She looked up toward the high ceilings where a cluster of crystalline instruments floated in the air and played ethereal tunes. The lights danced off of them as they moved, casting glimmering reflections along the floor and walls.

Nia took in the room, filled with servants who were talking, laughing, and dancing. It struck her that she should take time to get to know more of them. It didn't make sense to ignore them while they shared a dwelling.

A hissed swear word behind Nia signified Uma entering the room, her magic trays floating behind her. "So many here already and I haven't even got the cheeses out!"

"Can I help you?"

Uma waved her off. "A fine offer, but Neilos would have my head if I pulled you away from his party, or caused you to damage that dress."

"You don't get any time off tonight?"

"I don't want it." Uma's face soured as she made her declaration. "I hate noise. I hate dancing. Keeping busy is the only thing that saves my sanity when he holds these twittering parties. Now, off with you."

Nia left Uma to her bustling and instead searched the room for Enitan. She felt a hand on her shoulder a moment later and turned to meet Neilos's amber eyes.

"Welcome," he said warmly. "Is it to your liking?"

"It's enchanting," Nia conceded.

Neilos smiled slowly. "Well then, I hope you will allow yourself to be enchanted." He laughed loudly, seeing the sudden shift in Nia's expression. "Not literally, of course, but do enjoy the party."

A long exhale escaped Nia as she watched him hurry to mingle with the crowd. That wasn't so bad. She had been worried he would press for more of her time, but he seemed very busy socializing with everyone else. She wouldn't have to fumble and try to stay eloquent. Wouldn't have to worry what might happen if she let her guard down.

"Wow."

Nia turned once more to find the source of the surprised voice. Enitan stood a ways off, gaping. Heat instantly entered Nia's cheeks. Maybe the dress was a bit much.

"Wow?" Nia echoed as they approached one another. "How do I interpret that?"

"Oh, it's a good thing," Enitan fumbled. "You just, well, that dress really suits you."

"Thank you." Nia smiled and wondered if it would be appropriate to ask him for a dance. Even though Enitan had said she should find him for just that, she wasn't sure if dancing with the head guard was acceptable, even if he was off duty.

"Dance with me?" Enitan asked first, sparing Nia the predicament.

"I don't really do this," Nia warned, surprised at the lack of anxiety she felt over the prospect. "So, if you don't mind looking foolish with me, I'm all yours."

Enitan flashed a wide grin. "I would look foolish anyway. Even better with someone else."

They took to the floor. Neither of them had any idea what they were doing or any inclination to lead, but they fumbled through it anyway. The song was far more graceful than either of them. They laughed as they bumped into one another and tripped over their own and each other's feet. They weren't going to win any prizes for their dancing, but Nia couldn't remember the last time she had laughed so much.

"Thank you for being such an awful dancer," she teased in a pause between songs. "It puts me at ease."

"Thank you for being equally bad." Enitan put an arm around Nia's waist and pulled her off to the side, away from the other dancers. "I think I'll sit the next one out."

The room started to feel overly warm, but Nia couldn't say whether it was because of all the people or their dancing. Or maybe the way Enitan's hand was still on her waist.

"Do you mind if I get a drink?" Nia asked, face sore from smiling and out of breath from so much laughter and activity.

Enitan shook his head, his eyes alive with happiness. "Why don't I bring you one? You take it easy."

Nia beamed back. "How chivalrous of you. I'll be right here."

She flashed Enitan one last smile before he attempted to navigate through the crowd to the drink table. But before he made it there, she saw Neilos waving him over. She frowned. What could he want? Was he having Enitan return to his guard duties already?

She nudged her worries to the back of her mind and closed her eyes, listening to the sway of the music and breathing in the sweet aromas wafting through the room. It took no effort to sink into dreamlike bliss of it all when she dropped her walls and succumbed to it. She leaned against the cool stone wall, lulled into a sense of contentment.

Nia waited through one song. Then one more. She licked her dry lips—she really was quite thirsty and the dream was beginning to wear thin in Enitan's absence. Where was he? She opened her eyes and peered around the room, searching for the young guard's emerald-green uniform among the dancing lights and spinning pastels of elegant clothing.

At last, she spotted him and the room froze. He was surrounded by a group of ladies in shimmering gowns, telling jokes by the way they all laughed. They were completely captivated by him, just as she had been. Each of them—Enitan included—held crystal goblets in a rainbow of drink choices. He seemed to have forgotten all about her.

Heat and confusion shot through her. She had half a mind to march over and demand his attention. But, she didn't own him. It wasn't as though they had come to the ball together. When he asked her to save a dance for him, he was probably being charitable and now he was with the friends—and girls—he truly wanted to be with. The people who really knew him. After all, he was only allowed a little free time at the ball, and she had consumed most of it.

Suddenly feeling very foolish, she eyed the drink table and stalked towards it, ducking her head as tears of humiliation pricked the corners of her eyes.

The colorful liquids spread across the table gleamed like stained glass. There were so many choices, and she didn't trust a single one of them. Perhaps she should return to her room. Her desire for dancing was long gone.

"Don't worry—I didn't forget your drink of choice."

Nia started as Neilos appeared at her side. He gestured to the far end of the table where a few crystal goblets of water rested, evidentally untouched.

"I guess it's not a popular selection for these parties?" Nia asked, trying to force some kind of a smile and resist the urge to retreat from Neilos's presence. What had Neilos said to Enitan when he called him over earlier?

"No, not at all. But it doesn't seem you need it to enjoy yourself. You and my guard appeared to have a *marvelous* time."

He had been watching. Nia quickly moved to grab a goblet, assuring herself there was no reason to feel ashamed of dancing with Enitan. If Neilos didn't expressly forbid it, then she would socialize with anyone she chose. Besides, he only cautioned her not to distract Enitan from his duties. Right now, the guard was on his own time.

Nia steadied her hands and took a large gulp of the water. It was sweet and cold on her tongue. *Very* cold. The liquid shivered down her throat and into her chest. Perhaps she was more parched than she realized. She had been dancing hard.

Neilos stood with his arms lightly crossed, his amber eyes glinting. That same soft smile of confidence played on his perfectly sculpted lips. "Could I possibly have a turn with you on the floor now?"

"If you saw me, you know I'm no expert at it," Nia mumbled, her face flushing in spite of the water's chill. "Your feet might not make it out alive."

"Well, let's see how you fare with someone more experienced. Please, I insist."

Nia felt lightheaded. She took one more swig of water before allowing him to lead her to the center of the floor against her better judgment. Everyone parted ways for them, which only made Nia more nervous. She didn't need so many people paying attention to her. Neilos took Nia's hand carefully in his own and placed his other on her waist. The action brought butterflies, but not the kind that made her giddy. These were the nauseous, nervous kind. The swell of the music began once more, and he guided her movements. She had to admit, he was graceful, and helped her to appear the same. In her brilliant dress and with his captivating presence, Nia was sure they were a spectacle to behold. Still, she felt more comfortable when she was fumbling around with Enitan.

And why was it so cold?

After a few turns around the floor, Neilos prompted conversation. "Where are you from, Nia?"

"Ravenskeep." Nia surprised herself with how easily she answered. She didn't think of herself as a dishonest person, but she didn't like to reveal more than she needed to, either. Normally, she would be inclined to answer something vague like, "a village to the west" or "outside of the west kingdom."

"Do you have family there?"

"No. It's just me. I live alone." Again, spilling out more information than needed.

Neilos leaned forward slightly and asked, "Do you have anyone there who is dear to you?"

Why did this feel like an interrogation? "There's Magala. She owns a fruit cart. We look after each other."

"Anyone else?"

"No. Well, I mean, the villagers are important to me in a community sense, but I don't keep close ties with anyone."

"Is that because of your fortune stone?"

Cold burned down her spine, turning the ice within her to arctic temperatures.

He knew about the stone. However, the shock wasn't enough to keep her wayward words from spilling over like water from a freshly primed spout. "Yes. It's easier that way. I can't be taken advantage of if nobody knows." *Shut up, Nia.*

He dipped her low and Nia was certain her eyes betrayed her feelings.

"Are you surprised I know?" Neilos asked in a voice like silk. "You shouldn't be. There's little I don't know or can't find out." He leaned close and said in a harsh whisper "I've known the whole time."

Nia stopped dancing and forced her hands out of his, staring. The scene continued to play out around them, dazzling lights, scintillating colors, but her world had frozen.

"What do you want?" she asked, though the words seemed difficult to get out.

Neilos gave a light laugh. "Everything."

He left Nia then, resuming his flitting about the room, as though he hadn't just admitted to knowing Nia's biggest secret. She felt sick, hands reaching to support herself on a large marble column. If any of the servants noted her distress, they didn't show it. They only continued to dance. Where was Enitan? He must have returned to his guard duties, because he was nowhere to be found.

Everything about the room felt wrong. Nia's head whirled as she looked at the decorations, the dancers, the lights. Everything was so...perfect. Every movement of the dance was exacted with absolute precision, as though the ballroom guests were marionettes controlled by a grand master. Everyone wore the same manufactured smiles. There were no flaws in the music due to slipping fingers or misplaced breaths. Every light sparkled in just the right way. Nia was certain anything *that* perfect could only be a mask for the horrors hiding beyond the surface. The ghastly skeleton underneath the costume. She turned and fled from the ballroom, grateful that, if nothing else, nobody stopped her.

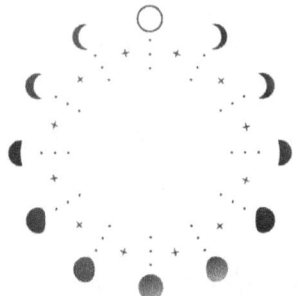

Chapter 16

Fifteen days until the Dark Moon

The already lengthy halls of the castle seemed to stretch endlessly as Nia rambled back to her rooms. Everything was off-kilter, as though her insides might come rushing out if she opened her mouth. So much of her already had. Neilos had stolen the truth from her. She would never be able to trust a drink in this cursed castle again.

She stumbled past a servant in the halls who observed her harried state with a furrowed brow. "Are you all right, miss?"

"No, I think I've been bewitched, or maybe drugged," Nia blurted. She gasped at her unrestrained words and quickened her pace, pushing past the servant who looked more confused, but didn't follow.

At last, she reached her room and shoved her way inside. She took several quick, shallow breaths and leaned against the bedpost, waiting for everything to stop spinning. Who could she talk to? Who could she trust? Antonia, maybe. Enitan? They were all loyal to Neilos, but seemed concerned for Nia too. Somebody here had to help her.

The dress that had been so exquisite just a short time ago now felt confining and dirty. Nia struggled out of it, not caring when she heard the snap of threads, and cast it aside, ignoring that she felt even colder in only her undergarments. Not even unicorn embroidery was enough to keep her in that dress while knowing it was a gift from Neilos.

Several minutes passed, and the panic in Nia's body began to even out. Her chest felt less constricted, and her breathing eased. Her body still felt so blasted cold! A warm bath would set everything right.

Nia started upon seeing an unexpected figure in the washroom. She relaxed when she realized it was Antonia.

Except...

Antonia wasn't moving.

Panic surged, the acrid burn of acid in Nia's throat bringing the first hint of heat to her frigid body. Antonia slumped over the marble countertop, the magic basin half-filled while the water bubbled up from nowhere.

"Antonia?" Nia rushed to her and gently shook her shoulders. Her head lulled and Nia caught her as she fell and buckled to her knees. "Antonia!"

For the moment, Nia forgot her own woes. She needed to get Antonia to a bed, a chair. Something.

Nia felt a scrape against her arm where she cradled Antonia's head. She carefully pushed back the dark strands of hair at the nape of her neck. A wind-up key?

The bile resting at the base of her throat threatened to escape her entirely. It looked so abnormal.

So wrong.

Nia tried to wrap her head around it. This was a magic castle. Was Antonia no more than a wind-up doll, enchanted to serve? She took a slow breath, forcing herself to calm. It didn't sound as crazy as it would have when Nia first got here. And, more importantly, doll or not, Antonia was kind to Nia, and she would do what she could to help her.

Perhaps all Antonia needed was to be wound up again.

With careful fingers, Nia turned the tiny key. Once. Twice. Three times. She continued to turn until the mechanism started to feel tight, and then turned once more.

Snap.

Nia was holding the key in her shaking fingers. *I broke it!* What would happen to Antonia?

Antonia released a loud, rasping gasp. Color rushed into her cheeks and her eyes popped open. "You broke it."

"I didn't mean—"

Antonia sat up and grasped Nia's hands, smiling. "You broke the spell!"

"Spell?"

"Everyone in this castle is under one, to some extent. Except you, of course. And that's only because Neilos knows you have to give him the stone of your own will."

Antonia knew about the stone. Did that mean...even Enitan? Was his kindness towards her all fabricated? No, it couldn't be.

"Do you remember anything?" Nia wanted to straight out ask how much of it was real but couldn't bring herself to do it.

"I remember everything. Sometimes I was even in control."

"What do you mean?"

Antonia tipped her head, thoughtfully. "Neilos allows some degree of free will. Basically, as long as we aren't doing anything that might foil his plans, we are ourselves. But his magic kicks in anytime we consider acting out of line. We still have to perform our assigned jobs."

"So, what was your job?"

"Simply to care for you. There were many times I wanted to tell you what was happening, to warn you. But I never could." Antonia's gaze drifted to the water bowl, almost wistfully. "I was trying to drown myself."

Nia gasped and Antonia continued, unperturbed by her revelation. "Obviously I wasn't supposed to do that."

"So, what Neilos told me about preparing magical elixirs wasn't true?"

"Oh, that part is true. I still make magical remedies when needed. When did he mention that?"

"He said something about a memory elixir...I declined."

Her eyes widened briefly. "I'm glad you didn't take him up on the offer. I'm sure you have many precious memories."

Nia struggled to take everything in, especially while she felt so out of sorts. Now, at least, Nia felt she could talk to Antonia without fear of her suspicions being used against her. And if Antonia was experienced with magical remedies and elixirs, maybe she would know what was happening to Nia. "I drank something. I thought it was water, but I started giving Neilos all the information he asked for. I couldn't help it."

"It was veritas water," Antonia said instantly, her face hard. "He had me prepare a batch before the party tonight. You're cold?"

"Yes," Nia said.

"You'll feel that way for the next thirteen hours or so. I would avoid talking to people until then. Otherwise, you'll have no secrets. Just stay here. I'll see to it you get anything you need."

"But you're free now," Nia said in awe. "Don't you want to get out?"

"I couldn't if I tried. Not until the dark moon when Neilos rests his enchantments. The best thing we can do now is pretend nothing has changed. I have to behave as though I'm still under the spell, and you have to do the same."

"And when the dark moon comes?"

"We run for it."

Nia now knew without asking that Neilos had no intention of letting her leave. Not if she asked. Not when the dark moon came. She was trapped unless she gave him what he wanted, which was the stone. Of course it was the stone. Anyone who had ever taken an interest in Nia did so because of that rock. Lucky, indeed.

"Now that you know everyone is controlled," Antonia warned, "Please be extra careful about who you speak to and what you say. Everything will get back to Neilos."

Nia nodded, hating that her carefree conversations with Enitan could no longer be carefree. She would have to guard every word. Had she already said too much?

"I'll find a way to free everyone," Nia said, her voice firm with determination.

Antonia met her words with a sad smile. "That's a wonderful thought. But I don't see how it's possible with a man as powerful as Neilos in control."

Nia still had nearly two weeks left in this place before the dark moon. No matter how hopeless it appeared, she was going to try.

Antonia came to Nia's room early, her mouth stretched into a tight frown. "He's insisting you join him for breakfast today."

Nia shivered. "I don't think I can. Not without giving something away."

"You have to try, Nia. Please. If you don't join him, he'll suspect something." Antonia rushed to the wardrobe and chose a dress on Nia's behalf, seeming to instinctively know Nia wasn't in the mood for choosing her own.

"Do you really believe he wouldn't expect me to be suspicious of the veritas water? Does he think I'm that stupid?"

"He probably thinks you wouldn't have enough evidence to act on, especially because he doesn't know I confirmed the use of veritas water. In isolation with nobody to validate their worries, most people would probably just assume the dancing went to their head and try to brush it off as nothing."

She busied herself with Nia's hair, turning the mess of curls from her restless night into something more presentable. "The veritas water should have worn off by now, but it's different for everyone.

There could be lingering effects. Try to keep as much truth in your conversation as you can."

Nia steeled herself. Overnight, Neilos had gone from a man she was just slightly suspicious of to a man who had his entire castle under magical imprisonment. Still, she could put on an act. She'd spent her whole life protecting herself and doing whatever she needed to survive. Compared to her life before the fortune stone, this was easy. All she had to do was keep up the ruse. With the stone secure in her pocket, she could only hope the conversation would turn in her favor.

"Ok," Nia said, "I'll see you after breakfast."

Neilos was always watching with those oddly piercing eyes, but he seemed to be observing Nia even more carefully now. "Did you enjoy the party? I didn't see you leave."

Nia worked to keep her voice calm, but not monotone. "I'm not used to that much excitement, so I left early."

"You look unwell. Did you sleep poorly?"

"I was a little cold." Nia gave an inward cringe at her answer. Was the veritas water still in effect to some degree? Antonia did warn her that she should avoid people. "Antonia got me more blankets, so it was fine." Oh no. She shouldn't have mentioned Antonia. If he asked about her more then she might say too much.

He smiled. "Has Antonia been taking care of you sufficiently?"

"Oh yes. She has been wonderful." At least she could say that without restraint. Antonia had taken care of Nia's every need since she'd arrived, as long as Nia allowed her to.

"Do you like being here?"

Nia couldn't bite off the words. "No."

The stone warmed, urging her to say more. Something that would smooth over her harsh reply. "I miss my village and the magic is unsettling." This shouldn't be surprising news to him, but he still might not like hearing it. Or maybe it was precisely what he wanted to hear. He could have more leverage on her if he knew she was eager to leave. He had something she wanted—her freedom.

Neilos sighed and closed his eyes. "While I'm unhappy to hear you aren't enjoying your stay, I do appreciate the honesty. And I suppose I understand. This must be so very different from what you're used to. And," He gave a sly smile, "Not having your lucky stone must be *very* disconcerting."

So, he didn't know she had the stone with her? Bless her luck for that. Thankfully, she could give a truthful answer about how it felt not to have it. "It is. I've had it since I was a child. It's like missing a limb."

"I would very much like to see it. Perhaps you could—"

"Master!"

Both Nia and Neilos turned sharply to the door as Enitan burst in. Nia's heart raced as her luck vanished. Enitan couldn't be here now!

"To what do we owe the rude interruption?" Neilos raised his eyebrows, his tone acrid.

"I'm sorry, master, but there's some kind of dragon or beast outside the castle."

Nia was curious about the dragon, but even more focused on the way Enitan didn't spare her a glance as he entered the room. It stung more than she expected it would.

Neilos waved a dismissive hand. "Let it be. It can't get through my enchantments."

"I think you should assess the situation, sir. It doesn't seem normal."

Look at me, Enitan. He didn't.

"Very well," Neilos sighed. "If you'll excuse me, Nia." He pushed up from his chair and retreated with Enitan.

If nothing else, the creature got her away from Neilos and his questions. Even if her good fortune disappeared, Enitan's timing was lucky. Nia vacated her place at the table the instant Neilos and Enitan slipped out the door. She raced towards her room but stopped short when she heard the sound. The familiarity of the low, rumbling roar sent an arrow of foreboding through her. She chanced a glance out the window and couldn't stop the shriek that fled from her lips. The shadowscale? Here? For the first time since arriving, she was grateful for Neilos's enchantments. While they kept Nia here, they also kept the shadowscale out. She moved away from the windows, terror seeping in. Even if the enchantments could keep it at bay, she didn't want to risk it seeing her here.

"What a terrible beast."

Nia jumped at Uma's sudden appearance at her side. The castle's cook stared out the window, her eyes dark and distant. "My grandfather was killed by one, so I'm told."

"I'm sorry," Nia said. "They're awful creatures."

"Raving mad," Uma agreed. "I wonder who this one is after."

Still compelled by the veritas water, Nia said, "I think it's after me."

"You?"

"One was chasing me before I ended up here. It's how I got into this whole mess."

The windows lit with flames and Nia and Uma both jumped back. "What the bloody—" Uma didn't finish her interjection as another roar pierced the air.

"Are we burning down?" Nia asked, alarm in her voice. "Do we need to get somewhere safe?"

But through the flickering flames, Nia saw the sky. The shadowscale circled, looking disorientated. The castle appeared unharmed. Were the flames only a trick to disguise the castle? At last, the shadowscale resumed its flight and disappeared from the skies. Nia's chest and lungs opened up once more and she held a hand to her heart, sighing in heavy relief. The flames extinguished a moment later.

"Well, the master knows his stuff. I'll give 'im that." Uma mused. "Don't suppose you would help me in the kitchens again, would you?"

"I can't, I'm waiting for veritas water to wear off." Nia gasped and shoved her hands over her mouth.

"Why in the blazes did you drink veritas water?" Uma demanded.

Nia dashed up the stairs before she could let anything else loose, hands still clamped tightly over her mouth. She stopped short, realizing a fatal problem. Uma must be under Neilos's control, just like everyone else. If he had all of the servants gathering information, Uma would likely tell Neilos what Nia had said the moment she saw him. There would be no more playing dumb. That would lead to him asking who revealed the information about the veritas water to Nia, which would then implicate Antonia.

Nia knew one thing she could do. She turned and hurried back down the stairs.

"Uma! Wait!"

Uma turned, her eyes narrowed. "You've got some explaining to do," she said. "Veritas water?"

"I'm going to break your curse," Nia blurted. That wretched veritas water!

"What!" Uma's eyes widened, but she responded exactly as Nia hoped; Uma's hair was too short to hide a key on the back of her head like Antonia's, but she reached behind her back and used both hands to cover the spot where her apron was knotted. Nia rushed at her. Uma was tall, with arms strong from working, but Nia was swift and determined. The hard part would be doing this before anyone else showed up.

Nia jumped on Uma's back and clutched her in a vise-like grip.

"GET OFF!" Uma shrieked. She backed hard against the wall, sending pain through Nia's shoulder, but it also threw Uma's balance. She couldn't protect the cursed winding key *and* throw Nia.

Nia pried at Uma's hands and felt the hard key beneath the apron's knot. She gripped and twisted as hard as she could.

Snap.

Uma relaxed at once, panting heavily, and Nia hopped off her.

"You...you really did it," Uma gasped. And then, to Nia's surprise, Uma began to cry. Ugly, unrestrained wailing that echoed through the hall.

Nia shushed her, "Please, not so loud!"

Uma stifled her cries, still blubbering softly. "T-thank you," she muttered. "Go, quickly. Stay in your room until that blasted water wears off."

"Please don't tell Neilos I know about it," Nia implored.

"Of course not. I'm no idiot. Get!"

Nia once more ascended the stairs, her heart racing. Had she really done Antonia and Uma favors by breaking their curses? How long would it be before Neilos found out? And what sort of punishment would he dole out once he knew? Still, with Uma's grateful tears, Nia got the feeling the castle's cook would take whatever hand fate dealt over being imprisoned in her own body again.

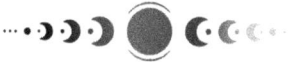

Nia was all fluttering nerves and jitters when she returned to her room. Had she really just done that?

"That was too long for breakfast," Antonia said warily. "What happened down there?"

"I broke Uma's curse!"

"What?"

Nia explained everything to Antonia—the shadowscale, the blurting everything to Uma, breaking the curse. She flopped down on her bed, emotional exhaustion wearing her down at last. "I can't believe I broke two curses in less than twenty-four hours."

"I'll forever be grateful, and Uma too, I'm sure. But I think it would be better if you didn't break any more for now. It's risky enough with us carrying on the facade, but the more people who have their curses broken, the more danger we're all in. Someone is bound to do something careless and unravel everything."

"I know." Nia admitted. "But I can't stand the thought of everyone being cursed." She thought again of Enitan and wondered how much of that kind smile was his own.

"We'll find a way. But our odds are better if we leave everyone else as they are until we have a respectable plan. As for you, you're not going anywhere until that veritas water is out of your system."

Nia certainly wasn't going to disagree with that.

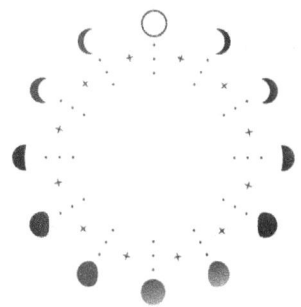

Chapter 17

Thirteen days until the Dark Moon

After the veritas water had worn off, Nia felt reborn. She no longer needed to question her instincts—she had been right about Neilos. There were less than two weeks left until the dark moon, but every day in the castle was another day too long, and she didn't trust Neilos to remain true to his word. He didn't go through all of this trouble to keep her here just to let her go without getting what he wanted.

She no longer dined with Neilos. So far, he hadn't requested an invitation, and she hoped she could count on that for a while longer. She knew eventually he would request her presence, but the longer he held off the better.

Nia hurried to the kitchen—she had business with Uma. She nearly changed directions when she glimpsed Enitan down the hall, but instead she squared her shoulders and continued forward.

"Hello, Enitan," she said, her voice cool. He had been avoiding her ever since the ball, but she wouldn't do the same to him.

"Hello, Nia," his reply carried an equal coolness, though his eyes betrayed his discomfort. He inclined his head in a quick, dismissive nod and hurried out the nearest door, which happened to lead to a secluded balcony. Nia rolled her eyes. Whatever game they were playing, it was getting ridiculous. She knew he didn't have any business to attend to out there. She followed him.

He whipped around, and Nia felt a small sense of satisfaction at the way his jaw dropped when he saw her.

"What's wrong? Did you think I would just keep letting you dismiss me?"

He started to form a word, but snapped his mouth shut and adopted a moody stride towards the balcony railing. For a wild moment, Nia thought he was going to jump over it. They were only on the second floor so he would probably survive the fall, but the thought of him going to such lengths to avoid her was unnerving. Thankfully, instead of jumping, he merely leaned forward and rested his elbows on the rails, gazing out over the castle grounds. Manes and tales...the man looked good even when he was sulking.

Nia strolled up alongside him and leaned back, facing the opposite direction. His view of the grounds was probably better than her view of the door, but her pride wouldn't let her share in it. She closed her eyes for a moment and listened to the birds, who sounded far too cheerful.

"Did you enjoy the ball?" Enitan asked at last.

Nia didn't miss the hostility in his tone. She snorted in response. Why was he angry? She was the one who should be angry. If he hadn't left her, maybe she wouldn't have drunk the veritas water. If he had been by her side, maybe she wouldn't have had to dance with Neilos.

Nia finally responded. "I had a riveting time. Didn't you notice?"

"It was hard to tell. You were with Neilos and hardly paid me a second glance."

Nia turned to face him, staring. "*You* were the one who left *me*."

He let go of the railing and straightened, slipping his hands into his pockets. "Neilos requested I not initiate. He wouldn't have done anything if you were the one seeking me out."

How was Nia to know that? He seemed perfectly content to let the other ladies entertain him. "I suppose you wanted me to giggle and curtsy like all the other girls swarming around you?"

"I wanted you to find me and carry on a conversation. Dance some more. Something."

"Well, then why didn't you try to get my attention? After you walked away it was like I became invisible."

He ran a flustered hand over his braids. "I was aware of you all night. Up until I had to leave for my shift, I knew every place you went in that ballroom, whether you could see that or not. I wanted to—" He stopped, shoulders stiff and face flushed with frustration.

It dawned on her that because of his curse, he probably couldn't come back to her no matter how he wanted to. He *wanted* to. Nia let this sink in and work through the gears in her mind. Was he really saying he was as fixated on her as she was with him? That he hoped for...more? But did he really, or was this more of Neilos's puppet games?

She should say something. The silence between them was worse than anything.

She wanted to tell him how attractive she found him—not just physically, but as a whole. Her heart gravitated towards him in ways she couldn't deny. But Enitan was cursed. Even her attraction might be a product of that. At the end of the day, anything he did was to further Neilos's goals. So instead of saying the things she wanted to say, Nia said softly, "I'm leaving as soon as the dark moon hits."

When he didn't respond, she glanced up at him. His jaw was hard.

"You're still set on leaving?" he asked at last. Something in his voice caressed her heart. "What do you have left to go back to?"

She couldn't tell Enitan about the stone. She couldn't tell him she was afraid of Neilos. Afraid of this place. Instead, she chose the safe answer. "Ravenskeep is my home. I can't stay here."

Enitan grasped her by the shoulders and turned her to face him. The wistful look in his eyes left her with a sudden desire to hold him close. But she didn't. Instead, she took a step away from him, shaking free from his grasp, and defied the pounding heart in her chest.

"Please consider staying." He pleaded.

Why did it feel so different when Enitan was the one requesting it? Her mind bucked against the thought when it was Neilos, but with Enitan, she found it harder to be dismissive. For him, she wanted to say yes. And that scared her even more. For all she knew, it was another manipulation. Neilos's will with Enitan's voice. She wanted to help Enitan, but she was certain falling for a cursed man would only break her heart in the end. So instead, she squared her shoulders and lifted her chin.

"If anyone in this castle wants me to stay, they'll have to make me."

"I wish you didn't say that."

Nia had a feeling there was more to his words than his own emotions, and she suspected she didn't have long before she found out what he meant.

"I have to head back to my post. Neilos won't let me stay away for long." Enitan's gaze lingered on her, as though begging Nia to understand. Contrary to his words, it didn't seem he wanted to leave, which both pleased and frustrated Nia. She couldn't trust that anything he showed was genuine.

When he at last pulled away, Nia sprang forward on an impulse and threw her arms around him. Her hands wandered over his back. He pulled away from her, a dozen questions in his eyes. But he didn't seek her touch again. She wished he would.

"Be safe, Enitan," Nia said, turning away quickly and rushing back inside the castle corridor before Enitan could question her actions.

He had pulled away from her embrace and did not return it. True, she had sprung it on him, and he was probably confused, but a fluttering, wistful part of her yearned for him to reciprocate. More importantly, she hadn't accomplished what she hoped to achieve with the embrace to begin with.

She hadn't felt a key.

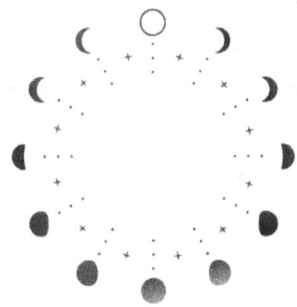

Chapter 18

Thirteen days until the Dark Moon

"There are many ways to place a curse. Enitan may not have a key at all." Antonia gave Nia an uneasy glance. "Miss, you'd better stop that, or you'll wear clean through the floor."

Nia continued her restless pacing in spite of Antonia's concern. "How could he not have a key? How am I supposed to break the curse if I can't find any marking of it? And why would Enitan's curse be different from everyone else's? It doesn't make sense."

"Neilos has it in for the boy." Uma piped up from her spot by the end table with a silver tray of food. She had come on the pretense of bringing Nia a meal, but that excuse wouldn't hold for long. She would need to leave soon.

"What could he possibly have against Enitan?" It made no sense. Enitan seemed fairly harmless. And if Neilos put Enitan in charge of the relics, he must trust him.

Uma tsked. "Did you know he used to be my kitchen boy? Neilos ripped him right out from under me. But it didn't seem like he was doing it to give him a chance of higher status. He was angry."

Nia raised her eyebrows. "You don't know why?" Nia at last stopped turning around the room and seated herself on the edge of her bed, listless as she picked at some stray lint on the comforter.

Uma shook her head. "No idea. But I wish I had him back. He was good help. Not that I don't appreciate you, Nia," Uma quickly amended.

Neilos must have been keeping Enitan under his watch. That was the only explanation. Nia was determined to break Enitan's curse, even if it meant he wasn't interested in her anymore. Her heart squeezed. If he wanted nothing more to do with her once his curse was broken, that was his right. She couldn't allow someone to remain stripped of their will for the sake of maintaining a relationship.

Antonia seated herself beside Nia with a little basket of hairpins and began fussing with Nia's hair.

"You don't have to do that anymore, Antonia. I'm sure Neilos won't notice the difference." Nia would miss Antonia's pretty hairstyles, but she wasn't bound to serve anymore.

Antonia gave a gentle smile and pinned back an errant curl. "Please, let me. I truly do enjoy this."

Nia's heart warmed. It did feel good to be cared for. If Antonia really didn't mind, she wasn't going to complain. Where would all the castle's occupants go when they were no longer bound to Neilos? Perhaps they could all find homes in Ravenskeep. Of course, Nia still had no idea how to free them all and keep Neilos at bay for good. Her stomach twisted.

Uma crossed her arms and glanced off at nothing in particular. "Our number one priority should be getting you out of here safely." Her voice had an edge of fear in it. "Neilos is running out of time, and I don't like to think of what he'll do if you don't give him what he wants." She jerked her gaze to Nia, eyes fierce. "You *won't* give it to him, will you?"

"No," Nia replied firmly.

Uma nodded. "Good. Last thing that beast of a man needs is more luck."

Antonia's brows were pinched with worry. "I agree with Uma. He'll start becoming more desperate. Have you noticed any changes in Neilos's behavior?"

Nia shook her head. "No, not really."

It was strange that Neilos hadn't said anything more to her about the stone after the night of the ball. She had an even greater concern for what might happen to her friends if he found them out. Everything was too quiet. Perhaps it was good that Enitan had all but ignored her these past few days so he wouldn't have any reason to be implicated. Nia pushed aside the weight that settled on her heart at the thought of Enitan and what their future might bring.

Nia tapped a moody foot. "What does Neilos do all day, anyway? He can't possibly spend all his time lounging in the gardens or entertaining guests for dinner."

"He spends a lot of time in his study," Uma replied with a huff. "Gets downright grumpy if I interrupt him with a meal. And nobody is ever allowed inside. I always have to leave the tray outside the door."

Well, that was interesting. What was he working on in there that he didn't want anybody else to know about? For some reason Nia had assumed the servants knew most of Neilos's secrets. After all, if he had them all cursed to do his bidding, what reason did he have to keep them guarded?

Antonia placed one last pin in Nia's hair then shooed Uma and Nia off the bed so she could busy herself with making it up. "He also has several servants giving him intel and following leads. Whereabouts of magical objects and things like that."

"He sends them on dangerous missions. Never does his own dirty work." Uma took up a chair and seated herself in a very unladylike position. "I swear he'll never be happy. Always looking for the next thing he can claim."

And a fortune stone was of particular interest. Nia was sure if he didn't get what he wanted from her, he would go after someone else. He was probably keeping tabs on other potential holders at that very moment.

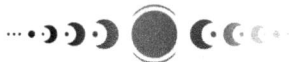

Nia couldn't sleep that night. With every second in the castle, she tipped closer to her end. Besides that, the castle's inhabitants were suffering, held prisoner in their own bodies. She could wait it out until the dark moon, but Neilos would be expecting her to try and leave on that night. She needed a way to break the wards on the castle and get herself and the others out while Neilos didn't anticipate it. Something told her she would find more of the castle's secrets if she could just go back to the library. But it wouldn't be open so late—poor Perla had to sleep in her own bed sometimes.

But Spencer's tunnels would lead there.

Nia considered the grate in her room. She could access the tunnels directly through there. But she would need to shrink down much smaller than she was comfortable with to get in that way. The thought sent an unsettled shiver through her. If she was going to eat magic chocolate anyway it probably shouldn't matter what size she ended up, but she suspected less was better.

With the stone assisting, she had no trouble making it to the gardens unnoticed.

When she arrived at the grate, she gave it a solid tug just as Spencer had done and it came away easily. She produced the chocolate from her pocket and took just a small nibble—enough to help her feel slightly less claustrophobic. It was tempting to do more but it seemed too much like playing with fire. She made her way inside.

As she crawled through, she tried to imagine where she was in the castle so she would have some sense of timing and orientation. She knew the grates for the first floor were located beneath her, whereas the grates in the remaining floors were located above her. So, at the very least, she knew when she had reached the second floor. Just two more floors to go.

Nia grew more spooked the longer she stayed in the tunnels, so it was a relief when she peered through one of the grates and saw grand shelves full of books.

The library grate was dusty, and she coughed as she shoved it aside. She stifled the coughing and listened, hoping the space truly was empty. Coughing from the vents would certainly cause someone to investigate. When she heard no sound, she squeezed her way through the vent. While it was larger than the one in her room, it wasn't a pleasant fit; She was nearly back to her normal size.

The library cast off any sense of coziness in the quiet of night. It was a maze of shadows, and the many shelves seemed like the perfect place for someone—or something—to lie in wait. Why hadn't she thought to bring a torch? She fumbled through the darkness, but as she walked past one of the wall sconces it lit on its own and the others followed. While the light brought relief, Nia hoped the door was solid enough to not allow any light to sneak through cracks or gaps.

She made her way to Perla's desk and snooped around until she found the glowing orb she had used to break the magic ward. She threw the orb as she had seen Perla do, and the ward shattered. Those books were likely going to go berserk again. What was she going to do when that happened? They didn't want to hurt her, at least, not last time. Hopefully, they still felt that way.

They're just books, Nia.

She inhaled and moved forward.

The moment she stepped into the space the pages fluttered. This time she didn't swat them away. After setting the orb down so she could break the ward again if needed, Nia remained still and let the flurry come, maintaining deep breathing to remain calm. After several minutes, the books seemed to settle. They floated away, allowing her more space. While she could still feel their curiosity and excitement, they seemed to have adjusted to her presence. She was able to explore their titles now.

Where to start? Nia didn't know the first thing about enchanted castles, or even what she should be looking for. Could she ask the books?

"Does one of you know," Nia began, her voice timid, "How to break an enchantment?"

The pages fluttered again, and several volumes flew off the shelves, each one vying for her attention. She tried to make out the titles in the chaos:

From Human to Beast

Magical Meals to Delight and Devour

Dispel and Defy: The Art of Breaking Magical Spells

The Uncharmed Life: Creating and Breaking Love Enchantments

Nia paused at that one. Something was especially unsettling about the thought of Neilos having books on love enchantments.

"I guess I should have been more specific," she said, laughing in spite of herself. However, she did have the stone, which should help her find exactly what she needed. "I need to find out how to break Neilos's wards around the castle."

The stone grew warm, and a book flew into her hands. She frowned as she read the title:

Echoes of Misfortune: A Guide to Cursed Artifacts

"Not really what I wanted," Nia muttered. She often felt the stone had a mind of its own, and if she didn't know any better, she would think it didn't *want* her to leave the castle. Most of the time, it gave her exactly what she sought, but sometimes the answers came to her in roundabout ways. Perhaps this was one of those times. She flipped the book open and began to read.

One might curse an object for many reasons: to dispel an enemy. To protect something. To execute revenge. It is important to note that a cursed object could be anything. It could be a candlestick, an article of clothing, or even a book.

Nia couldn't stop the unsettled shiver that flooded her with goosebumps. The book could be cursed. *Anything* in this library could be. At the sudden chime of a clock Nia nearly jumped out of her skin and the book slipped from her hands, floating in front of her. She couldn't do this tonight. Not when she was so spooked. Even with the stone helping her, she felt curses were far out of her element. Perhaps Uma or Antonia would have more insight, or it might even be safer to consult with Perla before dashing out on her own.

Nia didn't want to touch the book again, but she couldn't leave it out of place. Although, maybe touching it wasn't necessary.

"Could you go back please?" she asked.

The book floated lazily back in place on the shelf. Nia picked up the orb and returned it to its place, took another nibble of chocolate, and hurried back into the tunnels, securing the grate in place.

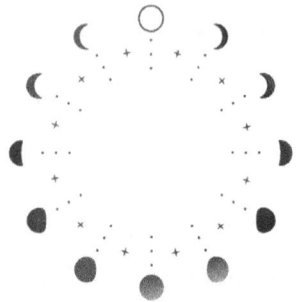

Chapter 19

Nia's mind swam, wondering what else she might be able to uncover. She should have had a clearer goal in mind before she decided to sneak around. She was wasting time.

She paused at one intersection in the tunnels, thinking she heard voices. She tuned her ears in. Who was awake so late? Curious, she followed the low chatter until she saw a beam of light shimmering through another grate up ahead. It looked like they were stuffing pillows. Nia waited, listening as a female servant launched into a tirade.

"I can't believe we're doing this in the middle of the night. Surely there are other pillows in the castle! He's in such a bad mood lately. He throws things around like a spoiled toddler when he doesn't get his way. It was shredded pillows today, but last week it was every vase in his study. Every time the master interacts with that Nia girl, I have more messes to clean up."

Nia's ears burned.

"The master's taken quite an interest in her," said another voice, her tone thoughtful.

"Well, are you surprised? She's a pretty young thing, isn't she?" A third voice.

Nia was grateful she was alone so nobody could see her discomfort.

The first lady let out an irritated tsk. "Come now, you should know the master well enough by now to know romance isn't what attracts him."

"Keep your voice down," the second voice said, an audible tremor in her words.

"Well, it's true, isn't it? If she's captured his attention there's likely m—"

"Stop! You'll—"

Through the spaces in the grate, Nia saw the first woman jerk forward, a throaty gargle emitting from her. Because of the way she was hunched over, it was easy for Nia to see the way her eyes bulged and the froth oozing from the corners of her mouth. Nia recoiled, her stomach churning. This had to be the curse at play, keeping the poor servant from saying more against her master.

"Oh, Issa! Get it together!" The third woman shrieked. "I don't want to have to call him here!" There was a clatter and retreating footsteps.

Was she going for Neilos? Nia had a feeling if anyone would notice her in this tunnel, it would be him. And she absolutely did not want that. She retreated, scrambling over the rough surface, the woman's wild face and wretched noises still flashing in her mind. The location of the grates shifted. First floor, then.

She continued as fast as she could manage, when at once, she felt the stone's influence go dark. But that never happened in the castle except for when…

She peered through the next grate and her breath went still. She was over Enitan's room. Enitan was always attractive, but in the glow of moonlight while he slept he looked angelic. His dark eyelashes nearly brushed his cheeks—how could he have such great eyelashes? If she had been closer to him, she wasn't sure she'd be able to resist the urge to brush her fingers against his cheek. Her fingertips tingled at the thought and her face warmed.

The tunnels began to shrink. Fast. Too fast.

Her luck—and the effects of the chocolate—were gone.

Nia yelped as she grew, the walls squeezing impossibly tight around her. She was flat on her belly, her arms pinned to her sides with her shoulders at an odd angle. It was hard to breathe. She gasped for whatever air she could get and at last it seemed she had reached her full size. It didn't do her much good, however. She may as well have been cemented in place. She couldn't maneuver herself enough to get more of the chocolate out of her pocket.

Tears sprung forth, fueled by a mix of anger and terror. As far as Nia knew, the only one who used these tunnels was Spencer, and Spencer didn't even exist anymore. The speculo was locked away. If she cried out, perhaps someone else would find her. And then she would face the humiliation of confronting Neilos yet again in the middle of doing something she shouldn't. She squirmed with the vague hope of inching free, but all the action brought her was more pain. She would get help from the stone once Enitan left his room, but what state would she be in by then? She was already feeling dizzy from her inability to get a full breath.

Nia pushed her pride aside. Whatever fate awaited her when Neilos found out had to be better than suffocating in a cramped tunnel.

"Help." The sound came out soft and weak. The combination of her awkward position and the tight squeeze made it impossible to pull in the air and force for a proper yell.

Nia began to feel an even tighter compression, but this came from within rather than the pressure surrounding her exterior. Her lungs pinched. Her stomach clenched. Blackness swarmed around her as her breath came in quick, pitched gasps.

The world stilled around her. A light burst into the tunnel. Nia shut her eyes against the brightness and opened them again slowly, squinting to locate the source. Was someone coming to her rescue after all?

Nia's mouth dropped open, and her eyes grew large. There, just an inch from the tip of her nose, was a tiny, ethereal creature. It was no bigger than a pea, shrouded in bright, golden light. It peered at her with midnight-blue eyes.

Nia dared to do no more than take in whatever wisps of breath she could, and even that bordered on risk. She had a great respect for small creatures, especially magical ones. After all, spiders and wasps could kill a human despite their minute size, and that was without magic in the equation. This manifestation, no matter how beautiful and benign it appeared, was nothing to be trifled with.

Something passed between Nia and the creature. It wasn't words. It wasn't action. It simply was. The little wisp closed its eyes and ever so gently floated forward and brushed against Nia's nose. A sense of overwhelming calm flowed throughout her. Her mind and vision cleared. The creature looked at her again, its eyes expectant. Then, with a flash it was gone, but the sense of serenity it brought remained.

Nia attempted a slow, calming inhalation, but stopped as the tunnels squeezed around her. *Think, Nia. You can get out of this.*

She could move her legs. If she could make enough noise, it might wake Enitan up. If he left to investigate—which she was certain he would—the stone would help her again.

She kicked. Her first attempt didn't have much force behind it as it was still difficult to move much at all, but she had to try harder. She kicked again and again until at last Enitan's eyes popped open. He sat up, staring in confusion. Nia flushed and closed her eyes as he reached for his uniform and began to shed his night clothes—she wouldn't peek. She kept her eyes shut tight until she heard the soft click of his door.

Luck flowed through her again. She could feel the confident suggestion. *Try the grate.*

She bashed her head against the grate. The metal hurt, and she wondered if it would leave any marks or bruising, but she did it again and again as she felt it giving way. It clattered to the floor of Enitan's room.

She wouldn't be able to fit through the grate, but she could use that space. She wiggled and shimmied until she was able to get her shoulder over the empty space and used that to twist her body further. Soon she managed to get an arm free, dangling in the air. She panted from the effort and giggled with the delirious thought of Enitan waking up to see someone's arm waving from his ceiling. With her arm free, she twisted and inched until she was able to get the shrinking chocolate from her pocket.

"Hah!" Her triumphant laugh was breathy, but she popped the chocolate into her mouth and felt sweet relief as she shrunk down again. She took in several gulps of air. She could likely fit through the grate opening now, and it was tempting to do just that so she could get out of the tunnels, but if Enitan came back and found her in his room, which would complicate things further, the stone wouldn't be able to assist her. Instead, she scrambled the rest of the way through the tunnels and nearly cried with relief when she reached the garden grate.

Nia yawned as she tiptoed through the quiet halls. After so much excitement she was ready for the comfort of her bed. A flickering light through a sliver in one of the doors caught her attention. Who else was awake now? She told herself to just ignore it and go to bed—no need to tempt fate again tonight. But in the end, curiosity got the better of her and she peered inside the room as she passed. It was empty.

Her luck left her.

Enitan must be returning to his chambers. Too tired to explain herself to him if he saw her, Nia instead hurried inside the room, closing the door behind her.

The room glowed with candlelight and appeared to be some kind of study. The space was all burgundy and gold with brass sconces. Every surface save for a velvet chair by the desk was covered in books of every size. Nia worried for a moment that they might jump out at her like the ones in the library, but their pages remained still.

Enitan's receding footsteps met her ears, and a moment later her luck returned.

It would be wise for her to retreat from the study before the occupant found her in it, but something drew her eyes to the desk and a delicate volume laying open on it. She could see a peek of its cover—a pale blue, just like...

Like a fortune stone.

In the dim light she could make out handwriting. With timid steps she approached for a better look.

Her eyes scanned the open page.

Katrina Rowlands—DECEASED.

The word "deceased" had been written in red ink and splattered slightly, as though the quill had been slammed forcefully to the page. The scrawl seemed to carry an undercurrent of fury. The thought of what could have made Neilos so angry forced Nia into an involuntary shudder.

The book next to the pale-blue one caught her eye. The thick, leather-bound tome looked ancient, its cover scratched and worn dull. It had been dyed royal blue but much of the color had faded. Odd symbols were etched into its surface, and she could just barely make out the faded title: *Of Worlds Beyond*.

Curious, she opened it, careful with the delicate, yellowed pages. It had sketchy, black and white illustrations of landscapes, creatures, flora, and fauna. Some of it looked familiar, while others were entirely foreign to her. She read the heading of the page she was currently on: *Melodia—the land of violet foliage.*

Most of the plants on Melodia are colored in shades of purple. The beings in this world are humanoid, mostly peaceful, and rather curious. They do not appear to have magic use and may be upset by it. Not recommended for sorcerers who like to show off. Recommended for an under-the-radar visit.

The text continued with notes about the culture and history. Every few pages another world was described. What was this book? She turned back to the beginning and found the following note:

This text to be used for holders of the fortune stones as a reference to their travels to other worlds.

She paused seeing "holders of the fortune stones." And what was this about other worlds?

Take heed never to abuse this power. The fortune stone holder, in combination with the wanderer's ring, may use the following words to travel:

"I whom fortune smiles upon
Wish to visit worlds bygone
With my hands I make my fate
Let me open up the gate"

After saying these words, simply speak the name of the world you wish to visit.

Was this book really saying there were other worlds and ways to visit them? Why holders of the fortune stone, specifically? She flipped through pages again, scanning the different worlds and struggling to take it all in. She stopped short at a page that was different from the rest. It was scribbled with darkness. She read the name: *Nihilnoctus.*

Beneath the name was only a short description:

Nothing. This world is a cold void, free of magic, free of life. Stay away.

She backed away from the book, letting it fall closed, and as she did so light from the hallway flooded the room. She nearly screamed when she turned and came face-to-face with Neilos, holding more books under his arm. He didn't look angry, and that was somehow more unsettling.

"Did you discover anything of interest?"

"I-I'm sorry," Nia stammered. She remembered the light coming through the door when she first arrived and quickly said, "I saw the door ajar, and I just got curious." She hoped he would buy that and not suspect she had come here to hide.

His eyes flicked almost imperceptibly to the open book on the desk and then back to Nia, a perfect smile in place.

"Please join me for dinner tomorrow, Nia. I have some things I'd like to discuss with you."

That wasn't what she had expected. People generally don't extend dinner invitations to someone they just found sneaking around in their study. Antonia and Uma's warnings to be careful flashed through Nia's mind. But what was "careful" in this situation? Joining him for dinner wasn't appealing, but was it even more dangerous to refuse? If she attended, she could at least play coy and try to work the situation in her favor. If she declined it might further anger him.

"That would be lovely," Nia lied.

"Excellent. I shall see you then. Now, if you don't mind, I was right in the middle of something."

"Yes, of course. Sorry to trouble you."

Nia retreated from the study, head reeling with everything she had read...and the fact that Neilos no doubt suspected she'd read it.

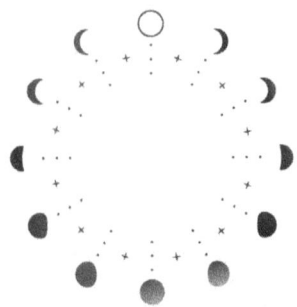

Chapter 20

Twelve days until the Dark Moon

"Oh, Nia! What can I help you with?" Perla always looked as though she'd been caught unaware. Her braid was as frizzy as ever and she smoothed the front of her dress in a vain attempt to minimize its wrinkles.

Nia traced her finger through imaginary dust on the library's reception desk. The castle never even approached the idea of dirty. "I saw a creature. I was wondering if you could help me identify it." She had stewed all night over the tiny, mysterious being that saved her, as well as everything she found in Neilos's study. She wasn't sure if she was ready to face the revelations in the study yet, so researching the creature seemed a safer way to distract her from the looming dinner with Neilos.

Perla's wide eyes shone with curiosity. "Where? Here in the castle?"

"Yes." No need to tell her the particulars.

Perla hopped up from her seat and disappeared for several minutes. Nia would have wondered if she left the library altogether if not for the occasional rustling she heard. When she returned, she carried a perilously tall stack of books that completely blocked her head from view. Nia rushed to assist before they all toppled.

"Thanks," Perla said breathlessly, pushing her glasses up on her nose. "Ok, let's see...can you describe it for me?"

Nia closed her eyes to focus on the image of the creature in her mind's eye. It was so delicate. So small. So lovely. She did her best to describe it to Perla, with its large eyes and angelic light.

Perla handed Nia a stack of books while she kept the rest and the two of them flipped through, searching for something to match the description.

"Oh, um, I do think you should read that turquoise book there. You may find something useful." Perla didn't look at Nia when she said it. She seemed engrossed in the book she was perusing.

Nia picked up the book Perla indicated, its rich turquoise cover standing out among the others. She flipped the book open and skimmed the pages. She furrowed her brow. "This is a book about castle architecture."

"Really? Check the index. There might be something there."

With an inward shrug, Nia flipped to the index, a thin, yellowed sheet of paper fluttered out. Perla was still absorbed in her current read, so Nia picked up the paper and opened it with careful fingers. It looked like a map.

A map of the castle.

Nia stole another glance at Perla and when she was certain the young librarian wasn't paying attention, she bent down, deftly folded the map and tucked it into her shoe. A map of the castle could be useful, and she intended to examine it in more detail later. Perla was closing her book just as Nia sat up again.

"It must be very rare to come by." Perla rested an elbow on the table and squished her cheek onto her hand. "I've never heard of anything like that." She perked up again and swapped her book for a lighter volume entitled *Rarities of the Magical Realm*.

After a few moments of silent page flipping, Perla let out an excited squeak and whipped the open book around into Nia's face. "Is this what you saw?" This was the most animated Nia had ever seen her.

Nia scrutinized the sketch on the page. The artwork couldn't come close to capturing the creature's essence, but there was no mistaking what it was intended to be.

"Yes, that's it!"

Before Nia could read about it, Perla yanked the book back and summarized the text, "It's called a Prelude. As I thought, sightings are extremely rare."

A Prelude. Nia wondered what it was a prelude to.

"What does it say about it?" Nia asked, watching Perla's eyes dart back and forth along the page.

Perla's face fell. "Oh."

"What?" It did not sound like a good "oh."

Perla gave a nervous, breathy laugh and closed the book, hoisting it under her arm and stacking up the others on the table. "Well, I'm sure it's just a story. Silly superstitions and things like that."

Nia stepped in front of the librarian, her voice unyielding. "Perla, what did it say?"

Perla cast her eyes to the side and sighed. "It says according to legend the Prelude only appears to those who will soon meet death."

Nia still felt as though her brain was shrouded in mist after her visit to the library. She tried to clear it with a wisp of sensibility. Perla was right—it was just superstition. How could any creature know when an otherwise healthy person was close to dying?

Unless the creature was the one who heralded death to begin with.

No, what a silly thought.

She found herself outside of her room, but suddenly she didn't feel like being alone. Where might Enitan be at this time of day? Probably in the relic room, where she wasn't supposed to go.

"Well," she whispered to the empty hallway, "If I'm going to die soon anyway, I may as well do what I want."

When she entered the relic room (after coaxing the door to open for her once more), she found it empty. At first, this disappointed her. She truly wanted the comfort of company right now. But then, she saw it as an opportunity. If Enitan wasn't there, he couldn't tell her to leave. She could study the room and the objects within it. And she would still have luck on her side. She stepped tentatively forward into the darkness.

Something caught Nia's attention. She turned toward one of the pedestals, expecting to see a glow or gleam, but she couldn't make out the object in the shadows. Yet, the pull of it was irresistible. She approached, straining to see. A ring? It had a wide copper band, and the center of it was set in, as though a round bauble should have rested there. It was otherwise unremarkable, and Nia couldn't imagine what Neilos would want with a seemingly broken piece of jewelry.

Curiosity propelled her actions. "Ring," she called into the space. Yellow light illuminated it. She wished she knew what that meant.

The ring called to Nia as though it were always meant to be hers. She had never been tempted by theft, save for the food she stole as a child just to make it through another day. But now she found herself compelled to take the ring with very little consideration to its owner. Neilos hadn't done anything to earn that sort of respect. And the pull of the ring, winking at her in the dark, was oh so tantalizing.

She strode to the pedestal where the trinket rested and plucked it up. She paused for several heartbeats, expecting something to happen, but nothing did. She slid the ring on her pointer finger. It was much too large. The ring grew hot and shrank, hugging Nia's finger in a perfect fit.

"Manes and tails," she whispered, tugging the ring off again. She loosed a sigh when it came off without difficulty. She had expected it to remain on her finger and reveal that it was full of dark magic after all. Still, she didn't trust wearing it again.

As Nia reached out to place it back on the pedestal, she paused. She didn't want to return it. It felt so natural in her grasp. Instead, she slipped it into her pocket. She would find a more secure place for it later.

With the temptation of taking the ring already realized, it left her free to focus on her original task again. She walked the circle of objects, examining each item in the dim light so she could call it out. "Skull." Green. "Coin." Blue. "Dagger." Green. "Book." Yellow. "Ruby." Yellow. "Bow and arrow." Blue.

"Blue...green...yellow..." she whispered. What do these objects have in common?

Nia approached one of the darker areas of the room, squinting to make out another object on a pedestal. It was a crystal vial, the base shaped like a heart. Filled with...

Nia reeled. Was that blood? Please don't let that be blood.

"Vial," Nia whispered. Emerald light washed over the object at once.

"Who's here?"

The voice barked through the room with such force that Nia almost didn't recognize it.

"Enitan! It's just me."

"Nia?" Surprise coated his tone, and he quickly approached. He grabbed her arm and pulled her roughly away from the vial. Nia gaped at him, bewildered that he handled her with such force.

His face softened in an instant, along with his grip. "I'm sorry," he said. "Really, I am. But you need to go."

"It's my fault." Nia allowed him to usher her away. "You already told me to stay away. I'm sorry." She should have known better. What if it had been Neilos who found her instead of Enitan? Enitan likely would have been in trouble for leaving his post unsecured, and she really should have put that ring back. She was being foolish with her own safety and Enitan's. Her face burned.

They climbed back down the ladder, and Nia felt less claustrophobic once they were out of the room. Really, how did Enitan manage to spend so much time there?

Enitan's face wore a shadow of frustration, but he blew out a breath and calmed. "I know I locked the door that time. After you got in before, I never leave without checking. How did you get in?"

Nia couldn't lie to him, but she couldn't tell him about the stone, either. But it wasn't fair for him to think she got in because he did something wrong. She averted her gaze. "I'm not completely sure. The door just opens for me when I want it to." She quickly added, "Please don't tell Neilos."

He ran a hand over his braids, brow pinched. "If he doesn't ask, I won't tell." The words came out strained. "I can't imagine him asking about you going to the room, so we can only hope."

"Would he be upset?"

Instead of answering her question, Enitan gently placed his hands on Nia's shoulders, his brown eyes staring straight into hers. "Please, Nia. Don't let me catch you in that room again." His voice was an urgent plea. He looked almost fearful.

"Why can't you just explain it to me?" Nia asked, relishing his touch in spite of the circumstances. "Is it dangerous? Do you not trust me?"

"I trust you. But it's my charge to protect what's in that room. I just can't predict what'll happen. If you did anything wrong in there, even if it was an accident, I have a duty."

He stated it as though it were inviolable. As though he would *have* to take action against her if she rebelled. And, under Neilos's curse, that was probably true. She suppressed a shiver.

"Ok," Nia relented. "Can you at least tell me what the vial was?" She couldn't stop herself from asking.

"A cursed object," Enitan spat. "That's all you need to know."

Cursed. Like so many other things in the castle. Like Enitan. Did that mean the other green-lit objects were cursed as well? If the vial and other objects truly were cursed, then the smartest thing she could do was heed Enitan's instruction to stay away.

As Nia dressed for dinner, intuition told her she should keep the ring close. Obviously, she couldn't wear it in plain sight in front of Neilos, but she sensed leaving it behind would be equally precarious. She slipped it into the pouch with the stone underneath her dress. She wasn't going to put the mysterious magical object on her finger again, but she couldn't bring herself to leave it behind where others might discover it, either. Again, she felt the strange stirring of feeling like it was meant for her.

Nia's stomach complained at her the whole way to the dining hall. She had been so anxious about her dinner with Neilos and caught up in the castle's mysteries that she hadn't eaten all day. Maybe that was a good thing. It meant she could distract herself with eating and not focus too much on what else was going on. Even if she wasn't looking forward to the time with the castle's master, she could always look forward to Uma's cooking.

She entered the dining hall without knocking or waiting to be invited. After knowing what Neilos had done, she was past the point of showing him respect. Perhaps she was being too rash—even if she despised the man, she still had to keep up appearances, not only for her own safety, but for Uma and Antonia's. She could keep up the charade for a little while longer for their sakes. Still, her rudeness didn't seem to matter; Neilos was nowhere in sight.

She noted that only two chairs were present at the long table this evening—one on each end. While it felt more awkward for conversation, at least it meant she didn't have to be too close to Neilos. The thought of being near him made her skin crawl. She took the seat at the end closest to the door, feeling more secure that way.

Nia looked around at the light streaming in through the stained-glass windows. Everything in this space was completely pristine. Not a scratch or smudge on anything in it. She picked up her spoon and noted her own reflection. Though distorted, she was a changed person, too. She no longer bore the scars on the outside she had come in with. By outward appearances, she was a perfect creature.

She frowned and put the spoon back down. Perfection had never been at the forefront of her desires. She only wanted contentment, and she didn't need perfection for that. Neilos, on the other hand, seemed averse to accepting anything less than perfection, or at least, his version of perfection.

At last, Neilos entered, looking as elegant and otherworldly as always. Nia's luck dissipated, and she caught a flash of Enitan's emerald-green uniform as he moved to stand guard outside of the door. Her luck would be of no use tonight. The thought stirred her insides as she glanced at the castle's master.

Servants followed shortly after Neilos's arrival, bringing goblets and decanters. Nia stared with distaste at the water that was poured for her. She certainly wasn't going to take *that* chance again. Then, noticing Neilos's gaze upon her, she took the goblet with careful fingers and pretended to take a sip.

Neilos clapped and more servants entered with silver platters of food. As always, there was far more than the two of them could eat, and it all smelled divine. While the drinks earned Nia's suspicions, she was less concerned about the food with Uma running the kitchens. When Neilos motioned for Nia to eat, she wasn't shy about helping herself to spiced vegetables, fluffy rolls, roasted chicken, and mashed potatoes. Neilos couldn't have known she hadn't eaten all day, but the hearty meal was certainly fortuitous.

"So, Nia," Neilos began.

Nia's fork stopped halfway to her mouth when she noticed he'd hardly eaten a thing. He noticed her pause. "Oh, please continue. Don't stop on my account."

She swallowed the bite she was working on, suddenly wary. Maybe he had done something to the food after all. Uma was no longer under his command, but what if he had asked her to enchant the food in some way and Uma didn't do it? Nia wouldn't know how to respond to whatever he had requested in order to maintain the ruse. Surely Uma would have given her a warning so she could act accordingly. She was just being paranoid.

Neilos sighed and took a deliberate bite of his food. "See? You are so suspicious of everything."

You gave me veritas water, Nia wanted to say. But he didn't know that she knew, so she sealed the thought away from her lips.

"I have provided you with food, shelter, amusement, practically everything you could want."

Was this how he was going to play it? Was he going to demand the stone simply because he felt she owed it to him? He would have to do better than that. "Yes, I thank you for your generosity."

"Still," he said, swirling his goblet. "You have never settled during your visit. In spite of everything I have done to make you comfortable, you don't want to stay. I can't help but wonder precisely what it is you have to go back to."

Nia formed a hasty reply. "I have a village. Family and friends."

Not all of that was true. Not anymore.

Neilos chuckled. "I know who you are, Nia. You're an orphan. You live alone."

Her breath constricted.

"You've spent most of your life in hiding. Haven't you ever wondered what else you could achieve? What you could obtain? With the stone at your disposal, you don't have to live the way you do."

"I know that," Nia couldn't help saying.

Neilos leaned back, his posture casual. "So then *why*? I struggle to comprehend it."

"I just prefer to keep things simple." Nia resumed her eating, fixating on her plate so she didn't have to look at him.

"I asked you here because I have a proposition."

Nia didn't want to hear it, but she gave him her attention anyway.

"I want you to be my queen."

Nia's fork clattered against her plate with a sharp tang. She fumbled to retrieve it as she swallowed the bile that instantly rose to her throat. She forced herself to ask, "Queen of *what*?"

"Of everything."

A beat of silence.

Nia's thoughts turned to Enitan outside of the door. Was he hearing this? Would he care?

Neilos broke the quiet. "Just think of it. With my vast power and your stone, we would be unmatched. Unstoppable. The universe would be at our disposal. Have you ever dreamed of such power?"

Nia knew better than to mistake his proposal as romance. He was building an empire, and she was merely another tool in its creation. For the smallest moment, Nia did imagine it. What would it be like to have anything and everything she wanted? To have access to limitless magic? With the help of the stone, they really would have all things their way. But Nia could never rule at the side of this creature. Never. The world he wanted and the world Nia imagined would no doubt be very different. If Nia stayed with him, she would be at his beck and call. She was nothing more than a vehicle for him to access the stone's power and make sure nobody else could have it.

He. Could. Not. Be. Serious.

She nearly inquired whether he was really that stupid, but instead she said, "Neilos, I appreciate that you've taken good care of me, but I can't." It was nearing the end of the month. Was this his last resort?

His sigh was wistful. "I've tried so very hard to make you happy. I hope you will at least consider it. You could have a home. And friends, perhaps? Surely, you've made friends here."

Flames licked Nia's insides and burned brighter. Hotter. How dare he try to manipulate her and pretend he had anything but his own greed in mind.

"I can't," she repeated. A whisper inside told her she was treading on dangerous ground to refuse him so strongly. Even so, she couldn't stop her voice from saying. "My answer will not change. On the night of the dark moon, I'm going home."

And she saw it. The instant his mask slipped to reveal the cold, cruel, selfish creature he tried to hide with pretty words and silken gestures. The temperature in the room dropped several degrees. His eyes sharp as a predator's.

"I see," he said softly. It was somehow worse than if he had yelled.

She felt as though she'd been backed into a corner, but she couldn't predict what he would do. Nia took another bite of potatoes. It was easier to appear cool in the situation while eating. She chewed carefully, contemplating her next move.

Squish.

The texture of the food in her mouth turned cold and rubbery, the taste foul. Nia spat it out at once and stared in revulsion at the half-mutilated frog on the table, one webbed foot still twitching. Nia retched. She leaped from her chair but didn't make it two steps before she doubled over on the floor. She closed her eyes as she vomited to avoid seeing the remains of whatever else it was she just ate.

Neilos's laugh resonated off the walls. Nia wasn't sure how long it continued. Her head was spinning, her stomach heaving. The only sound was Nia's panting and sobbing until footsteps came closer to her across the stone floor. Neilos grasped the top of Nia's hair and forced her face upward to look at him.

His words were clipped, absent of any trace of the satin charm he had shown. "I will make your life a living nightmare. By the time I am done with you, you will *beg* me to take that stone off your hands."

He let her head drop and turned away from her. She heard a croak and looked up at the table long enough to see the massacred frog hopping away. She covered her mouth to suppress another gag as Neilos strode away, his head thrown back in cruel laughter.

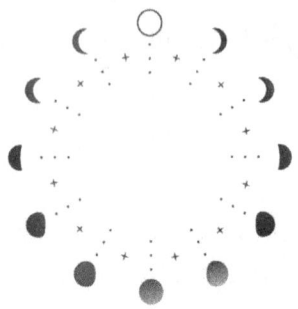

Chapter 21

"Nia. Nia!"

Enitan's strong hands were on Nia's shoulders as she curled on the cold floor of the dining hall. He helped her to an upright position as his eyes darted over her. He pulled her close to his chest and the motion took her by surprise. She buried her face into his uniform and cried.

"I'm sorry," he murmured. "I'm so sorry." He stroked her hair, and it seemed to light a fire in her chest.

She had wished for a moment like this with Enitan countless times before. Had imagined it while she drifted off to sleep at night. Pictured it happening in various places around the castle. But she had never wanted it to happen under such awful circumstances. The fact that Enitan was even allowed to comfort her at that moment meant he was still a card in his master's hand, played only to further manipulate her. She nearly pushed him away, but he seemed to sense it because he only held her tighter. Nia closed her eyes. She would pretend for a little while.

"I wanted to go to you sooner," Enitan said. "But—"

The words cut off and he grew rigid, reminding Nia of Antonia frozen over the wash basin or the servant who went into convulsions when attempting to speak ill of her master.

"It's ok, Enitan," Nia said numbly. She gently moved her head from his chest and began to get to her feet. Enitan caught her wrists and drew her back to him, searching her face. Was the longing she saw in his eyes for her, or did he long only to be free of his situation? Like everyone else, did he think Nia and her stone were the answer to all his problems?

As his face drew closer to hers, she almost didn't care what the reason was. She wanted to melt into the security of him. The warmth of him. But just as it seemed their lips might touch, she tilted her head downward. Enitan ran his thumbs across her cheeks and pressed his forehead to hers.

"Enitan," Nia whispered, her voice choking with emotion, "Why doesn't my fortune stone work around you?"

He pulled back, just slightly, and she turned her gaze upward to meet his surprised eyes. "You mean you've had the stone with you in the castle this whole time?"

Nia gave a slow nod. Perhaps she shouldn't have revealed that to him.

His brow furrowed and he shook his head. "If it doesn't work around me, I'm not sure why."

After a few moments of heavy silence between them, Enitan slowly rose to his feet and extended a hand, which Nia gratefully accepted. She couldn't ignore how secure her hand felt within his.

When he pleaded with her to let him escort her back to her room, she didn't refuse, even if it was all part of Neilos's twisted game.

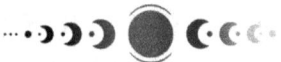

If Nia thought she knew who Neilos was after learning he cursed the castle's inhabitants, she was wrong. The events of dinner left no room to doubt how twisted he was. She gagged again at the thought of the frog.

Antonia thrust a cup of tea towards Nia and a minty aroma swirled around her face. Nia had recounted the story of dinner to her friend moments before.

"Drink it," Antonia demanded. "You'll feel better."

"What does it do?" Nia didn't trust that anything in the castle was simple anymore.

"It's just an herbal mint tea. I promise." Antonia's voice was soothing and her eyes were full of compassion.

Nia accepted the tea and took a grateful sip. The strong mint brew erased the memory of the amphibian on her tongue. Some of the tension left her shoulders.

Antonia tucked a wisp of her shiny black hair behind her ear. "He's an evil man. We have to get you out of here."

"We have to get you *all* out of here." Nia couldn't stand the thought of leaving them all behind to suffer while she walked free. It wasn't fair for her alone to be spared. The longing in Enitan's eyes played across her mind again.

Antonia gave Nia a smile full of pity. "How would we do that? There's no way we could escape with everyone. You are the owner of a fortune stone, which he absolutely cannot get. You're the most important one to remove from this place now."

"Don't say that!" Nia stood so abruptly that most of the tea splashed onto the bed. She sighed. "Don't clean that, Antonia. I'll do it." She stole the towel that Antonia had immediately produced from her hands.

As she blotted up the tea, Nia said, "I'm not more important than anyone else. Just because someone gave me a rock years ago doesn't mean my life has more value."

Nia's heart pinched at her mention of Enitan's sacrifice.

"All lives are valuable," Antonia agreed. "And if Neilos gets what he wants, more lives will be destroyed. If you don't see the value of yourself, I'm sure you can at least see that we have to look after others, too."

Gentle Antonia, who spent most of her life looking after others. Even absent of Neilos's control she showed tender kindness and service to those around her. Nia didn't deserve her. She had spent most of her life locked away, avoiding others and thinking only of her own security. She hung her head. That was all the more reason to begin taking better care of other people. She couldn't change the years she had thrown away, but she could do better going forward.

Antonia's voice was urgent when she continued. "There is not much time left before the dark moon. I'm sure it's obvious to you that Neilos won't release you if you haven't promised him the stone."

Nia gave a silent nod.

"So, we need to formulate a plan to get you out the instant the enchantment goes down. Otherwise, you'll have at least another month of enduring his horrors."

Twelve days. Well, eleven and a half, to be specific. That was all the time she had to find a way to escape, and hopefully set several others free with her. Even if she alone could get free, she could return with the stone and its luck to help her after the dark moon. Antonia was right; if she couldn't save everyone, she had to at least save herself so she could come back in a better position. Maybe even on the night of the full moon when her luck was strongest. If they *all* remained in the castle, *nobody* was getting out.

"Ok," Nia said, her voice steady. "Let's get thinking."

Because Neilos was becoming bolder, Nia needed to do the same. Her luck would only wane more each day until the dark moon. She strode into the library and made a beeline for the librarian's desk. Perla, looked up in surprise.

"Can I hel—"

Nia pulled her from her chair and spun her around.

"Excuse me!" Perla squeaked as Nia grabbed the back of her head.

Just as Nia thought, she found the little wind up key hidden away in the stray curls at the base of the young woman's neck. Its brassy surface was almost the same shade as the librarian's hair, which made it difficult to spot. She grasped it and turned until she achieved the satisfying snap she was seeking.

Perla clapped her hands and bounced up and down, her two long braids flying. "Oh, hooray! I so hoped you would do that!" Her voice was girlish and full of energy. Not nearly as subdued as it had been on previous occasions.

"What?"

The young lady spoke in a rush. "As soon as I saw you come into the library, I knew you were the one who had the fortune stone. Except you were hiding it and that was probably making Neilos pretty mad. But I heard about the vines and the speculo told me about the tunnels and—"

"Wait, wait." Nia interrupted. "You've been talking to the speculo?"

"Well, when he was Spencer," she said, waving a dismissive hand. "He used to come here and tell me all sorts of things. I could never respond to him, but I think he wanted me to get the information back to you." She paused and took a deep breath. "Anyway, I tried to leave you hints where I could but that was really difficult under Neilos's curse."

"You're the one who left me the map," Nia stated. She had forgotten about it until that moment. It was safely stashed in a drawer in Nia's room.

"Yes! I was so happy you found it, although I don't really know what you can do with it. I just thought maybe knowing your way around the castle would—"

Nia had no choice but to cut her off again. "Listen, I'm so sorry to interrupt, but we don't have a lot of time. I'm trying to figure out how to escape from here on the night of the dark moon. I thought you might have resources."

Perla clapped her hands again. "I'm so happy you asked! When I heard you tried to escape by climbing the vines I remembered something." She rushed to one of the many bookshelves and produced a large volume, flipping through the pages. "Neilos always has ways to get through his traps, you see. He could just magic his way out of almost anything, of course, but he wanted alternate ways just in case. Kind of paranoid about losing his powers, I think. Ah, here it is!"

She hurried back to Nia's side and thrust the open book into her face. An image of a white, star-shaped flower stared back at her.

"You'll find flowers like these in the garden," she said. "If you eat one, the vines won't try to grab you."

Nia studied the flower, memorizing it so she could be certain to find the correct ones. "Are you sure?"

"It's what the book says," she said with a shrug.

"Thank you very much, Perla."

She held out her hand and grinned. "My pleasure. It's good to meet you for real."

Nia may have been bold enough to break Perla's curse in broad daylight, but that was still within the security of walls. The gardens were more exposed, leaving her feeling like a mouse out in the open while birds of prey circled overhead. She ventured toward the vines under what little security the darkness offered.

She was sure Neilos's magical wards would prevent escape even if she could get past the vines, but she wanted to test the flower so she would be ready when the moment came. If by chance she was able to slip by the wards and escape, even better, though she didn't count on it. She had located the flower earlier that day while it was still light—she didn't trust herself to find the right one in the dark. Still, when she found it growing up a trellis near the vines, she realized it wouldn't have been hard to find. The stark white flowers almost glowed.

Nia plucked one of the star-shaped blooms. Was she supposed to eat the whole thing, or would any amount suffice? Could she just eat a few petals? She wished she had brought the book with her to review the specific instructions. She supposed she should eat the whole thing—better safe than sorry. A flower wasn't the worst thing she could have eaten, but the idea was still odd.

She bit into the flower and ripped a petal loose with her teeth. It tasted like honied citrus, the rest of the pale bloom going down without difficulty.

The book hadn't said any waiting period was necessary for the flower to take effect, so she started towards the vines again. She halted. A strange sensation began in the pit of her stomach, as though something within was uncurling. Had she been tricked? What did it feel like to be poisoned? The feeling grew, crawling upward. Nia hunched over and gagged and coughed. White petals fell to the ground, but they couldn't have been the ones she just ate. These were still whole. She fell to her knees as she coughed up more and more of them, choking.

A strangled, horrified noise came out of her as thin, curling vines grew out of her mouth. Cursed. Those flowers must have been cursed! Nia tried to pull the vine out but it hurt. Her arms shot out to the sides against her will and she noticed the green tinge spreading across her flesh. Her screams were stolen by the ever-growing fauna, leaves sprouting from her fingertips.

And then it all stopped.

Nia ceased coughing up petals, the vines receded and vanished. Her green skin shifted to its usual shade. She took several breaths before she dared to look up. And when she did, Neilos stood, watching her with cruel amusement. How she wished she could erase that smile from his eyes!

"You're despicable," she said, her voice hoarse. She could still feel the phantom touch of the vines creeping over her.

Neilos tsked. "You were breaking the rules. Punishment should be expected. Consider yourself lucky that I stopped the curse before you became a permanent member of my garden."

Nia's bones turned to ice as she wondered how many of the trees surrounding the area started out as trees. It was only then that she noticed the shadowed figure beside Neilos.

"Perla?"

Perla stood as still as the other statues in the garden, her expression vacant. The bubbly life she exuded right after Nia broke her curse was nowhere to be found.

"What did you do to her?" Nia hissed.

"Only what she earned. I discovered she had been helping you."

Did he know Nia had broken her curse? Would he suspect anyone else was free of their enchantments? Once more she feared for Uma and Antonia.

"I'm not sure how she managed to defy me," Neilos mused, "But I do plan to find out."

He said nothing of a curse. So, he didn't know it was Nia. He may not even have suspected Nia's knowledge of the cursed inhabitants and was keeping that card close to his heart.

Neilos regarded the eerily still librarian. "Regardless, it will not happen again."

He swept his arm in a fluid motion and Nia watched, frozen in horror as Perla turned into a tree right where she stood. Nia couldn't help but notice the two long branches that twisted exactly like Perla's braids.

"I don't suppose you feel like giving me that stone yet?" Neilos asked, plucking one of the leaves from the newly formed tree.

"No," Nia said, not bothering to hide the shaking in her voice or the tears that formed. The truth was, she did want to give it to him. She wanted to end all of this. But she knew if she gave it to him, the nightmare would never truly end. It would become impossible to wake from. So, no matter how easy it seemed on the surface, she could not give in.

Neilos cast the leaf aside and ground it under his shoe. "Suit yourself."

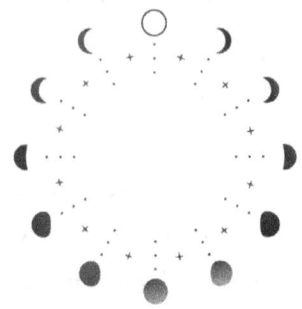

Chapter 22

10 days until the Dark Moon

Nia had asked Uma to stay away from her as much as possible over the next few days. After what happened to Perla, she wasn't going to risk harm coming to anyone else by helping her. Antonia was another matter, as she was supposed to be with Nia.

"You're sure he still doesn't suspect your curse is broken?" Nia helped Antonia smooth the quilt over her bed.

Antonia bit her lip. "If he suspects, he hasn't shown it. He has started asking me more questions about you, and I just answer or tell him I'll find out."

Nia started. Antonia hadn't been asking her questions. "Antonia, if he's expecting you to ask me things then you need to make sure you do it. If he asked you to do it directly, you can't refuse, or he'll know."

Antonia stepped around the grand bed and took Nia's hands in her own. Her touch was smooth and soothingly cool. "Please don't worry. I'm used to his prying questions and I've gotten very good about answering them in ways that don't draw suspicion or give too much information. I can handle Neilos." Her lips curved slightly upward.

Nia returned Antonia's smile but couldn't shake the feeling that *nobody* could truly handle Neilos. He was simply biding his time, and heaven help anyone who was in the vicinity when that thread of patience finally snapped.

At that moment, Nia's luck vanished.

Nia eyed the door. "I'll be right back, Antonia. There's something I need to look into."

"All right. Do take care."

As Nia suspected, Enitan was in the hall. He paced fretfully outside her door. Nia closed it softly as she stepped out to join him and asked, "What are you doing here?"

He stared at her, but his eyes were a maelstrom of so many emotions that she couldn't begin to sift through them. The dancing light of the mismatched shadows reflected off his gaze in a way that made it feel more like a puzzle than anything. Her spine tingled at the memory of how it felt to be secure in his arms and she wished more than anything for him to hold her like that again.

"Nia, I have to—"

His words cut off with a strangled noise, just as Nia had witnessed before. She suspected it happened any time he tried to counter Neilos's command and his torment became her own. She couldn't overpower Neilos's curse, but perhaps she could soothe Enitan.

As Enitan continued to grapple with his words, Nia placed her hands on either side of his face. "Enitan, look at me."

His eyes met hers and it seemed the shadows left them. The boy who saved her life was still in there.

Nia swallowed, choosing careful words, as though her voice could ignite embers of the same warmth he made her feel. "It's all right. I know you're not yourself right now. I understand." She couldn't tell him everything she knew, or he would report it straight back to Neilos.

He closed his eyes and took a deep breath. "I need you to come with me."

Nia's heart thumped. Should she go with him? He wasn't barred from asking her, which meant it fit into Neilos's whims. But as she'd seen with Perla, sometimes there were loopholes. He had wanted to tell her something—maybe he could show her something instead and that was what he wanted now.

"Ok. I'll come with you."

He extended his hand, and she took it, relishing the feeling. More make believe, she knew. But somehow, she couldn't help it.

As Nia followed Enitan through the castle, a chill rushed up her spine. It was too quiet. The air too still. Something was wrong. A compulsion to return to her room came over her, but if something was amiss, she couldn't simply hide, and she wouldn't abandon Enitan.

She tried to work out where they were going, unable to shake the feeling she'd walked this route before. Then the realization struck her like a bolt.

"Enitan," she froze, his name a shocked whisper. "Why are you taking me back to the ocean door?" He couldn't help it, but the betrayal stung her nevertheless. She pulled to remove her hand from his, but he tightened his grip, his expression stoic.

Nia whirled around as a shadow fell over her. Neilos stood a breath away, his eyes colder than a winter's midnight.

Nia struggled against Enitan's grip. "Let go!"

The spot where Enitan held her throbbed with pain. Whatever conflict she'd seen in his expression earlier was gone. In that moment he was no more than a lifeless tin soldier in Neilos's army. He couldn't help even if he wanted to, and the realization shattered her.

Neilos gazed at Nia with a twisted smile. "He won't help you but having him as my spy has been very useful. He told me what happened when he brought you here before."

She thrashed, strengthened by a rush of fear and adrenaline. She managed to free her arm and bolted, but Neilos grabbed her by the hair. Nia shrieked and landed a blow to Neilos's stomach. She took satisfaction in the look of pained surprise that marred his perfect features, but it was short-lived. He released her hair only to catch her up by the shoulders and slam her against the door.

And Enitan only stared.

"Enitan also told me something very interesting. You've had the stone with you the whole time. You have it right now, don't you? Bequeath it to me, and this will all be over." His amber eyes glinted.

"I don't know what you're—"

"DO NOT LIE TO ME!"

His roaring shook the halls and Nia shuddered away from him. She wished Enitan would leave so the stone could aid her.

As though reading her thoughts, Neilos continued. "I know it's here. It is taking me twice the energy it normally does to keep my servants in line."

Even without Enitan's presence, her luck was weakening as the dark moon grew nearer, and Neilos's magic was so strong. She hated to think what would happen without the stone working against him in some way.

"Bequeath me the stone," Neilos said again.

How had she ever found this man beautiful? All she saw before her was a monster. A tyrant. A being who used others and cast them aside at his whims. Whose heart was as cold as the bowels of the castle he tried to pretend was more than a prison.

Nia swallowed and her answer resonated through the room. "Never."

"So be it." Neilos opened the door with a wave of his hand and the sea breeze swept Nia up in a coil of terror once more.

"Help, Enitan!" Nia knew it was a fruitless plea as her poor emerald soldier stood motionless, but the cry broke free from her lips all the same.

Neilos shoved her over the threshold onto the beach's rough sand and the door closed with a boom, trapping them outdoors. She scrambled to her feet, her back to the ocean. She would not turn around and let the fear overcome her.

"Whether you bequeath the stone to me or not, I will take it. You will not use it against me a moment more."

This was it. Now that he knew she had the stone, there were no more games. No more pretenses. But that also meant she no longer needed to be so cautious.

Luck, don't fail me now.

She jumped out of the way just as a cyclone of sand, shells, and sea glass sprayed up into the area she had just been. It swirled into sharp points as Neilos attempted to hit her with the magically manipulated sand again. Nia continued to dodge with close calls that could only be considered luck. His fury was building and fortunate or not, she wasn't sure how long she could keep this up.

He attempted to ensnare her with seaweed on the shore that he enchanted into serpentlike compliance, but he missed her limbs by a fraction every time the slimy green strands attempted to bind them. Nia picked up a heavy rock and hurled it towards Neilos's head and it found its mark.

He howled and Nia retreated for the door. If she could just make it back inside the castle...

A fury of coastal debris ripped across her skin and clothes, slashing thousands of tiny fissures into her. She shrieked and shielded herself as another torrent came. She'd been careless in her retreat, and it seemed Neilos's rage made him stronger. After another slash of the torrential beach cyclone, it was over. Nia felt the weight of the stone leave her as the sandstorm cut across her waist. Neilos had the stone in hand before Nia could so much as attempt to retrieve it. He flung her into the foamy sand.

Nia stood on trembling legs, giving Neilos a fierce glare as the waves washed over her ankles. The saltwater licked her broken skin like tiny flames. Surely, he couldn't control the waves, too. But as the next wave flooded around her stinging knees, Nia was less sure.

"Do you remember," Neilos asked, "The state of your body when you arrived at the castle?"

She could never forget. He had healed her of every physical malady. She didn't answer but continued to maintain steady eye contact.

He didn't seem troubled by her lack of response and continued, "When you came to me your body was broken, but I healed it. Including," he said with a sinister curl of his lips, "The progressive healing of your lungs, which were damaged after the flood from your childhood."

She shivered as another wave crashed, this time soaking her up to her thighs and sending the skirt of her dress billowing atop the water. There was no point in reminding him her lungs hadn't fully healed yet, even if the improvement was remarkable.

Neilos stretched out his hand. "Because you don't seem to appreciate my gift, I'll take it back."

The air left her.

Her breath stuttered and the familiar burning in her lungs took hold. She had forgotten what it was like when every breath was a struggle, and for a moment she feared she would pass out then and there, leaving her body to be taken by the sea.

Get a grip, Nia.

She endeavored to recall the many books she'd read about peaceful outings at the seaside so she could narrow in on something positive. Collecting seashells. Warbling seabirds. Calming waters lapping gently.

And Enitan.

Thoughts of him broke momentarily through the chill of fear. When he brought her here the first time, he had been excited. To him, it wasn't a fearful place, and perhaps she could believe that if she tried to borrow his perspective. She imagined him standing in front of her again with his warm brown eyes, free of Neilos's darkness. There must be beautiful things about the sea, if she could just calm herself enough to notice them. She held her ground and clamped her teeth together to hide the quiver in her lip.

The next wave went over her head, whipping her hair around her face in tangles and knocking her to her knees. Her already wounded skin scraped along the sandy surface and the pull of the undertow threatened to take more. The wave receded and she sputtered, coughing out salty water as she struggled upright. She felt disoriented and her eyes burned. Her dress clung to her, heavy and restrictive.

Neilos stood on the shore, untouched by the waves, not one flaming-red hair out of place. He smirked at her as another wave pulled her under. Nia wasn't prepared for how quickly they came.

Air. She needed air!

She scrambled towards the sand, desperate to make it there before the next wave came. A strange force yanked her upward and she found herself flying over the waters. She flailed above the choppy surface of the sea. She could no longer see the bottom. Her heart pounded and her vision spun. If he dropped her here, she would drown.

"Has this persuaded you?" Neilos asked. His voice should have been drowned out by distance, wind, and waves, instead it resounded right in Nia's ear. She swatted at the side of her head as though he were a venomous insect. But his wretched words continued.

"Your stone can't help you now. Surely you know what will happen if I release you here. But if you give me what I want, I'm willing to overlook your defiance and pretend it never happened."

At last Nia found her voice. "My *defiance*?" she barked. "You mean defending my possession of something that was never yours to begin with?" She narrowed her eyes, hoping he could clearly discern her intent. "I will not give you what you want."

Nia fell into the sea.

Down, down, down she plummeted, as though a stone had been tied to her ankle. The weight of the water crushed her from all sides while her lacerations burned, and it was all she could do not to open her mouth to scream. She always feared she would die like her parents did, but a little part of her had never truly thought that's how it would happen.

And then an odd feeling of calm struck her. Neilos wouldn't let her die. If he did, he would not only be cursed for life, but the stone would be rendered useless. Nothing more than a pretty trinket. Men like Neilos didn't let go of their obsessions so easily—not even for revenge.

Nia closed her eyes as she drifted downward. She let the cradle of the waves rock her body. For a moment, she actually felt serene. All she had to do was wait. She forced herself not to think about the growing pressure in her chest and throat. Her senses screamed for her to take a breath, but Nia concentrated on the feeling of simply being.

Her mother was singing. Some of her earliest memories were of being rocked and sung to by her mother. This wouldn't be such a bad way to go out, would it?

Golden leaves in trees

Piercing skies of blue
Darling, none of these
Are cherished more than you...

As Nia lost herself in the lullaby, the blue-green light behind her eyes grew brighter and brighter, and she felt as though she was being pulled upward. Had she died?

Her head broke the surface. She took a breath as though it was her first, and gulped in several more after that, even as each inhalation seared her scarred lungs. She opened her eyes, blinking into the blinding sky above. Before she could orient herself, she was pulled back to shore where Neilos let her slam to the ground, scraping her battered skin in the process.

He crouched down beside her as she coughed up water and sand. "You think you've beaten me?" He hissed. "You think that because I won't kill you, you've won?"

Nia refused to look at him and kept her gaze fixated on the sand. She noticed a pearly, purple shell and tried to imagine what it would be like to collect them. Wasn't that a thing people enjoyed on the beach?

"You will regret forcing my hand, Nia." Neilos's voice was that of a viper, each word oozing with venom and carrying a promise of the deadly bite to come. If what he had just done wasn't his worst, Nia hated to think what he might do when he felt truly forced. After all, there were so many horrors humans could endure without actually succumbing to death.

Nia was back in her room. Her ears roared with the sudden quiet. She lay panting on her bed in her wet dress, shivering violently. She summoned the strength to roll herself to the ground to strip her clothing and crawl to the washroom. She leaned over the side of the tub, letting steam waft over her as the basin filled. Every inch of her stung as though someone continuously used her as a pincushion. She wished Antonia was around to assist. Her fingers were red and numb, and every breath reignited the hot coals in her lungs. Her knees were scraped raw and had tiny pebbles and grains of sand lodged in the skin. Her body shook from both cold and shock.

But she was still alive.

As disconcerting as it was having Neilos fling her to and fro as though he owned her, all she cared about now was that she was away from him. She would take any small reprieve she could get. She set her jaw, determined that she would not appear weak the next time she saw him, even though the thought of him sent a new wave of shivers through her.

For the moment, the nightmare was over, but Nia feared her waking reality was about to get far worse than anything her mind had ever concocted.

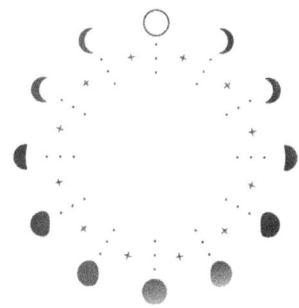

Chapter 23

9 days until the Dark Moon

Nia hit the ground with a force that set her teeth on edge. Had she fallen out of bed? She tried to make sense of what was happening in her freshly awakened state. This was not her room. This was the long, echoing throne room where she met Neilos for the first time. She pulled her robe tighter around herself, feeling disarmed and exposed. *Manes and tails*...what stupid game was Neilos playing now?

The door slammed as he strode in, and she flinched. Neilos was alone.

"Good morning," he said, as though he hadn't just transported Nia out of bed and into this room against her will.

"Don't be coy. Just tell me what you're doing and get it over with." After surviving the ocean, Nia felt bolder, and she reminded herself of her vow to appear strong in front of him. But she didn't like the way Neilos suddenly curled his lips. An all-knowing smirk playing across his features.

"So eager. Very well. I don't mind getting right to the point."

He circled around her, looking as pristine as ever. Nia was sure he brought her here in her just-awakened state so he could feel even more superior. She crossed her arms and stood taller, tilting her head up at him with narrowed eyes. He only looked more amused by this, and it infuriated her.

He held his hands behind his back and gazed towards one of the stained-glass windows. "I want the stone's power, Nia."

Nia snorted. "Oh really? This is the first time you've mentioned it."

He brushed a speck of lint off his sleeve as though it was her remark. "Thus far my attempts to persuade you have been unsuccessful. But I could still do worse."

Persuade. What an interesting word choice from a man who had essentially tortured her because he didn't immediately get his way.

"You can do whatever you want to me, Neilos. I won't give you the stone." It both thrilled and terrified her to say it. She would never give him his way, but the thought of what else he might do loomed over her and threatened to devour any courage she managed to show.

Neilos breathed a laugh. "Precisely. You don't care what happens to you, and you know I won't kill you." He gave her a steely glance. "Are you naive enough to assume I have no leverage?"

There was another loud sound as the doors at the other end of the long room flung open. Enitan stepped in holding a thrashing, protesting individual. Someone Nia knew all too well.

"Magala?" The words came out near breathless. Nia turned icy cold. What would he do to her dear friend? She could endure her own pain, but she could not bear to see Magala harmed in any way.

All thought of strong appearances forgotten, Nia rushed towards Magala but was halted by Enitan before she could get too close. Her emotions lurched, but she only gave him a moment of attention before turning to her friend.

"Are you hurt, Mag?"

"Nothing I can't handle," Magala said, her voice coming raspier than usual. "I'm so happy you're safe, Nia. When I saw your house I—"

Her words were cut off when Enitan delivered a blow to her side.

"Magala!" He may as well have hit Nia for the pain that stabbed her heart. Controlling Enitan. Hurting Magala. It was all too much.

She whirled to face Neilos. "Let her go," Nia demanded. "This doesn't involve her in any way."

"Oh, but it does now," Neilos purred. "She's part of a valuable trade. Her life for the stone."

Oh no. Not this. Nia's lungs burned as her breathing grew more intense.

Magala thrust herself forward as much as she could while being restrained. "If you give him that stone, I'll curse you until the day I die! Do you hear me, Nia?" Magala's voice echoed through the great hall.

Neilos laughed. "If she doesn't give me the stone, the day you die is already upon you."

Nia clenched her teeth and spun to face Neilos. "If you hurt her, I will *never* bequeath the stone to you."

Neilos tilted his head to the side. "So you've said. But what if she is the first of many? It does not matter to me how many I kill to get what I want. But I suspect it matters to you."

At once Enitan thrust Magala to the ground and unsheathed his sword. He held it to his own throat, no hint of emotion on his features. Magala attempted to run but howled as Enitan threw a heavily booted foot down on her leg, sword still dangerously poised for his own blood.

"Do you want to kiss him or kill him?" Neilos taunted.

Nia's blood turned arctic. Neilos wasn't bluffing—he would really kill Magala. And Enitan. And many more until she said the words needed to transfer the stone to him. But how many more would he destroy with the stone in his hands? Nothing would be able to stop him. There was no winning in this situation. But at least if she gave him the stone she would still have her friends by her side, for however long Neilos let them live after that.

"Please," Nia choked out through the lump in her throat. "I beg you not to do this. There must be something—anything else at all—I could offer." She wasn't foolish enough to believe her pleas would amount to anything. But she didn't know what else to do.

Neilos flicked his wrist and one of the large stained-glass windows high above them shattered, causing Nia to stumble as she attempted to avoid the jagged fragments raining down. A shard caught Enitan's temple, which seemed to break him momentarily out of his stupor. His eyes widened just the slightest and he removed his boot. Magala seized the opportunity and broke free. Nia sprinted after her and grabbed her arm. She would take her to the tunnels. She—

Magala flew into the air and Enitan slammed against the stone wall. Nia gripped Magala's sleeve fiercely, attempting to pull her back to the ground.

"This is all very entertaining," Neilos said lazily, "But my patience has long expired."

A great gust of wind ripped Nia away from Magala and they both cried out. But while Nia was bashed to the floor across the room, Magala remained airborne and flew swiftly, at Neilos's bidding, towards the shattered open window.

"Don't!" Nia shrieked, her throat straining from the force of her yell. The ceilings in this room were so high. Magala would never survive a fall from that window.

"This is your last chance." While Neilos's voice was soft, it carried across the chamber.

"Nia." Magala's voice was firm. "Do. Not."

Nia met her gaze and saw the resolution there. The acceptance. The reassurance. Nia knew Magala. She wasn't just trying to appear heroic. She truly was willing to trade her life to keep the stone out of Neilos's hands, and she would despise Nia in an instant if she gave into his desires.

"Neilos...don't!" Enitan's words growled free, and his efforts would cost him.

The castle's master gave his guard a bored expression. "I will deal with your insubordination later." He waved his hand again and Enitan's head bashed back against the wall. He jerked and fell unconscious.

Hot tears came in a flood and Nia clenched her fists at her side, her heart threatening to burst. Still, she stood resolute.

"Very well then," Neilos spat. He pulled his arm back and threw it forward, sending Magala flying out the window.

Nia's scream filled the room in a million echoes, but Magala would never utter another sound.

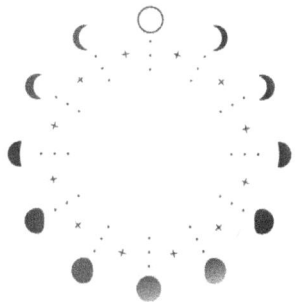

Chapter 24

Neilos magically transported Nia back to the bed in her room again. He wouldn't even let her see Magala, although she wasn't entirely sure she wanted to. Still, she felt responsible for her dear friend's death, and Nia owed it to her to view the aftermath, to be a witness to the entirety of Neilos's cruel deed. Magala deserved so much better.

Apart from that, what would happen to Enitan now? How long would it be before Neilos killed him, too? It seemed like Enitan was becoming stronger and building resistance to his curse, and Nia was certain that would only make Neilos target him with more intensity.

Nia sprung up from the bed and ran to the door. It was locked. She released an agonized cry and threw herself against it. All her action gave her was a throbbing shoulder. Hot tears erupted from her eyes as she raged around her room, throwing vases, knocking over her nightstand, ripping little lace doilies and trimmings from wherever she could find them. She shoved her face into her pillow and screamed over and over as the cushion absorbed her tears.

The passage of time became meaningless as she unleashed her sorrows. She wasn't sure how long it had been when she finally looked up and became aware of the world around her again. Her room was shadowed, and it felt very late. Nia couldn't say whether it was actually dark outside or if Neilos had removed the enchanted light from her room as another form of torment. Antonia hadn't come at all today. Was she ok? Nia sprang up and tried the door again.

Still locked.

Of course Neilos would trap and isolate her in her grief. He wanted to make this hurt as much as he could. But if he had done something to Antonia...

No. As far as Neilos knew, Antonia was still under his curse. He had figured out Perla, though. Maybe that was only because she had found sneaky ways to leave hints even while under his curse. Coupled with Enitan's momentary awareness, this would make Neilos more cautious and mindful of his servants' actions.

Nia threw her shoulder against the door again, but it didn't budge. She ran to her vanity seeking a hairpin from the drawer. Once, she had lost her key to the stone's box. It left her in a state of panic, and she broke the whole box open. Vowing to never be put in that position again, she learned how to pick locks.

As Nia yanked the drawer open, a tiny glass vial rolled around inside. A scrap of paper with Antonia's handwriting read, "Veritas water. Just in case."

Nia would inquire about that as soon as she found Antonia, but at that moment she focused on the task at hand and secured a hairpin.

The pin slid into the keyhole, but Nia drew back with a yelp as a current of magic shot through her. There would be no picking that lock.

Her eyes fell to the decorative grate in her room and for a moment everything seemed to stop.

Painful air surged into her lungs again and her mind came back to life. She hurried to the grate and fell to her knees, grasping the intricate panel and giving a hard tug. The force of the panel popping free threw her backwards. Nia jumped up and fumbled through her dresser, shouting in triumph when she found a small piece of Spencer's chocolate.

As she hurried to swallow the shrinking chocolate, her thoughts turned to Neilos, and a determined flame sparked within her. She would set the castle free and make him atone for his actions.

Or she would die trying.

Nia smoothed the map out again, studying the details. There had to be something missing, or perhaps the map Perla left for her was out of date. An ache filled her as she remembered Perla's current state. With any luck she would help her soon.

The first time Nia came to the crystal pool she had been enchanted. It was a vision pulled straight from her most beautiful dreams. But now she could feel the echoes of fairies and the haunted whisperings of her conversation with Neilos. The dream was closer to a nightmare.

Nia followed the walls of the cave-like space, searching for anything that looked off. Prying her fingers through every crack and crevice. Kicking up the dust beneath her feet in hopes of unearthing a trap door. There was nothing. No sign of a dungeon entrance. But the plans in the library had been accurate to everything else. This was her only lead. She closed her eyes and took several steadying breaths, willing whatever forces existed around her to show her the way.

Her eyes popped open and her gaze fixated on the crystal pool. She approached it with caution, marveling again at its glassy surface. The bottom, full of pastel pebbles and white sand, was easily visible. Her breath hitched and she became acutely aware of the pain in her lungs. She took several shuddering breaths.

This was not the ocean. This was not a river or even a stream. It was merely a pool. There were no waves or currents to decide her destiny for her. Just still, calm waters. Her breathing still burned, but it steadied.

Unsure precisely what prompted her to do it, Nia removed her shoes and stripped down to her undergarments. She dove into the pool.

It was just as warm and pleasant as she remembered and for a moment, she lost herself in its comfort. Only when her lungs reminded her did she recall she was underwater. She steadied herself before she could overthink it. *This is not the ocean.*

She swam downward. The pool did not appear deep from above, but now it seemed she might never reach the bottom. She swam back towards the surface, desperately needing a breath, but the world seemed to shift, and she was no longer sure where up was. Her lungs begged for air but there was none to give. Why was the water always threatening to undo her?

Yet, the bottom of the pool still glimmered, compelling, beckoning even. Nia propelled herself once more towards it and thrust her hands into the sand. She began to dig. And dig. And dig. A force sucked her under. Her head broke through to fresh oxygen and she gulped and gasped.

When her breathing returned to normal her surroundings took shape. There was no mistaking it—she was in the dungeons.

How deep did these dungeons descend? Nia was sure she had been navigating the steps for at least twenty minutes. She halted, wondering for a moment if this was an endless labyrinth and she would never get away. Her teeth chattered and she wished she had something to dry her hair and clothes.

At last, the steps ended. It was pitch dark, and the lantern Nia had pilfered from the tunnel's entrance seemed to be fighting a losing battle. Was it just her imagination, or was it flickering? Her heart hammered at the thought of getting lost here in the dark. *Turn around*, her head screamed. *Go back while you still can.*

Then she heard it—a light tinkling sound, like bells. But oh so soft and delicate. She knew that sound, but from where? She gulped and ignored her dying lantern, following the noise.

Her eyes strained. Was that a glow up ahead? When she reached the source, she let out a coarse breath. Before her were several hanging cages, each one full of pixies. Nia heard the tinkling sound again and located the culprit—the tiny lilac pixie she met at the cave pond. Nia's insides seared hot. So, he hadn't let them go after all. The pixie's light was dim, its color pale.

"I'm getting you out. All of you."

She examined the lock—it looked ordinary enough. Neilos probably saw no need to use anything other than an ordinary cage on such small creatures. She set her lantern down and pulled a pin from her hair. She fumbled to find the lock again—her lantern really didn't do much good on the ground. As if sensing the predicament, the pixie closed its eyes and strained, glowing brighter and allowing Nia to see better. She braced herself as she pushed the pin in, waiting for another magic shock, but none came. She probed and twisted with her pin in the lock until she heard the satisfying click she had been waiting for.

The pixie walked onto Nia's hands and Nia was horrified at how cold it felt. How could the tiny things survive this way? She cupped the pixie close to her chest.

"Let's get your friends out now, ok?"

One by one, Nia picked each lock, setting the miserable creatures free. Most of them seemed too weak to fly, so they seated themselves on Nia instead. Neilos would pay for this. Somehow.

When the last creature was free, Nia said, "I'm looking for the speculo. Do you know where he's kept?"

One of the pixies gestured to Nia's left. Again, all she could see was darkness, but she picked up her lantern once more and followed, dozens of chilled pixies clinging to every inch of her. Nia shivered, wondering how any creature could survive long in this place.

At last, she came to the cell she sought, with a shadowed form crouched at the far end.

"You've finally come," the speculo said, its whispering voice laced with amusement. Nia could only imagine what he thought of her as she stood there, still damp from the pool and shivering in her undergarments. She pretended not to care.

"You knew I would come?"

"A person like you always seeks the truth, in one way or another."

What did it mean by "a person like you"? What did the speculo see in her that Nia herself did not?

"I want to make a deal," Nia said, voice firm as she broke free of her thoughts.

"Ah, straight to the chase. What is it you seek?"

"Two things." Nia wondered what the creature might ask for in return. "First, I want to know how to break Enitan's curse."

The speculo seemed unphased by this. "And the second?"

"I want to know how to get out of the barrier."

The creature gave a raspy laugh. "And what do you offer me?"

"Your freedom. You help me, and I'll get you out."

"And what, dear child, makes you think you can get me out?"

"There's an object in the relic room. A mask. It can help you go unnoticed. Enitan will help me get it. Once his curse is broken, I know he will." In truth, Nia could get the mask without Enitan's assistance. But the speculo didn't need to know that.

"Ah, very clever. My escape is contingent on you first getting one of the things you seek. If Enitan isn't free, then neither am I. I see."

"Do we have a deal?"

The silence grew heavier as the speculo considered the offer. "Normally, this would be a one-for-one deal. You have two requests and only offer one. But," the creature laughed again. "Ruining Neilos is reward enough for the second. You have your deal."

The creature extended its arm, and a silvery hand loosed from the dark, heavy robes. Nia marveled at its...skin? She wasn't sure what to call it. It looked like a hand formed from a mirror. She grasped the creature's hand and gave it a firm shake.

"Now we are bound. The first answer is a simple one. You spoke earlier of a relic room?"

"On the seventh floor."

"That's the one. In that room, you'll find a heart shaped vial."

Nia remembered. The light shining off its scarlet surface was still etched into the crevices of her mind. A cursed object, Enitan had said.

The speculo continued, "The heart holds Enitan's curse. It must be broken with another cursed object, and the blood spilled onto a blessed object in order to remove the curse."

Blessed object. Cursed object. Nia's head spun. "How do I know what's what?" Surely Neilos had several of each in that room. Then it dawned on Nia. "The colored lights?"

"Yes. Good." The speculo nodded. "Green is cursed, bringing nothing but woe. Blue is blessed, bringing only fortune. Yellow is neither blessed nor cursed and depends on the one who wields it."

Nia heated at the idea of Neilos's cruelty. All this time he forced Enitan to guard his own ticket out. What was it like for Enitan each day, having the key to his freedom so close but being unable to reach it? Not only that but forced to drive away anyone who might be able to help him?

"Thank you," said Nia. "Now, the barrier?"

The creature tilted its head. "If you kill Neilos, his barriers will come down."

"I could have worked that out myself!" She steadied herself and blew out a stinging breath. "Is there really no other way? The legends say a fortune stone can get a person through magical barriers, but I couldn't do it."

The speculo chuckled. "That is a question you'll have to ask the stone. It could have gotten you out but chose not to."

"How could you possibly know that?" There was no way. The stone always helped Nia get what she needed. It wouldn't have kept her trapped in this place.

"When I'm near the stone, I can hear its whisperings and sense its magic dealings. I am unsure of the reasons, but I am certain it refused to let you through."

Nia wasn't sure how to process this new information about the fortune stone. It could have gotten her out the whole time, but chose not to? It didn't make any sense.

"You have your answers," the speculo rasped. "See to it you don't neglect our bargain."

"I won't. As soon as I can, I'll get you out." Nia paused. "I get the feeling you know more than anyone else in this castle. I need to know...can you tell me why Neilos wants the stone so badly? He doesn't seem like he needs extra luck, so I have a feeling there's more than that."

"You are pushing your luck with your questions. What else can you offer me?"

"I could still change my mind about freeing you."

The speculo released a harsh laugh. "No, you could not. If you renege on our deal, I will reveal all I can about you and the stone to Neilos, and I suspect you do not want that. Still," The speculo pressed the fingertips of its strange hands together, "This information may help you work against Neilos, which is an offering unto itself. So, I shall tell you."

Nia waited, unsure if the speculo's pause was due to thinking or simply being dramatic.

At last, it said, "Do you recall the origins of the stones?"

Nia searched the crevices of her mind. She probably should have researched them more, given that she owned one. But she hadn't cared about the origin when she was a child and by the time she was older it was so much a part of her life that she didn't think twice about it. "Forged by sorcerers, or something like that?"

The speculo nodded. "Twenty powerful sorcerers created the stones in hopes of keeping their families safe for generations long after they were gone. Together, they grew more powerful and studied ancient magic thought to be long forgotten. The knowledge and power they possessed was dangerous and otherworldly.

"Soon, whispers of their workings traveled through the land and the people became anxious. While the sorcerers saw themselves as scholars and intended only to build their knowledge and foundations, the rest of the world did not see it that way.

"The people began to attack the sorcerers and their families. Nowhere was safe. It's said that one sorceress, in a desperate attempt to protect her infant child, forged a gateway to another universe as an escape route. Working with the others, they created the wanderer's ring as a way to open these gateways to find a safe haven. They continued world hopping and taking notes to find the right place to start over."

"Why did they make it so only a holder of the fortune stone could use it?" Nia asked.

"Because, as I said, the stones were initially only passed to family members, and only to those thought to be worthy. If they limited the ring's access to only stone holders, they felt it would help ensure the ability to hop worlds was never abused. A person cannot even touch that ring if they are not a fortune stone holder." The speculo chuckled. "So of course, you had no trouble picking it up."

Nia's eyes widened. The ring from the relic room was the wanderer's ring? And how did the speculo know she took it? More importantly, if only the holder of a stone could touch it, how did Neilos get it?

"Do not look so surprised. I can sense the ring's presence, as I can with all magical objects. Surely you felt something special about the ring when you saw it."

Nia felt the ring burning from where it was tied around her waist. No wonder she had been so drawn to it. In a way, it truly was meant for her. However, if it really was a gateway to other worlds, she had no intention of using it for that purpose.

"Can I ask you just one more question?"

The speculo chuckled once more. "As I have nothing better to do, I will humor you, child."

"Neilos said magic is drawn to me." Nia thought of the pixies, the magic books, all the little creatures that paid her a visit over the years. "I've found that to be true. Why?"

"Why do you think?" The speculo said it as though the answer should be obvious.

"The stone," Nia said matter-of-factly. She might have known. Such an object would undoubtedly attract magic.

"No," The speculo countered. "Think again."

"I have no idea," Nia frowned, entirely uninterested in the creature's riddles. "There's nothing special about me. Especially without the stone."

A long sigh escaped the speculo's mouth. "The magic is drawn to you because you don't want it. You don't seek to possess. To use. To manipulate. You want to coexist without using it to your advantage. And so, the magic feels free to be what it is. In short, it is not the stone, but it is your heart, which is the very reason I'm willing to give leniency in my bargains with you. I cannot deny the appeal of your aura."

This wasn't the answer Nia anticipated. "So, it's really just...me?"

The speculo barked out another raspy laugh. "There is no 'just' about it. But yes, it is you."

Nia wasn't sure if she believed him. But what reason did he have to lie?

A shiver on Nia's shoulder brought her back to the present. She still needed to release the pixies. "Thank you for all the information. I have to go before Neilos notices I'm gone."

The speculo reached once more through the bars. "I suspect you'll need more of this. It's the last I have, so use it wisely."

The silvery light the speculo generated cast a shimmering glow on the surface of the shrinking chocolate he offered.

"Thank you!" Nia stuffed it into her pocket, feeling a warm flood of relief. If Neilos was keeping her under lock and key, she wasn't sure how she was going to get around.

The speculo moved away from the bars to crouch in the shadows once more. "Do not forget about me."

"I swear I will not."

Nia's first order of business was to release the pixies. She led them to the garden grate. The gaps left by its twisted vine design were large enough for the tiny creatures to escape through.

"I don't know if you'll be able to get free of Neilos's ward." Nia suspected that's why he was able to capture them again the first time he pretended to set them free. "If you can't, I need you all to hide really well until the night of the dark moon, ok? It's just a few days away." She hoped Neilos would be too occupied with the stone and Nia to notice the pixies were missing.

The pixies nodded and tinkled in excitement and flew with haste through the openings of the grate into the moonlight.

The lilac pixie hovered in front of Nia's face and gave her a grateful kiss on the tip of her nose before soaring away after her friends. While it was obvious the pixies were weakened, they still knew how to make a quick exit. Hopefully the sunlight and flowers would rejuvenate them in the morning. As for Nia, she needed to get back to her room.

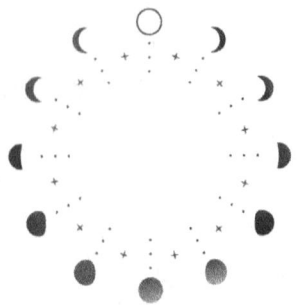

Chapter 25

Eight days until the Dark Moon

Nia was surprised when the door to her room opened early the next morning. She braced herself but relaxed when she recognized the figure coming through the door.

"Uma!"

Nia raced forward to embrace her, nearly knocking the tray out of her hands. Nia's stomach rumbled and she realized she hadn't eaten for the past day other than a few nibbles of shrinking chocolate. The offering on the tray was a dried out, crumbling roll and a bruised apple.

"I'm sorry." Uma's voice was woeful. "He told me this was all I'm allowed to bring you."

Nia picked up the apple and took a bite. It was mealy and dry, but her stomach wanted more anyway. "It's ok, Uma. Thank you for bringing what you could."

"I shouldn't stay. He instructed me to bring the food and leave."

"Of course," Nia said hastily. "Do what you have to do. But it's good to see you, Uma."

Uma smiled back, the corners of her eyes watering. "Take care, Nia. I'll keep doing what I can."

The door swung open again just moments after Uma departed and Nia was greeted with another familiar face. Antonia gave Nia a smile laced with tired sorrow. As soon as the door clicked shut Antonia was at Nia's side, pulling her into an embrace. Nia let the dry roll fall to her tray with a thud and her eyes misted with tears at the compassion in the gesture.

"Oh, Nia. I heard about your friend. I'm so, so sorry. I wanted to see you sooner, but Neilos wouldn't allow it. Are you ok?"

Nia gave an honest answer. "No." She couldn't be ok after what happened to Magala. And all she'd been able to do since then was worry about what might happen to everyone else. At times the pressure of it was so much she wished she could just forget any of this happened. Antonia seated herself on the edge of the bed and motioned for Nia to join her. It opened the floodgate and Nia cried tears she didn't know she had left. Antonia sat and stroked her hair, allowing Nia to simply feel what she needed.

After a few moments Nia spoke, voice quivering. "She was the one person in my village I felt secure around with the fortune stone. I gave her a little piece of it."

Antonia stiffened. "She had a piece of your stone?"

"Just a tiny one."

"And Neilos killed her. Do you know what that means?"

Nia wiped her eyes. "Neilos is a monster?"

Antonia shook her head, her expression brightening. "It means his luck is cursed."

She was right. Neilos's luck would have started to turn the wrong direction as soon as Magala died. But Nia frowned. "It would only be a little. Barely noticeable, I'm sure. It was such a small shard," Antonia gave a rueful smile. "Sometimes just a little is all it takes. Magala may yet be avenged." It was too much to hope for, but Nia did like the sound of that.

"Thank you," Nia said with a sniff. Now that she'd purged her own sorrows, Nia became more aware of Antonia. The shadows under her eyes became apparent and it was taking more effort than usual for the kind servant to maintain her straight posture. How had Nia not noticed before how tired her friend looked? Antonia would never admit it, but Nia was certain Neilos was taking a toll on her as he became more desperate. He had to be pressuring her for information.

"Antonia, you need to make sure you're getting enough rest. I'm worried. Why don't you go back to your room?"

"That's very kind of you, but I want to set to work on finding a cure for Perla. If I stay in your room Neilos will assume I'm attending to you and your things, which is what I've been asked to do."

Guilt stabbed through Nia. The weight of responsibility for what happened to the young librarian hung like a cloud over her. "How can I help?"

Antonia waved a dismissive hand. "All you need to do is stay safe. Besides, I can work faster on my own. I'll be fine. But," Antonia hesitated. "There is something I want to give you. I was waiting for the right time, but I have a feeling it's better to give it to you sooner."

Nia noted the slight tremor in Antonia's hands.

"What's wrong?" She hoped her friend wasn't doing anything to put herself in greater danger.

"If Neilos doesn't know about my curse, it's only a matter of time before he does. And when that happens, well, I don't really want to know."

Antonia pulled something out of her apron pocket and pressed a lumpy ball into Nia's hands. It was mint green and speckled with traces of lavender and periwinkle. "Hang on to that until the time is right."

"What is it?"

"Neilos's gaze is far-reaching due to his abilities. When you eat this, you will be invisible to him for exactly twelve hours. This should give you plenty of time to get away from the castle."

Nia examined the object—it felt light and delicate in her hands. "But what about you? Do you have one too?"

Antonia shook her head. "The ingredients are hard to come by and the process takes several days. This was only for you."

"No, I can't do that. He'll kill you." Nia was certain as soon as Neilos learned what Antonia did it would be the end of her.

"I knew what sort of person I was taking up with when I came to work here. I chose it anyway and I reaped what I sowed."

"You didn't choose to be magically imprisoned."

Antonia smiled. "Even so, you freed me, and I want to do the same for you. Now that I have my own mind again, I'm going to make Neilos pay by taking away the thing he wants most. Don't deny me that."

Nia closed her fist around the ball, her eyes misty. "Thank you. I'll keep it safe." She slipped it into her pillowcase and Antonia gave an approving nod.

An odd flashing green light suddenly peeked out from the pocket Antonia had produced the ball from just moments before.

Nia's eyebrows furrowed. "What's that?"

"I..." Antonia's voice carried a slight quiver. "I'm being summoned."

"By Neilos? Now?"

Antonia stood, smoothing the bedding where she had been. She gave Nia a weary smile. "I'm sure it's nothing. Some silly new plot to get more information from you. It'll be all right."

Nia walked her friend to the door, worry needling at her. "You'll come back right away after you've spoken with him?"

"Of course. Don't worry."

Nia wasn't sure how many circles she made around her room. The evening hours drew on as she waited for Antonia to return. Something had to have gone wrong. What if Neilos hurt her? What if he learned of her broken curse and was placing her under a new one? What if she met a similar fate to Perla's?

At last, Nia heard the creak of her door.

"Thank goodness. I was starting to worr—" Nia cut off her words when she saw it was not Antonia who had entered, but Neilos. His narrowed eyes glinted.

"I suppose you think you're clever," he said, the sneer heavy in his voice. "How long ago did you break Antonia's curse?"

Nia clenched her jaw to steady the trembling as dread filled her chest.

Not Antonia. Please not her too.

"Where is she?" Nia demanded, ignoring Neilos's question.

Neilos cast something down at Nia's feet and she gasped. Lying cold on the floor was a little rag doll with long, raven hair, and a dress that exactly matched the one Antonia had been wearing.

"Just try breaking *that* curse," Neilos spat. "You should have left well enough alone."

Nia grabbed the doll, horrified. "Please, turn her back."

"Bestow the stone to me."

"I won't," Nia whispered. In her heart she plead apologies to Antonia.

"Enjoy your doll," Neilos said with a huff. The echo of the heavy door as he slammed it mirrored the heavy grief in Nia's heart.

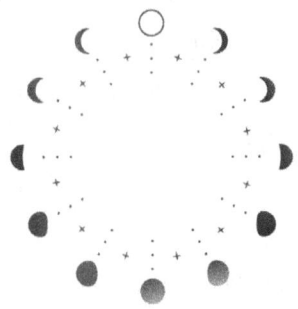

Chapter 26

Two days until the Dark Moon

Two days. Well, thirty-one hours, if she wanted to be precise. That was all the time Nia had left to come up with a plan. She wasn't sure she had it in her anymore. She turned her bleary eyes toward the little doll propped up on her bed. Antonia, Perla, Magala… How many more would suffer? And while Enitan may be in fine physical health, he suffered at his master's hands every day.

Nia refused to be a pawn in Neilos's game any longer. It was time to flip the board.

She changed into a velvety, long-sleeve dress, making sure to choose one that was snug at the wrists. She raced to her nightstand drawer to produce the black chain necklace she found in the tunnels and stuffed it carefully into her sleeve, just far enough in to conceal it. Next, she raided the drawer for the little bottle of veritas water, whispering thanks to Antonia as she slipped it into her other sleeve. She ran to the door, half expecting to find it locked. But this time it was open. She grabbed the first servant she saw—a teenage boy—by the shoulder and demanded, "Where is Neilos's room?"

The boy looked at her with a glimmer of fear in his eyes, but he told her where to go.

Nia reached the ornate doorway of his chambers, encrusted in emerald serpents. How fitting. If anyone was a snake, it was Neilos. If he wasn't here, she'd scour the entire castle to find him.

A moment after her hand touched the handle the door opened of its own accord. Whisked inside as if by a strong wind, she swallowed a scream. Nia didn't want to appear intimidated or scared. She came to a sudden stop, hair billowing around her face.

The room was shadowed, lit only by candlelight. The flames gave dancing hints of the deep greens and golds of the room. Neilos reclined in an armchair at the side of his bed, as though he'd been anticipating her. Perhaps he had. He swirled a large goblet of dark liquid in his hand.

"Ah, Nia. To what do I owe this...*pleasure*."

The malice and thinly veiled sarcasm behind his words bit into her. But she kept her resolve and assessed the situation. How could she make this work?

"I'm through with games, Neilos." Nia took a deep breath, fighting nausea as she made her next move. "What could you offer me as your queen?"

He arched a brow, and his posture straightened. "You assume that proposition still stands?"

"It's the only way we both get what we want."

He stood from the chair, placed his goblet on the side table and prowled closer to her. "And what is it you want, Nia?" His amber eyes seemed to glow. He leaned in close to her and tipped her chin up with one slender finger, his devil smile playing in the flickering light. "Is it my power? Or do you simply find *me* irresistible?"

Nia's pulse quickened, the raging survival instinct to flee growing stronger within her. He was definitely toying with her. But she had to follow through.

Manes and tails...respond, Nia!

"I—I just..."

He laughed and drew back. "You loathe me. Any fool could see that, and I am no fool." He circled her, making her feel more like prey than ever. "But we truly would make a pair."

Nia fought the bile and coarse words rising in her throat and said nothing.

After studying her for a moment, he waved a lazy hand. "Very well. I will indulge you. Allow me to be transparent about precisely what I can offer."

Nia waited. She was certain she wouldn't like whatever he had to say next.

"My mother was a witch. My father was fae."

Nia's breath stilled. That explained...everything.

"Their only desire was to conquer the world, but they learned of creatures with the means to strip them of their magic. They wanted a vessel to temporarily transfer their powers into if something should go wrong. That's all I was to them. A shell. A container. They didn't even pretend to love me and made my purpose clear. What they didn't know was that I spent my solitude in learning. I already had tremendous magic ability from both bloodlines, and I grew stronger."

Nia remained silent. She couldn't even begin to find the words.

"When I was five, the day finally came when they needed to use me. But magic beings must keep some of their power in order to survive. When they began the transfer, I took it all. Every. Last. Drop. They perished, powerless. Their power, combined with my skill has made me what you see today. Best of all, they had already laid the groundwork for me to have a kingdom."

How could he speak so casually of causing his parents' deaths? Even if he didn't feel loved by them, how could he consume their lives without a thought at five years of age? The creature was born without compassion.

He regarded her, a hint of a smile on his perfect lips. "My reach stretches far beyond these castle walls. The rulers in the lands North, West, South, East. All belong to me. Merely my puppets."

Nia knew what that meant. All the corrupt decisions by these leaders were orchestrated by Neilos. The refusals to trade. The attacks. She stifled the fire burning inside of her, instead returning Neilos's gaze, impassive. "Why are you telling me this?" she asked at last. Why did she need to know of his past?

"I'm pulling back the curtain. I want you to understand exactly how much more you could have."

Nia's eyes traveled to the goblet again. She needed to keep him talking while she figured out a way to get close to it. To keep him believing they were entering into some kind of negotiation. "I've never been interested in power. What else can you offer?"

"Perhaps it is simply your limited mortal perspective. You don't even comprehend what it is you're resisting." Something sparked in his eyes. A ball of violet lightning formed in his hands, and he shot it towards the goblet on the end table. The liquid burst into purple light and the goblet soared into Neilos's hand. He smirked. "You're certain you don't want this power? I dare you to deny it after having a taste."

Nia stepped back. "No." Farce or not, she wouldn't go near that.

He gripped Nia behind the head and shoved her against his chest to hold her in place as he forced the goblet to her lips. She struggled against him, but it was no use. The instant a drop of the unearthly liquid touched her tongue the remainder of it sucked into her. Molten ice slithered down her throat, through her chest, spreading through her stomach and outward through her limbs. A crackling sensation filled her body—forceful, but not painful.

He released her and she stumbled backwards, trembling.

"What did..."

"I gave you my power. Half of it. We are now equals."

He was lying. Why would he do that? As power-hungry as Neilos was, Nia was sure he wouldn't share. But what if he was telling the truth?

"I don't want it," Nia insisted. She held her body rigid, afraid of what she might inadvertently do if she really did hold such power.

"Don't be proud. Go on, try it."

Nia could feel it as he said it, flowing through her. The power to create. To destroy. To control. She could sculpt worlds. Shape destinies. The power was begging her to release it and finally she could no longer resist. She let a spark flow from her fingertips and a delicate sprinkle of glowing flowers cascaded out before her. She made them dance. Another movement of her hands, and they were singing. She bathed them in moonlight and falling stars.

She could do whatever she wanted.

She glanced at Neilos, who watched her every move with intensity. Nia knew better than to try and use her powers on him. He was experienced—she was not. Though he may say they were equals, he still held the upper hand.

"Isn't it marvelous?" he asked. "Just imagine it. It could be yours to keep forever, if you choose."

And heaven help her, Nia was tempted. She felt grand. She was unstoppable. What could she do with such power? She could feed her entire village. She could set her friends free and let them live like royalty. And Enitan...

There would be no Enitan.

Not if she chose this. She would be Neilos's queen and forced to do his bidding. Nia knew where this power led. She would be used. Manipulated. Yes, she and Neilos and the stone would be an unstoppable force, but to what end?

She let the power fizzle at her fingertips, her arms falling to her sides. "Take it back."

"What absolute fool would choose to give this up?" Neilos asked with a deadly quiet. "When you could have everything you desire at a literal snap of your fingers, why would you say no?"

"Because I don't want it. It's really that simple."

Red heat burst to life around her, burning to her core. She shrank under the energy of Neilos's anger, fearing it would end her then and there.

"You dare defy me? I am the greatest force in the universe," Neilos snarled. "There is none greater than me."

Nia felt the lie in his words. Who created the fairies? The rivers? The mountains? And even Nia herself. Not Neilos. Nia knew that much. "There are hands greater than yours," Nia said softly. "There must be. And it's in those hands I place my fate."

Neilos shot a heated stare in Nia's direction, then lifted the goblet once more, beckoning her close. Her heart raced as she gripped the goblet. As Neilos lifted his hand and ripped his power back from her, she feigned a loss of balance and stumbled to the floor with the goblet, even as it refilled itself. Crouching over it with her back to Neilos, she loosed the vial from her sleeve and emptied its contents. A moment later the goblet flew from the floor into Neilos's waiting hand.

He sneered down at her. "Pathetic."

Indeed, she felt small and empty. A hollow shell. But she reminded herself the power was never hers, and the consequences of keeping it would reach far beyond herself. No matter how intoxicating it may have been at that moment, this was as it should be.

She watched with wide eyes and bated breath as Neilos tipped the goblet back, claiming his power once more.

"I believe," Neilos hissed, "That an extended stay is in order. Though don't expect the same comfort I was gracious enough to give you."

It was now or never.

Before Neilos could say another word, Nia blurted, "Where is my fortune stone?"

"It's in a vault in the floor of the snake pit." The answer was immediate.

Neilos froze.

Nia pressed forward. "Where's the key?"

"The ravens have it." He hissed and clamped his hands over his mouth. And suddenly he was raging towards Nia. "Curse you! What did you do?"

"Will you really drop your wards on the night of the dark moon?" Nia spouted her question as he used his magic to throw her against his dresser. Still, even through the wave of pain she caught his involuntary answer.

"Yes. I can't maintain the spell infinitely, so I must take one night a month to replenish. I chose the one night a holder of the fortune stone could not best me."

Nia scrambled away as he fired magic at her in blind fury. Somehow his shots weren't connecting. As though he was simply unlucky. He ran to her instead, evidently ready to fight her tooth and nail if that's what was required.

She pressed her back to the wall and, hands behind her back, she slipped the black necklace from her sleeve and waited, heart drumming, until he was nearly upon her. She sprung forward and threw the necklace over his head.

As the cursed jewelry fell into place around Neilos's neck, he jerked to a halt, his expression one of sheer surprise. His lips struggled to move, but he finally ground out, "How?"

Nia needed to move quickly, unsure of how long the necklace would hold someone as powerful as Neilos. But she couldn't resist one final jab. "Magala had an earring made of a chip of the fortune stone. I bestowed it to her."

The eyes of the half witch, half fae monster before her grew rounder still.

"That's right. You cursed yourself the moment you killed her."

Nia ran.

"Nia, what—"

Nia barreled past a stunned Uma with her floating trays behind her. She skidded to a stop, an idea striking her.

In between heavy breaths Nia said, "Need food. For Ravens. Meat." Oh, her lungs burned!

"I have some scraps here, but what on earth—"

"Hurry!"

Uma opened a tray and shoved a few greasy leftovers into Nia's hands. Nia called a hasty "thank you" over her shoulder as she continued to the gardens.

It was dark. The ravens may be tucked away for the night somewhere, but Nia searched for them anyway. She held the bits of meat in the air.

"Where are you, birds! Come and get it!"

Large insects—in the darkness Nia could only assume they were moths—flitted past. The breeze rustled and the crickets chirped, but no ravens.

A caw sounded loudly in Nia's ear and she shrieked in surprise. Two inky black shadows flapped beside her and landed on the ground, seeming to wait in expectation.

Nia crouched down and held out the scraps, but pulled her hand away as the birds drew near. "Uh-uh. This food comes with a condition. I'll let you have this, but in return you need to bring me something."

She felt crazy talking to birds as though they could understand. But she'd always had an affinity for animals, and she had to rely on that now. She sensed that she'd need to give them the food first if she wanted to win them over, so she held out her hands and let them pick the scraps clean.

"There now," she said. "Neilos said he gave you a key. Can you please bring it to me? It's really important."

After a pause, the ravens vanished.

The night turned cold.

Nia tasted the crackle of magic for a split second before she was whisked away. It took her a moment to process her new surroundings. She shivered as her eyes adjusted to the darkness. This was…

"Ah," said a raspy voice. "You've come back. But you don't appear ready to uphold our bargain."

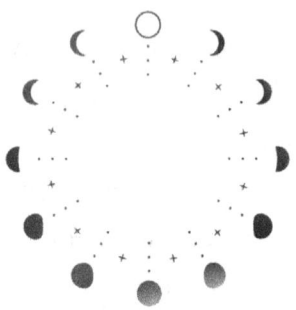

Chapter 27

An undetermined amount of time before the Dark Moon

Nia stared at the shadowed form in the cell across from her. The speculo.

"I'm in the dungeons?" she asked, voice barely more than a whisper.

"It would appear so."

She sank to the floor. She had been so close. She truly thought the necklace would have bought her more time. If she was here, she couldn't protect anyone. She couldn't escape. She couldn't even release the speculo as she had promised.

"I don't have the mask." Her voice was flat and hoarse. "I'm sorry. I should have come sooner."

"You could make it up to me," the speculo said, surprising Nia with the hint of amusement in its voice. "Tell me your darkest secret, and we shall consider it an even trade."

Nia shook her head and sunk to the floor, not in the mood for this kind of conversation. If this situation taught her anything it's that her secrets were valuable. If she had been allowed to keep more of them, perhaps this would have been avoided.

"I'll think of another way," Nia insisted. "I promised to get you out and I will."

The speculo wheezed a laugh. "Good luck."

Luck. Nia had that in short supply at the moment. "You and all your secrets," Nia said, her voice flooded with irritation, "I don't suppose you know how I can get out?"

"Have you tried simply opening the door?"

Nia stilled. Could it really be that easy? Her heartbeat hammered as she reached for the bars. A jolt ran through her and she yelped as a magic force flung her against the back wall of the cell.

She scrambled to her feet, her fists balled and shoulders tight. "You knew this cell was enchanted. Why on earth would you tell me to do that?"

The creature spoke in a voice heavy with amusement. "I had to discover it myself. It seemed fair to let you do the same. Particularly because you do not have my mask."

Evidently the speculo wasn't above petty grudges. Nia scowled at its shadowed figure, sensing this would be a long night.

Nia paced endless circles around the cell, looking for some kind of weakness to exploit. What time was it now? The dark moon was tomorrow night—or tonight, depending on how late it was. It was maddening not to know.

"Is that a good use of energy?" The speculo rasped. Nia prickled with irritation. It was strangely blase for a creature who may have lost its one ticket to freedom.

"Do you have any suggestions?" Nia's voice echoed harshly through the chambers.

"I do not."

"Then don't bother me!"

The creature chuckled but did not speak.

After a brief silence, Nia asked, "Shrinking chocolate?" The remainder of hers was secured in her room, but perhaps the speculo still carried some.

"I gave you the last I had."

She dropped to the floor, shivering as her skin met with the cold stone. She closed her eyes and put her head in her hands.

"Are you giving up?" the speculo asked.

"I'm. Thinking."

To the speculo's credit, it did not goad her.

Nia's eyes snapped open, and she jumped to her feet once more. "What was it Neilos said..."

"Neilos says a lot of things. Most of them not worth—"

"Shut up." Nia waved her hand at the creature, struggling to remember the exact phrasing Neilos had used. "Neilos said the gateway to other worlds could be opened by someone who had stewardship over the stone. Does that mean I don't have to actually have it with me to create the gateway? I just have to be the owner of it?"

The cloaked form of the speculo looked back at her in silence.

Nia sighed. "I'm sorry I told you to shut up, ok? Just...am I right?"

"It's much more entertaining for me if you figure it out for yourself."

Nia growled in frustration, but something in her core told her she was correct. She reached under her skirts for the pouch at her waist—turning away from the speculo as she did so—and found the ring. Its energy pulled and beckoned to her again and she slipped it on her finger. All she needed were the words to the spell. She had seen the book on Neilos's desk in his study. Felt its excitement when she approached... Would it be able to sense her here?

She thought about the worn leather cover, dyed royal blue. The markings etched in it. The title. What was it? In Worlds Beyond? No, Of. *Of Worlds Beyond.*

She put everything within her into feeling out the energy of that book. "Of Worlds Beyond!" Her voice echoed through the chambers, and she could sense the speculo's curiosity resting on her. "Of Worlds Beyond, If you can hear my call, please come here!"

Please, please work.

Nia held her focus on the details of the book, and at once she could feel it—the tiniest glimmer of excitement that grew by the second. The sound of flapping and dripping echoed in her ears. The book came to her cell, soggy, no doubt from entering through the pond. Nia hoped the text hadn't been damaged.

"Good work!" she exclaimed, and the book danced before the bars. "I need the page that talks about opening the gate. But be careful please. Don't rip your pages."

The wet book flipped through its pages delicately, and much slower than Nia would like. But it couldn't be helped. At last, the book stopped, and Nia skimmed the page until she found what she needed.

"I whom fortune smiles upon
Wish to visit worlds bygone
With my hands I make my fate
Let me open up the gate"

The air cracked and popped all around Nia. Purple sparks exploded from the ring, and she shielded her eyes. She heard the speculo's rasping gasp of surprise. She squinted through the bright light and gaped at the sight before her. Streams of what looked like lightning pulsed in the unmistakable shape of a door, handle and all.

This was what Neilos had sought. What he had killed for. The very thing he turned Nia's life upside down to possess. It was never about the stone itself for him. Nia wasn't sure she was ready to open the door, but she was running out of time. She reached towards the handle but before she could turn it, an echoing, whisper of a voice rushed past her ears.

Where do you wish to go?

She stilled. Her throat felt dry, but at last she managed to croak out, "Earth."

You are on Earth. Would you like to visit a different location on Earth?

"Yes."

State your desired location.

"Um."

Um is not a recognized response. State your desired location.

She nearly said Ravenskeep. She could go straight home. But if she did that, she would leave behind the stone and everyone else. And Enitan.

She had a choice to make. She could have the magic send her straight into the snake room. But she had no way of knowing whether she could make it to save Enitan after that. She might lose him forever.

State your desired location.

"Just give me a minute!" Nia growled.

She wrapped her arms around herself. This was crazy. Enitan was cursed. He might despise her. Even if he didn't, being with him meant she would never be able to use her stone in his presence. She could *never* have her luck and her soldier. She would forever live in a dark-moon state.

Even so, her thoughts overflowed with his warmth and laughter. The gentleness of his touch. The way she never had to question her worth when she was beside him. His selfless sacrifice of the fortune stone to save her, in spite of the great cost to himself. Her thoughts swam with Enitan, and her heart drowned in him.

She knew her choice.

State your desired location.

Nia took a breath. "Nia's room in Neilos's castle."

As you wish. Please step through the door.

It was as though the door opened into the universe. Midnight black and a rainbow of stars met her eyes. She gulped and stepped through, fearing she would be trapped in this space forever. But as soon as the door closed behind her, she stood in her room and the doorway vanished.

Nia's legs gave out and she collapsed. Was it the result of opening the gate? Perhaps the ring should be used sparingly, and rightfully so. Nobody should have easy access to that sort of power. She attempted to stand but her knees quivered like jelly. It was difficult to breathe. Her head swam in a dizzy fog and sweat appeared in beads across her forehead. If this was the side effect of transporting within the castle, what would happen if she traveled elsewhere?

There was no time to waste on recovery. Every second brought her closer to the dark moon and there was too much at stake.

She forced herself to her feet, using the bedpost to keep steady. She would break Enitan's curse, free the speculo, and get the stone. Once she had the stone, she would find a way to set everyone else free.

Her footing remained unsteady, but she managed by leaning on the furnishings for support. First, she opened her pillowcase and pulled out the herb ball from Antonia. There was also Antonia herself, staring out of her lifeless doll eyes. Nia stifled a sob. She couldn't leave Antonia, no matter what state she was in. She needed something to carry her with...

The wardrobe had always given Nia whatever she wanted for fashion. Perhaps a satchel would count as an accessory? She faced the wardrobe and said, "I need a satchel. Something I can move quickly with." Nia opened the wardrobe door, and a small leather satchel awaited. She stuffed the herb ball inside and returned to the bed to gently rest the doll inside the bag, hoping Antonia couldn't be injured in that form.

A light scratching on her door caught her ear and sent a shiver down her spine. She wasn't supposed to be here.

Just ignore it.

The sound continued, growing more frantic, and finally followed with a loud *caw!*

Could it really be?

Nia raced to open the door and one of the ravens flapped inside, clutching something in its curled foot.

"You got the key? Good bird!"

Nia held out her hand and the raven dropped a shining object. Nia frowned. It was not a key, but a tiny emerald.

"But, Neilos said there was a key." She tried not to let disappointment discourage her. It was only a bird, after all. It may have simply brought her a present as thanks for the food. Yet, as the creature stared at her with its beady eyes, it seemed to say, *trust me*.

"Well, all right," Nia said, stuffing the jewel in the pouch that formally held her stone and the ring. "Thank you. Hurry back outside before someone sees you."

Her next destination was the relic room with its magic door, and she could only hope she'd make it there before Neilos caught wind of her escape. She stole a glance at one of the hallway clocks as she rushed to her destination.

Three hours left.

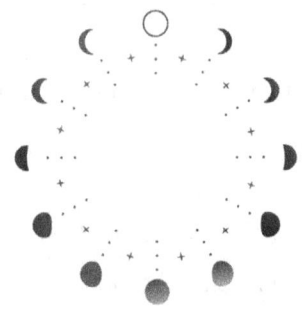

Chapter 28

3 hours before the Dark Moon

Nia didn't think it was possible, but the relic room was even more unsettling at night. She had pilfered one of the torches from the hallway to bring with her, but the space seemed to swallow up most of the light. Fortunately, she knew her target.

"Dagger," she said, just to be sure. The pedestal with the dagger illuminated green. She reached for it but stopped short. The dagger was a cursed object. Would something happen to her if she took it? Well, she couldn't imagine a life more cursed than it already was with Neilos on her tail. She took a breath and grabbed the object.

Nothing happened, at least, not that she could tell.

Next, she needed a blessed object. It would have to be large enough to rest the vial on. She searched the crevices of her mind, recalling the other objects she had seen.

"Scarf," she said at last. The scarf illuminated in deep-blue light. She hurried forward and grabbed it, then called for the final item.

"Vial."

There it was, bathed in emerald light. She lifted it from the pedestal, gripping it as tightly as she could manage with her still weakened body.

"Nia?"

Nia's breath stilled at the sight of Enitan's form in the entrance. Her heartbeat accelerated, and while her fear of being caught was a valid reason for that, she knew it was more. The relief of seeing him alive and well rushed through her like a warm summer wind. She'd imagined Neilos torturing him a thousand different ways since Magala's death. Her emerald soldier was here.

He stared at the vial in her hands and his eyes widened. "Put it back." His voice quivered with the slightest tremor of fear.

"Enitan—"

"PUT IT BACK NOW!"

Nia shook at the intensity of his words, a tone she didn't even know Enitan could take. She took a step back and clasped the vial all the harder, adrenaline bringing strength back to her limbs.

"I told you not to come back here." Enitan's voice filled with pain as he unsheathed his sword. He rushed forward and Nia scrambled into the shadows. She just had to break the vial in the way the speculo described.

Easier said than done. Enitan lunged at her, weapon poised to strike. Nia met his blow with the dagger. The force of her weapon against his did almost nothing to throw him off. He came at her again and she screamed as she dodged and sliced the dagger into his side. She never wanted to hurt him, but he was going to kill her.

Enitan groaned, but in an instant, his wound flashed with white light, and the slice appeared on Nia's own side. Ah, so that was the curse. She staggered and clutched her injury, her fingers coming away wet with blood. Not good. She already had little chance against Enitan, but this complicated things further.

"Stop, Enitan!" Nia cried. "I know this isn't you!" Whether or not he harbored feelings like Nia did, she knew he was at least a kind person at heart.

Indeed, horror flashed behind his eyes as he took in the sight of her blood-stained dress. He raised his sword again, arms shaking as he battled his orders and the dark magic enforcing them.

Nia dodged as he brought the blade down, clutching the three objects with all her might. An idea bloomed among the scattered thoughts in her frantic mind. What would he do if he didn't have his sword? If his directive was to stop her, surely, he would use other means. She wrapped the scarf around her hand and grabbed a large vase to her right. Enitan came forward again and she threw the vase, hitting her mark—the hand Enitan held his sword with.

He groaned and lost hold of his weapon. Nia kicked it into the darkness and dropped the dagger.

"Oh no!" she cried, hoping he would take the bait in his controlled state. Sure enough, he seized the dagger.

He pulled the dagger back, ready to bring it down upon Nia, in spite of knowing its curse. Neilos's cruel control compelled Enitan to attack anyone with the vial, even if it meant harm to his own person. Nia waited for the right moment as the blade came swiftly down towards her heart. She thrust the vial forward, clasped tightly in her scarf-wrapped hand.

Blade met glass, and the vial shattered, raining Enitan's once-contained blood down upon the scarf. Enitan fell back, the dagger clattering to the floor. He dropped to his knees and Nia rushed to him, ignoring the pain in her side.

"Enitan?" She searched for signs that his spell was broken. "Is it you? I mean, is it *all* of you?"

"Nia," he breathed, as though saying her name for the first time. "Nia!" He grasped her face in his hands, his touch all at once gentle and urgent as he drew her close. He kissed her, and Nia felt nothing but light in that room of darkness. After so many years as a prisoner in his own body, the first thing he chose to do with his freedom was kiss her. The knowledge engulfed Nia with dizzying joy.

Just as she came to herself enough to reciprocate, Enitan pulled away, running his thumbs down her cheeks. "Sorry, I just—"

"Don't apologize," Nia said breathlessly, "And don't stop."

Enitan didn't need to be told twice. While his first kiss was a spark, the second was a wildfire, and Nia let it consume her from head to toe.

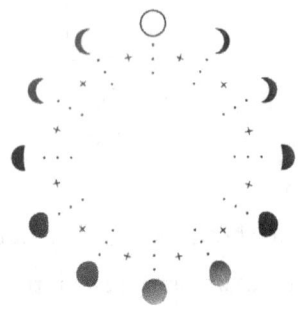

Chapter 29

The beautiful spell between them was broken too quickly when Enitan remembered Nia's wound.

"We have to take care of that," he said, brows knit together in concern.

"It's fine. I'm fine." In truth, it hurt a lot, and the amount of blood staining Nia's dress made her dizzy with dread.

"May I?" Enitan asked softly, gesturing toward the injury.

Nia flushed but nodded.

Enitan carefully ripped away the cloth of her dress at her side, but ever the gentleman, he exposed as little skin as possible. Nia reminded herself to breathe.

"Fortunately," he said, his voice slightly husky, "We already have what we need to take care of you. Can you hand me the scarf?"

Nia unwrapped the scarf from her hand and gave it to him. Curiously, any traces of his blood had vanished from the material.

Nia's breath hitched as Enitan wound the scarf around her middle with painstaking care.

"Sorry. It needs to be a little snug."

Nia shuddered as her blood once more soaked through the scarf. "Maybe I do need further treatment."

"It's ok," Enitan assured. "This is actually what we want."

Nia raised a quizzical brow. "You would make a terrible doctor."

"Trust me," he said, pressing a kiss to her forehead.

The scarf glowed, and a soothing warmth wrapped around the cut. Nia felt as though someone was smoothing balm over her skin. She relaxed her shoulders as the pain dissipated.

Enitan pulled back the scarf to examine her but didn't unwrap it. "There, see? All better." He cleared his throat, his face noticeably red even in the dim light. "You can unwrap it if you want, but if you'd rather leave it there to hide the tear that's ok."

Nia smiled, her own face growing hot. "Thank you."

It would have been a dream to stay sequestered with Enitan, but the urgency of the situation deprived them of that option. In a rush she explained the veritas water and the location of her stone.

Enitan stood at once and assisted Nia to her feet "Ok. Let's get you out of here then."

Nia scanned the items in the room, squinting against the shadows. "Wait. There's one more thing I have to do."

She located the mask and lifted it from its pedestal.

"What do you need that for?" Enitan asked.

"To free the speculo. That was part of our deal." She noticed the speculo's staff a few pedestals over and couldn't resist grabbing it too. Neilos had no right to keep it.

"That thing?" Enitan shook his head. "As much as I hate Neilos, I think he was right to lock the creature up. I don't like it in the castle."

Nia gave a coy smile. "Well, then you should be happy to know once I give it the mask, it will leave."

"Maybe," Enitan mused, "We should get the stone first. If you use the mask, you'll be hidden from Neilos."

"What about you?"

Enitan's dimple made its first appearance in a while. "As far as Neilos knows, I'm still his puppet guard. I can travel freely around the castle."

Nia was about to place the mask on her face when Enitan caught her arm. "Actually, let me test that thing first. I don't trust any of these relics."

The mask was on his face before Nia could argue with him. One second he was there, and then he was simply gone.

"Enitan?"

He reappeared in front of her, mask under his arm. "You couldn't see me at all? Or hear me?"

"Or smell you," she added, grinning.

"Or touch me," he murmured, suddenly running his fingers down her cheeks and leaving a trail of goosebumps. He then traced a thumb over her lower lip. "Or..."

She snatched the mask back and put it on before they ended up delaying this further...no matter how appealing the distraction might be. It didn't hurt that the mask hid her vibrant blush.

Enitan laughed. "Ok, ok. Let's go. Stay close to me."

"I gotta say, it's really weird not being able to see you," Enitan whispered.

The experience was strange for Nia, too. With the mask on, the world was tinged with glistening rainbows at the edges, and everything appeared slightly out of focus.

"Enitan!"

The sharp voice brought Nia to a halt. Enitan changed in his demeanor, appearing instantly stoic as Neilos stormed down the hallway. Nia struggled to take nervous breaths into her damaged lungs. The mask had worked on Enitan, but would it do the same for someone as powerful as Neilos?

Neilos caught Enitan by the collar of his uniform and Nia fought the urge to lash out against him. She ground her teeth.

"The girl is in the dungeons. Now that she's had some time there, perhaps she will be more pliable. See if you can persuade her. Charm her. Make her bequeath you the stone and then you will give it to me straight away."

"Yes, my master."

He sneered at Enitan, his teeth glinting. "And if she doesn't, I *will* kill you in front of her and relish every second of it. Report to me in two hours."

"Yes, my master."

Enitan remained the tin soldier, though Nia wasn't sure how he managed to maintain the facade. She herself was shaking, anger rolling through her like thunder.

Neilos shoved Enitan aside and continued down the corridor.

Enitan picked up his pace, apparently unphased, and Nia's heart clenched as she wondered how often he'd experienced such behavior from the master of the castle.

"Still with me, Nia?" he whispered. "We should hurry."

When they reached the door that led to the snake pit, Enitan opened it and stepped inside. "Uh...after you?" He motioned Nia in, and she slipped past him. As he stood waiting, she removed the mask and tapped him on the shoulder from behind.

He jumped and whipped around, relaxing when he saw her. She covered her mouth to stifle her laughter.

"Not cool," he said as he shut the door, although he was grinning. His face turned serious once more. "Are you sure that's a good idea?"

"You said Neilos is the only one who comes here, and we just saw him. If there's any sign of someone else coming, I'll put the mask back on."

He still seemed reticent but sighed. "All right. Shall we continue, my lady?"

Enitan laced his fingers through hers and drew her close, placing a quick kiss on the top of her head. The tender action conjured a new round of delighted butterflies in Nia's stomach.

He really did like her as much as she liked him. She sniffled, the realization bringing uncontrolled tears of relief to her eyes.

"Whoa, hey!" Enitan's eyes grew round. "What's wrong? Does it still hurt somewhere? We can use the scarf—"

Nia shook her head. "I'm just so glad I didn't imagine everything between us. I was afraid you wouldn't want anything to do with me after I broke your curse."

"All I wanted was you." He brushed Nia's tears away with his hands and his expression softened. "Not being able to tell you, and knowing I was helping Neilos hurt you, was torture."

"But it seems like you were able to help me sometimes, like when you tried to comfort the dragon. How did you do that?"

A shadow crossed Enitan's face. "I convinced him it played into his plans by saying you'd be more comfortable in the castle if I gained your trust. But in the end when he saw you weren't warming up to him, he used me against you. I'm sorry."

"You have nothing to apologize for. It wasn't your fault."

"I've been with him long enough that I should have known better."

"How long *have* you been with him?" Nia asked as they continued towards their destination, the speculo's staff still in her hand.

"Since I was ten years old."

Ten years old. That's how old he was when he gave Nia his fortune stone. He still didn't know. Nausea crept in and Nia dreaded knowing the rest of Enitan's story.

"How...how did you end up here?"

Enitan sighed and his fingertips brushed absently against his dragonfly pin. "My grandmother worked with Neilos when she was young. She had a fortune stone, passed down through our family for generations. Neilos didn't show his true colors right away and had her convinced he was going to change the world for the better, so she helped him. She even got the wanderer's ring for him. But of course, he wanted the stone for himself. I think due to his fae nature, he prefers to manipulate and make deals over using force to get what he wants."

Nia put the pieces together. "And she made a deal with him."

Enitan nodded. "My grandfather, who was grandma's closest friend at the time, sustained a life-threatening injury. Neilos promised to heal him if she would bestow the stone to Neilos in her old age. Of course she agreed.

"Years passed. My grandparents got married. Grandma began to see who Neilos really was. When the time came, she refused to give him the stone."

Given what Nia knew of Neilos, she imagined this didn't go over well. "He would have been furious."

Enitan's voice quieted, his eyes turning distant. "He was. He said their deal was now broken, and he re-injured my grandfather and made her watch as he suffered and died."

Nia couldn't contain her gasp. None of it should have surprised her, but it still hurt to hear it.

"And of course," Enitan gave a bitter laugh, "He wouldn't give up on trying to get her stone. He threatened the rest of her family. That's when she decided to bestow the stone to me. She told him she bestowed it to another member of the family, but he didn't know who. If he killed any of us, he took a risk."

"That was brilliant of her."

"She was an amazing woman."

His use of past tense didn't escape her. "Did Neilos…"

"She protected us, but Neilos had no incentive not to kill her without the stone. I was six at the time. I still miss her."

"I'm so sorry." Nia noticed his fingertips running along the pin again and made the connection. "That dragonfly was hers."

"Yes. Made with gems from her travels." He scoffed. "It was one possession Neilos let me keep, but in typical Neilos fashion he meant it as a mockery, to remind me of what I'd lost. He thought it was ironic for me to wear a symbol of good fortune when I had none. I'm just glad to have it."

They walked in silence for a few moments. Enitan's voice was subdued when he spoke again. "Neilos started causing disasters in our village in an attempt to uncover who had the stone. He looked for the survivors. The *lucky* ones. He caused the flood."

Nia's blood ran cold. Neilos was responsible for the destruction of her village and her parents' deaths. Her whole life—and the lives of many others—had been uprooted because of him.

"Neilos's previous observations, along with the fact that my parents and I survived and our house was undamaged, led him to conclude I had the stone." He paused and his voice grew soft. "But when he found me, I had just bequeathed the stone to a little girl."

Nia's breath hitched. But Enitan barreled on with his story before she could tell him the truth.

"He was livid, and he took it out on me. He kidnapped me and brought me to the castle, and in his blind rage he placed a curse on my grandmother's entire bloodline so we would never be able to experience the positive effects of a fortune stone again. The stones go null around us."

"That's why!" Nia exclaimed. "Whenever you're around me, the stone stops working."

Enitan ran a hand over his braids. "I'm so sorry. I remember you mentioning that. I didn't realize it happened all the time."

Nia shook her head. "It's not your fault." She gave a small laugh. "I'm happy to know it was Neilos's curse and not something you did on purpose." Somehow, she had always known there was no malicious intent on Enitan's part.

"Curses like that come at a price. His own luck was tarnished for the next several years, which was why you escaped his notice for so long."

"And why all the disasters started up again suddenly," Nia realized. "His time was up, so he began looking for the holder of a stone again."

"How *did* you get your stone?" Enitan asked. His question was one of sincere curiosity.

Nia froze and stared at the floor, leaning the staff against the wall. She had to tell him. If they were to have any kind of future together, she needed to be open with him.

Enitan stopped and Nia only glanced up long enough to note the concern in his eyes.

"Are you ok?" He asked.

Nia wrung her hands, still unable to make eye contact. "Do you remember anything about the girl you bequeathed the stone to?"

His brow furrowed. "There was so much going on and I was focused on saving her. I vaguely remember what she looked like. I don't even recall her name."

Nia swallowed and her voice quivered, heavy with emotion. "It was me, Enitan. You gave your stone to me." Her admission renewed her guilt and brought her to tears over the luck she felt she'd stolen from him. Over the enslaved life he lived under his cruel master. If he'd kept the stone, Neilos might never have ensnared him to begin with.

Enitan gazed at her with wide eyes. Nia waited for his anger or sorrow or bitterness. She deserved whatever response he threw at her and she was prepared to accept it. But instead, he pulled her in close, tipped her chin up, and in a tender voice said, "Then it was all worth it."

He swept her into his arms and kissed her until her tears stopped and her remorse fled. Until there was nothing left but warmth and light—those shining, glowing embers Enitan always seemed to ignite within her. Somehow, even without her stone, she was the luckiest girl in the world.

"Something seems different." Nia spoke in a hushed tone as they entered the chamber with the snakes. The back of her neck prickled, warning of danger.

"You're right." Enitan took a few steps forward, glancing around in full guard mode. "It feels off."

Shapes wormed out of the darkness, scraping across the stone. It was the snakes, but—

"Get back, Nia!" Enitan unsheathed his sword and swooped in front of her.

These were not the same creatures as before. Instead of the harmless reptiles Enitan had been so enchanted with, these snakes had an array of rattles and hoods and dripping fangs.

"Neilos must have increased his security after I made him tell me where the stone was," Nia guessed.

"Yeah, no kidding." Enitan's voice was tight as he assessed the situation.

The snakes covered the entirety of the floor, blanketing the stone tiles and the jewels that covered them.

The jewels.

Nia reached for her pouch and produced the emerald given to her by the raven. It did look much like the jewel inlays on the floor, but how was she supposed to find the right spot, especially with deadly serpents writhing over every inch?

"I could just start chopping heads," Enitan offered.

"I'd prefer not to kill them." It seemed unfair for the creatures to die. None of them asked to be there. They were yet another group of beings Neilos used for his designs.

Nia pulled the mask from where she had slipped it under the scarf at her waist. "They probably won't notice me if I put this on, but I'm not sure I could get through without stepping on one. They might still be able to strike me even if they can't see me." Nia was uncertain how the magic worked.

"I won't lie," Enitan said, "These snakes have me rattled."

"Did you *really* make a pun right now?"

"Sorry. Nerves."

Nia smirked at him and playfully said, "I can't stand your puns." The speculo's staff in her hand sent a shiver down her arm and the room at once felt cooler. Nia furrowed her brow.

Enitan distracted her from her confusion. "Aw, man. Do you really hate them?"

She grinned at him. "They're the worst."

The staff shivered again.

"Does it feel like it's getting chilly in here?" Enitan asked.

"Yes," Nia murmured. "It does."

The speculo dealt in secrets, truth, and lies. Enitan said before that the staff was useless, but maybe it did do something after all.

"Enitan," she said, "Tell a lie. A really good one."

"You're the most hideous woman I've ever laid eyes upon." He flashed her a look of pure adoration as he said it, which made it impossible to take him seriously.

Nevertheless, the staff rattled again and the drop in temperature was undeniable.

"Well, I think you're the most gorgeous man I've ever seen." At her honest declaration, the staff warmed along with the surrounding air.

Nia whooped and Enitan gave her a puzzled look.

"The staff!" She exclaimed. "When it detects the truth, it turns the air warmer. When it detects a lie, the air turns colder. If we make it cold enough, the snakes will be dormant, and we should be able to work around them unharmed."

Enitan wasted no time in executing the plan. "That's the worst idea you've ever had."

The room grew colder.

"I think Neilos has a beautiful heart." The words left a bitter taste on Nia's tongue and she wrinkled her nose.

The two of them shivered.

As their lies continued, the room grew colder and the snakes more sluggish. When her teeth began to chatter, Nia decided it was safe enough to seek out the vault. She and Enitan took a few cautious steps and proceeded with more confidence when the snakes did not stir.

Nia held up the emerald. "We're looking for a tile with jewels that match this one, I think."

With Nia using the staff and Enitan carefully using his sword, they shifted snakes aside, examining the stone tiles beneath. There were many green jewels, but not quite the right shade or sheen.

At last Nia came upon one that looked like a match. She had hoped the correct stone would have a jewel missing in the shape of the one she held, but the tile before her had every jewel in place. She shifted a few snakes over and crouched down for a closer examination. As she ran her fingertips over the jewels, one had a distinct hum to it. She picked at it, and it came away easily from the stone.

"I think I found it!"

At her exclamation, Enitan hurried to join her. Nia set the emerald into the newly created gap. Green light shone from the tile, and it cast itself aside, revealing a cavity beneath.

And the fortune stone.

Nia scooped it into her palm. She thought she might feel whole again, flooded with relief at having the stone with her once more. But while she was glad to retrieve it, the sensation wasn't what she expected. It certainly didn't compare to what stirred in her heart when her soldier nestled at her side.

Enitan replaced the tile and reclaimed the jewel. "If Neilos comes here looking for the stone, that'll delay him a bit longer. Let's get these serpents moving again and get out of here."

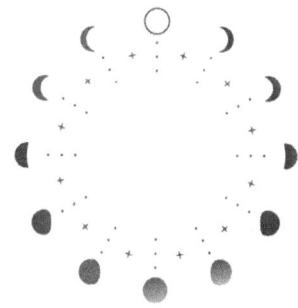

Chapter 30

The Dark Moon

Nia wasn't sure how to react to the genuine surprise the speculo exuded when she and Enitan returned to its cell. It must not have had much faith in her. "So, you did return," it rasped.

"I promised I would." Her eyes widened. "Wait, how can you see me with the mask?"

The speculo wheezed out a chuckle. "I see through lies."

"I hope you're talking to Nia," Enitan said. Nia couldn't help but giggle at his perplexed expression. The one-sided conversation would be bizarre to witness.

Nia grabbed a hairpin, sending curls cascading into her face. Her body tensed on impulse as she prepared to push it into the lock, remembering the shock she received earlier. But no shock came.

Just as Enitan had promised, the mask kept her undetected by the magic as well.

The door popped open and the speculo cackled its approval.

Nia removed the mask with reluctance. It had been useful. But she had the herbs from Antonia, so the speculo would need it more, and she'd made a deal. She extended it to the creature.

"Here's your ticket to freedom. I hope you use it well."

"I shall. Thank you, Nia. Perhaps we will meet again." It then turned its focus to Enitan, who held the creature's staff. "I believe you took something from me."

Enitan laughed nervously, thrusting the staff towards the speculo. "No hard feelings, right?"

No response, and Nia chuckled at Enitan's obvious discomfort when he saw the creature's silvery hands.

The speculo paused with the mask halfway to its hidden face. "Because I want to see you succeed, I must warn you about that ring. You may have noticed it took much energy to use it."

Nia nodded, even now feeling the lingering drain from its use.

"If you use it again within the week, you will likely die."

Nia and Enitan released a simultaneous gasp. Fortunately, Nia had no plans to use it again any time soon, if at all, but her curiosity prompted her to ask, "Why is that?"

"The ring was meant to be wielded by powerful sorcerers, not ordinary humans. In that same vein, should you ever feel compelled to use it again, you must only use it within this world. You would not have the power to return from another."

"But someone like Neilos could do it," Enitan surmised, his voice grim.

Nia put a hand to her chest. "Thank you for the warning. I won't misuse the ring, and I'll do whatever I can to keep Neilos from having it."

The speculo still hesitated. "There is one last gift I can give you." Nia watched in uneasy fascination as the speculo breathed out a curl of black smoke. It wrapped into a wispy ball and floated towards Nia's mouth.

"Get away from it, Nia," Enitan pulled her arm.

"Relax." The speculo's tone reminded Nia very much of Spencer in that moment. "If you say the name of the stone's location, it will remain hidden unless you speak it. You can only do this once, so be wise."

Nia nodded and swallowed before speaking the words clearly. "The stone is in the pouch at my waist."

The ball of smoke sucked into her, and she felt momentary heat as it whooshed down her throat. Then it was as though nothing had happened.

"It is done. Take care, little one." The speculo put on the mask, and that was the last Nia and Enitan saw of it.

All that remained was to leave. Nia and Enitan slipped into the gardens, which appeared empty, though it was difficult to say in the courtyard's flickering torch light.

"Stay on your guard," Enitan warned. "The ward will be down, but that doesn't mean there aren't other safeguards in place." He hesitated, then clasped Nia's hands in his and looked into Nia's eyes, his own troubled.

"What is it?"

"Leave without me."

Nia broke out of his grip. "Absolutely not. How could you even suggest it?"

"You can't use your stone when you're with me," Enitan's voice was uneven.

Nia clenched her skirt in her hands. "I can't use it with the dark moon anyway." Why was he saying this now? As far as she was concerned leaving him wasn't an option. He'd sacrificed so much as it was, and she refused to abandon him to an unknown fate at the hands of the castle's master.

He turned away from her. "The stone's magic will come back tomorrow. You can have your luck or me—not both. You deserve happiness."

A life with Enitan at her side meant she would forgo the effects of the stone. But she would gain so much more. She didn't want anything else.

Nia clutched Enitan's arm, turning him around to face her again. "No amount of luck would make me happy if I leave you behind. My mind is made up. Don't waste time with a senseless argument."

He sighed, and while Nia could tell he still struggled with the idea, he didn't press it further.

At once, Nia remembered the ball from Antonia. She had only given Nia one, but could Enitan have half? Antonia said it would last twelve hours. Could the time be split?

With haste, she grabbed the ball Antonia concocted and broke it into two pieces. "Eat this," she demanded, shoving half towards Enitan.

He balked away from it. "What is that?"

"A spell from Antonia. It will hide us from Neilos for six hours."

"How—"

"Just eat it! Do you trust me or not?"

Enitan raised his brows in surprise, but stuffed the concoction into his mouth, chewing as fast as he could. Nia did the same and was hit with a strong peppery flavor, followed by an herbal sweetness. She started as it popped and fizzed in her mouth and dissolved into a hot, buttery liquid. As she swallowed, warmth washed and tingled over her entire body. She was met with an unsettling sensation, as though her bones were liquifying, and then in an instant, she felt normal again.

"Do you think it worked?" she asked Enitan.

"It sure did something. I hope it doesn't repeat that little number on my digestive system later."

Nia rolled her eyes. "Let's go. Every second counts."

Enitan nodded his agreement, eyes scanning the garden. "Any idea of how to get over the wall?"

"Perla showed me how with the flowers, but…" Nia glanced in the direction of Perla's tree, her heart sinking. "I'm not sure if Neilos still has those flowers cursed. If he was anticipating my attempt to escape tonight, I wouldn't trust it."

Enitan darted in front of her as a rustling sound came from the shrubs ahead of them. A shadow emerged.

Nia strained her eyes in the darkness, unsure if she could trust what she saw.

"A griffin?" Enitan asked. "How did that thing get out?"

Nia rushed forward in spite of Enitan's exclaimed protests. "You waited for me? Thank you!"

The griffin clicked its beak, and Nia stroked the feathers on its neck. It bent once more for her, and she hopped on its back. "Enitan needs to come with us, too. Is that ok?"

The griffin remained low, turning its head slightly towards Enitan. Enitan hesitated, a mild frown on his face.

Nia reached one hand out for him. "It'll be ok. Trust me."

Her beautiful soldier stepped forward and climbed on the griffin, seating himself behind her with his hands around her waist.

Nia smiled and prepared herself for the flight. "Let's get out of here for real this time."

The griffin set off at a run and made a great leap. Enitan yelped in surprise when they lifted. Nia held her breath as the three of them approached the spot that sealed them in before. Neilos was compelled by veritas water when he said he had to remove his wards, but part of her still expected to meet resistance. So, the feeling was especially sweet when they went far beyond the walls and continued to fly over the forest beyond.

"We did it!" Nia gasped.

Enitan laughed and squeezed her a little tighter. For the moment at least, they were free of Neilos.

After a few minutes of flying, Nia had a stomach-churning realization. "We can't stay airborne."

"Why not?" Enitan asked. "I figured the griffin wouldn't last the whole journey, but a little longer shouldn't hurt."

"It's not that. I'm still a target of the shadowscale. I'm not comfortable being this exposed."

Enitan made a harsh exclamation. "Right. I forgot about that nightmare."

Nia leaned forward, wind whipping through her hair, and shouted, "Can you take us down, please?"

The griffin listened at once and they made their descent, weaving through the leafy tops of the trees. Once she and Enitan had dismounted, Nia threw her arms around the griffin's neck.

"Thank you so much, my friend. You're really free now. Stay away from the castle, ok?"

The griffin trilled softly and gave Nia a quick nuzzle before taking flight again. Nia watched until it was swallowed up in the inky black expanse of the night sky.

Enitan clasped Nia's hand in his. "Shall we griff-on with it?"

Nia smacked his arm, groaning, and they sought the cover of trees as they continued on their journey.

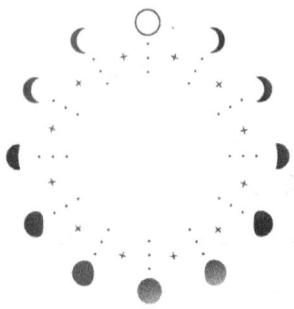

Chapter 31

"Relax a little." Enitan placed a gentle hand on Nia's cheek, directing her gaze to him after she had looked over her shoulder for the umpteenth time.

She leaned into the comfort of his touch. "I'm sorry. I keep expecting Neilos to pop out of the shadows. We must be nearing the end of Antonia's spell." She wasn't sure how long they had traveled, or if they had any time left at all.

"Even after that, he probably won't find us right away."

"But he *will* find us." Nia wasn't naive enough to believe he wouldn't.

Enitan's face turned somber. "Yes. He will. But with any luck, you'll have the stone's help again before that happens."

She stifled a yawn and couldn't deny the heaviness of her steps.

Enitan caught on in spite of her attempts to mask her exhaustion. "We should stop and sleep for a bit."

"No. I don't want to waste any of our time." If they fell asleep, they would snooze through the rest of Antonia's spell for certain—assuming their time hadn't expired already. She pictured the doll in her rucksack and her heart sank. She wouldn't squander Antonia's sacrifice.

Without warning, Enitan swept Nia into his arms.

She gripped the front of his uniform, though his arms were steady around her. "What are you doing?"

"Sleep. I got this."

Nia giggled. "You won't last long like this."

"You don't think I'm strong enough?" His lips formed a mock pout.

"You're plenty strong, but you're also human." He had to be as exhausted as she was.

Enitan's retort never formed as a force hit them.

Nia hit the ground. Her face scraped across dirt and pebbles and the sound of Enitan swearing met her ears. She spat out dirt and scrambled to her feet.

"Enitan! Are you ok?"

His arm twisted at an odd angle, and he cradled it gingerly. "Something hit me. It was like a ball of lightnin—"

His words were cut short by another burst flying in their direction. Nia already knew the identity of their assailant.

"He found us," she hissed. They bolted for the trees, but it would only buy them a little time, if any. Had Neilos been looking for them from the moment they ate the herb ball? He must have located them the instant it wore off. Now he came at them with cold fury, his scarlet hair even more vibrant in the dawn's light. For the first time, he didn't look pristine. He had snags in the delicate silk of his robes and his hairstyle, which normally gave the impression of planned chaos, flew fully untamed around his face. But what scared Nia most was the unhinged look in his eyes and the ice-cold contempt in their depths.

His next ball of lightning struck Nia in the leg. She cried out and fell to the side. Enitan was there immediately, helping her to her feet and pulling her into a run. Neilos was faster and struck Enitan down too.

Nia knew he wouldn't kill her—not without the stone.

But he would kill Enitan without a second thought.

She jumped into Enitan's arms, ignoring the pain in her leg, and wrapped herself around him. She would be his shield.

"Nia, don't." Enitan caught on immediately.

"I won't let him take you from me." Magala was dead. Perla and Antonia were trapped in dark states of magic that Nia didn't know whether she could free them from. Uma was a prisoner in the castle, living in danger every day. Not Enitan, too. She couldn't bear it, especially when she had just broken his curse. He deserved freedom. Happiness.

"Charming," Neilos spat. "You wasted no time in latching to each other after breaking his curse, I see. Scum attracts scum."

"I guess that's why you found us so easily, then." Enitan spoke through clenched teeth, not bothering to disguise his contempt for his former master.

Nia found herself ripped away from Enitan, flung through the air once more with Neilos as the cruel puppeteer. She fought against his spell, but it was like trying to swim through tar. The force of his magic kept her suspended and unable to return to Enitan.

Enitan unsheathed his sword and lunged at Neilos. Nia screamed as Neilos shot a bolt of green lightning straight through her soldier's chest.

Enitan groaned and fell to the ground, an eerie emerald glow blooming around him like a poison flower. His skin became wooden, and his clothing melded into the grain. The features Nia had so often admired became more chiseled, as though they were slowly being shaped and carved by an invisible hand. Enitan now resembled one of his wooden figures, except in a twist of Neilos's cruelty, Enitan had no face.

It was too much. Nia let out a wail as Enitan's wooden hands clawed desperately where his face should have been. He stumbled around and Nia rushed to him, grasping his arm firmly.

"Be still. I have you," she whispered, fresh tears running down her cheeks. Enitan stopped his grappling, but his form shook.

Nia whirled on Neilos. "Change him back." She surprised even herself with the force behind her voice. She didn't shout, but her words held strength nonetheless.

"Why should I?" Neilos asked. "He betrayed me."

"You did that to yourself. You might have had a loyal servant if you allowed him his freedom and behaved honorably. And you made the same mistake with everyone who came your way. Your grasp for control profited you nothing but a castle full of enemies."

Neilos's lips curled somewhere between a grin and a snarl. "And they shall pay dearly for their insubordination. There can be no doubt of that."

Nia's heart clenched. She should have tried harder. Should have freed more people. She and Enitan escaped, yes, but at what cost?

Now hundreds of others were in danger, and Enitan was no better off than before.

Neilos stared her down, eyes narrowed. "I've accepted you will not bequeath the stone to me. I've altered my desires. I simply want the object for my collection, and so that you can no longer benefit."

A life without her stone. Nia would have balked against the idea weeks ago, but it didn't mean as much to her as it used to. If she chose to live with Enitan by her side, she was giving up her luck anyway. And the stone would be nothing but a trinket to Neilos if she didn't bestow it to him. Giving up her luck seemed a fair trade if she could use it to her leverage.

"Fine. I'll make you a deal," Nia said at once.

Enitan lifted his head and shook it hard.

Nia ignored his wordless protests. "I'll give you the stone back, but I have conditions."

Neilos barked out a laugh. "You think you're going to bargain with me, girl? I can take it back myself."

"The speculo gave me a gift," she blurted. "You will never find the stone unless I tell you where it is. Never. No matter how much you want it, it will always elude you. Even if you send servants to find its location, you'll never be able to comprehend it. You'll live out the rest of your sorry immortal life not knowing where it is."

Neilos snarled, scrubbing a hand through his unkempt hair.

"And what, precisely, are your...conditions?" He spat out the last word. Nia imagined Neilos was not used to making concessions.

"First, you change him back. And heal him." Nia gestured towards Enitan. "I don't want a hair on his head left out of place."

"Fine." Neilos snarled.

"And second," Nia's heart rate sped, but she kept her voice solid. "You will release everyone in the castle. Every single person and creature. Free from your spells. Free from your walls. Antonia, Uma, and Perla and anyone else you cursed will be turned back to normal, and you won't harm anyone within the castle. You'll set your magical creatures free."

"Do not test me," Neilos stared her down. "I may get bad luck if I kill you, but Enitan's life will bring me no grief."

Nia raised her eyebrow. "You think my terms are unreasonable? How many fortune stones have you come across in your long lifetime?"

Enitan grasped Nia's sleeve, shaking his faceless wooden head with greater vehemence.

Nia clutched him close to her chest and brushed a soft whisper against his ear. "*Trust me.*"

Even if she gave Neilos the stone, he couldn't use it as long as it was bestowed to Nia. And Nia would never, ever bestow it to him. If she had to live out the remainder of her life in solitary exile to protect those she loved, so be it. Let Neilos have it. It would do him no good.

She gently eased herself from Enitan and directed her gaze at Neilos, lifting her chin. "Do we have a deal or not?"

"Fine."

"I want it bound. With magic." She didn't trust him to keep his word without a spell forcing him to do so.

Neilos loosed the sigh of a parent losing patience with a child, but extended his hand. "By my word I am bound."

Although the thought of touching him made her skin crawl, Nia accepted his hand, grasping it firmly. A tingling buzz shot through her, and she knew the deal was made.

"Release them. Now."

Neilos waved his hand in a slow, labored motion and Nia thought she felt the very earth shake beneath her feet. "Are you satisfied? They are all free."

Nia heard a shriek and a scuffle behind her and turned to see Antonia, one foot still in Nia's discarded satchel. Neilos must have spoken the truth if Antonia was herself again. Antonia's wide eyes took in the scene before her and she stood with a blaze in her expression, but just as she rushed forward Neilos waved a hand once more and she disappeared.

"What did you do?" Nia demanded.

"I sent her back to the castle. I may have given her freedom, but I won't have her interfering. Now, I believe we had a bargain."

Nia had to trust that the magic agreement would do its work and Neilos was telling the truth. She gestured towards Enitan, still trapped in his wooden form. "You're not done."

Another sigh, a snap of the fingers, and Enitan shifted back into his normal self. His eyes held a deep pain as he fixed them on Nia. She looked away, hoping this was enough to buy them time.

"Now, the stone's location. Fulfill your end of the deal." Neilos crossed his arms, impatience engraved in every aspect of his stance.

"It's in the pouch at my waist." As Nia spoke, inky smoke billowed out of her mouth and curled into Neilos's ear. She watched his expression darken as the location was made known to him, as though he was irritated the speculo's spell blinded him from such an obvious hiding place.

"Hand it over yourself, or I will take it from you." Neilos demanded. Nia did as she was asked, remembering their fight on the beach. She had no interest in repeating that without her luck.

Enitan groaned. But surely, he would forgive her once this was all over.

A smirk stretched across Neilos's face, and then something went horribly wrong. His eyes widened and shifted as his features softened. His stature diminished. Nia took a step backward as the shade of his hair deepened and spun into tight coils. Nia stared at the image of herself, only whereas the real Nia was battered and travel-worn, this Nia was pristine and elegant.

"What are you—"

A harsh laugh echoed through the trees, but with Nia's voice rather than that of Neilos.

"I learned an interesting truth from the speculo while I had it in my possession," the fake Nia drawled. "If I'm an exact copy of you, the stone won't know the difference."

Nia's eyes widened. "You're lying."

"I guess we'll find out, won't we?"

No. This couldn't be true. If so, the stone was as good as his. All he had to do was act as Nia and bestow the stone to Neilos—himself. Nia lunged forward, but Neilos threw her back against a tree, and she cried out as the rough bark scraped her skin.

"Careful," the imposter tsked. "I only need you alive long enough to bestow the stone. Once I've done that, you're useless to me."

Nia thought of everyone within her village. All the simple townsfolk living their lives in innocence. Even beyond her town, the whole world was in danger if Neilos got what he wanted. Multiple worlds, even. Nia took a shuddering breath, realizing they had to foil Neilos's misdeeds no matter what the cost.

Enitan raced forward before Nia could stop him. Neilos propelled him into the trees and Nia flinched as his skin tore, branches clawing at every inch of him.

"You said they would be unharmed!" Nia accused, whirling on Neilos with fire in her eyes. "That was our deal."

"Slow learners," Neilos said in his stolen voice. "You said those within the castle, which does not include my former guard at the moment. Now if you'll excuse me, my stone is waiting. Consider this a mercy."

He held the stone before him. "I Nia—"

Nia grasped a fallen branch and charged, swinging at her wretched doppelganger. Neilos screamed and whipped towards her, rage distorting his features. Nia flinched at seeing her face so contorted.

"You can't kill me yet," she said. "If you do, it's bad luck forever. I will fight you tooth and nail."

He acted as though he didn't hear her. "I Nia do bestow—"

She lunged, gripping the dark coils of her—his—hair and holding on like an alligator fastened to its prey. He whipped around and threw her to the ground. Nia thought perhaps they would be matched in strength since he took her form, but it seemed he was stronger. He was an immortal being, after all, and she a mere human. The wind rushed out of her, but she wouldn't allow herself time to recover. She stumbled to her feet again and attempted to kick him in the stomach. He shot a spell and Nia shrieked as the shock crackled through her. She collapsed, her body spent.

Enitan appeared with his sword at the ready. Neilos blocked his blow, but in defending himself he lost the stone. It flew into a nearby cluster of trees.

With a snarl, Neilos flourished his hand and a shining dart appeared. He threw it forward and it stuck into Enitan's chest. Enitan ripped it free and started towards Neilos once more, but his steps slowed, and he fell to his knees.

"Enitan," Nia called hoarsely, struggling to crawl to him. "What did you do to him?"

"Poison." Neilos sneered. "He'll be dead within the hour. Consider that a parting gift for your insolence."

"No, please!" Nia didn't restrain her tears. She had nothing left to barter with.

Neilos laughed and set off towards the tangle of trees and thick brush where the stone had fallen.

Enitan was curled in a tight ball on the forest floor, his breathing shallow and his skin drenched in sweat. Nia's heart begged her to go to him.

But then Neilos would get away with everything.

Blinking back her tears, Nia rushed for the trees but stopped short as she caught sight of a shape in the sky. She gasped and hid her face in the brush.

The shadowscale.

Everything clicked into place. She could kill two birds with one stone. She raced forward, ignoring the screaming pain within her body and lungs. Ignoring the warnings the speculo had given her earlier. She needed to get close enough.

Finally, she found him. She had to time her actions just right. Nia used the remaining strength within her to shout, "Neilos! Look up!"

He did, just in time for the shadowscale to fly overhead. Nia covered herself. Neilos's eyes widened, and he attempted to do the same, but it was already too late. The shadowscale found its mark, having no reason to believe Neilos wasn't its target when he wore Nia's skin.

Neilos ran, but the shadowscale was faster by far and swooped the cruel master of the castle into its talons, far away from the stone he sought.

As she ran forward, Nia stretched forth her hand that wore the wanderer's ring and chanted the words:

"I whom fortune smiles upon
Wish to visit worlds bygone
With my hands I make my fate
Let me open up the gate!"

She knew where Neilos belonged. He deserved a place without others to hurt. A place without feeling. A place without his precious things that mattered to him more than people or love or anything else.

Nia growled the words. "*Nihilnoctus.*"

The ring thrummed with energy and shot out a bolt, opening a portal in the sky ahead of the shadowscale, like a gaping mouth. The shadowscale had no time to react as it flew straight into it. Neilos's shouts, masked with Nia's voice, echoed through the air. The uncanny sound sent a cold shiver down her spine.

The portal snapped shut, the force of it causing Nia to stumble backwards. But then it was over. Nia would never have to worry about Neilos or the shadowscale ever again.

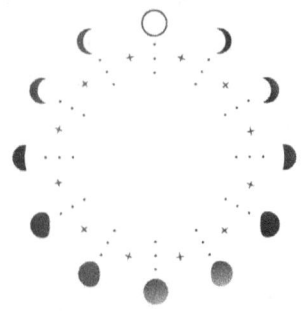

Chapter 32

Nia had no time to revel in her victory. It rang hollow and meaningless. She struggled back to Enitan—as fast as she could with her strength depleted—and brushed her fingers across his forehead. He was burning up.

"Neilos is gone, Enitan," Nia whispered, sniffling as she collapsed at his side, her energy spent. "We did it."

He gave her the barest hint of a smile, but then convulsed, clutching his chest.

"No, Enitan, please." Nia lifted her head and frantically examined the plants around them. Surely, she could find something that would help. But there was nothing, and even if she spotted anything useful, she lacked the strength to retrieve it. Even the small exertion of lifting her head took a toll on her.

There was only one thing left to do: comfort him. She grasped his hand lightly and held it to her cheek, singing in a weak voice.

Golden leaves in trees

Piercing skies of blue
Darling, none of these
Are cherished more than you...

His breathing slowed and grew soft as the brush of a feather. For a moment, she feared his breath had ceased altogether. But as she leaned in close, it fluttered against her cheek—just barely.

Her own life was failing as her vision rippled like murky water. If Enitan was going to die maybe it was a mercy that she wouldn't be far behind. She only wished she could have at least saved him. The fate of worlds hardly seemed to matter if Enitan couldn't be part of it.

Nia curled at his side and a tear slid down her cheek as her breathing faltered. A soft padding sound danced across her ears, but she couldn't find the strength to open her eyes and see what sort of creature approached. A gentle touch grazed her cheek, and warmth like the first beam of springtime sun spread throughout Nia. But it wasn't a hand. It was a...

Nia's eyes snapped open.

"Manes and tails!" She exclaimed as her energy returned, magically restored by the apparition before her. Her heartbeat sped and new breath expanded her lungs.

She must have died. She was being ushered into the next life by a unicorn. There was no other explanation. She scrambled to her feet, utterly incapable of grace in the moment. Nia had waited her entire life for this, but all she cared about now was the young man growing closer to death each passing second.

"Please," she begged, the tears now a free-flowing river. "Can you save him?"

The unicorn walked with perfect grace to Enitan's side and seemed to contemplate him, as if determining where to heal. Only then did Nia notice the teensy, shining creature floating in the air, staring at her with dark, curious eyes. The prelude? Nia had been on the verge of death moments ago. Is that why it came?

"Did you guide it to me?" Nia asked, gesturing towards the unicorn.

The prelude gave the tiniest nod.

"Thank you." Nia's voice was choked with emotion. The prelude nuzzled her nose as it did before, then winked away. Nia understood, then. The prelude wasn't a herald of death, but perhaps visited those who stood on its brink. That one, like so many other magical creatures, seemed to favor Nia.

Nia redirected her attention to the unicorn, which bent low to tap its horn to Enitan's chest. Nia shielded her eyes as a flash of rippling, silver light burst forth. When she could see again, she laughed. How could she do anything else at the sight of Enitan gaping at the unicorn as though it were a twenty-foot-tall monster?

She rushed to him as he began to rise, and the force of her embrace sent him back to the ground. She kissed him frantically and his arms encircled her. He pushed her away with a wide grin.

"I hate to stop you," he whispered, his dimple pronounced. "But you'll regret it if you miss this." He spun her towards the unicorn, who was standing by as if waiting for her to make the next move. Manes and tails, Enitan was right! Nia stood and brushed off her dirtied skirts, knowing full well that even if they were spotless, the brilliant white of the unicorn's coat would make her own clothing appear dull.

"Thank you so much for saving us," she said, her voice quivering. She covered her mouth, tears and hushed laughter spilling from her as her mind finally caught up with what she was seeing. She looked at Enitan in disbelief and he beamed back at her.

"I told you they're real," she whispered, staring in awe at the creature.

Enitan gave a quiet chuckle. "I don't know what's better—seeing the unicorn or seeing you see the unicorn."

"Oh, trust me, the unicorn is better. Now shut up and stop distracting me."

Nia watched its every movement, noting each shining hair, every graceful ripple of skin. It gave off a light of its own. The white flowers blooming in the surrounding forest dulled in comparison. Were its hooves cloven or not? She strained to get a better look, wanting to note every detail of the dream before her. The unicorn looked straight at them. Straight into Nia's eyes.

Don't run away yet. Please don't run. Nia prayed.

The unicorn continued gazing at Nia, soul to soul. Finally, it extended into what was very clearly a bow, then righted itself and took its leave into the cover of the trees. A hush fell over the entire forest.

"Life is funny," Nia said at last, certain the unicorn was now well out of view. "In all my years of having the fortune stone, I never saw one. Not once. And now, it shows itself. When I'm just me. Just Nia."

"You're not 'just' Nia." Enitan said, giving her hand a squeeze. "You are the same wonderful Nia who has always deserved to see a unicorn and just never knew it. The Nia who unicorns bow to."

Nia laughed. "That sounds pretty epic."

"It is. You are."

Enitan swept Nia into his arms and took her breath away with his lips once more.

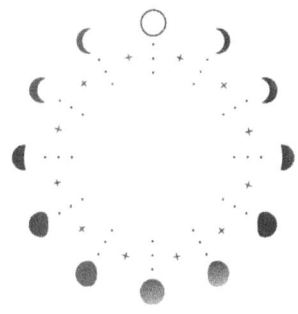

Chapter 33

"So...this is home." Nia gave a sheepish grin as she gestured towards the rubble.

Enitan gaped at the remains of Nia's cottage. "I'm so sorry."

"It's all right. The nice thing about living a simple life is that you don't have much to lose." Oddly, Nia wasn't upset about it. She had no cherished objects aside from the stone, which they had found in the brush before continuing. With nothing remaining to cling to, she could start over again without too much trouble.

Enitan helped her sift through the rubble to clear a path to what was once the kitchen. Other than being folded over at one corner, the rug was the one thing in the house that appeared undisturbed. Nia pulled it back the rest of the way and found the box as though nothing happened. She opened it and set the stone inside. She would have no use for it today, because she didn't plan to leave Enitan's side for an instant.

She smiled at him. "Let's go into town."

For once, Nia didn't hide. She didn't grasp for a phantom stone in her pocket to aid her in being unnoticed. She strode down the cobblestone streets with Enitan at her side. She didn't shrink away from the curious glances of townsfolk. The breeze across her uncloaked face made her smile, but the grin faded from her lips as soon as they reached Magala's cart. It was empty, save for a few rotted produce remains.

A vendor at a nearby shop approached, her brow furrowed. "You're Nia, right? Magala hasn't been at her cart for weeks. Nobody at her house, either."

Nia's heart grew heavy, and she attempted to steady her voice as she replied, "She passed away. She fell from a great height." Perhaps someday Nia would relay all the details and expose everything about Neilos, but for now, she didn't want to taint the air with his name. Enitan gave her hand a gentle squeeze.

The woman's hand flew to her chest, sorrow plainly written across her face. Everyone loved Magala, and the town lost much of its color and spark without her. Nia didn't attempt to stop the gentle tears that now rolled down her cheeks.

"Hold on, I'll be right back," the woman said, her voice shaking slightly. She disappeared into her shop, and Nia and Enitan exchanged a puzzled glance.

When the woman returned, she produced a piece of parchment. Her eyes watered. "She instructed me to give this to you after her death. I never imagined it would come this soon."

Nia took the parchment with trembling hands.

Dear Nia,

If you're reading this, I guess I've moved on to my next adventure. Nothing would give this old woman more joy than to see you happy. I'd like you to have my cart, if you want it. Continue bringing fortune to this town. My house is also yours for the taking. Get out of that lonely little hut of yours and start living among people. Don't just shove them along after they've made their purchases. Chat with them. Get to know them. They'll love you. And don't you be sad for me. I'm living it up wherever I am.

Love,

Magala

P.S. Meet a handsome man!

Nia laughed through her tears at the last line and gave Enitan a shy glance. *Mission accomplished, Mag.*

"Why are you smiling at me like that?"

"No reason." She folded the parchment carefully and cradled it against her heart. "Anyway, it appears my dear friend is looking after me even now."

Over the weeks Nia learned more about the town and its needs. Famine was still a threat across the land, but with Neilos out of the picture, conditions were becoming ripe for successful crops again. Nia, of course, had no problem stocking Magala's cart, but she tried to help other carts and shops in stealthy ways too. She wished she could give each of them a piece of the stone.

They held a memorial for Magala and Nia did her best to live up to her name and her wishes. She was actually starting to make friends.

The dark moon was that night, and Nia did not feel afraid.

"Never mind. I can't do this."

Enitan turned away from where his hand hovered over the door on the forest-green house. He attempted to retreat, but Nia stood in front of him, pressing her hands against his chest.

"You *can* do this. And you will."

It wasn't difficult tracking Enitan's parents down, especially with the fortune stone helping Nia find all the right contacts in his old village. As it turned out, they lived only a few miles from his parents' current residence.

Enitan ran his hands over his dark rows of braids. "What am I supposed to say to them? I haven't seen them in so long. They won't even recognize me."

He looked like a deer at the mercy of a hunter's bow, ready to take a desperate leap into the thicket. She hadn't considered how strange it must feel for him after living without them for so long. Her heart softened and she placed a gentle hand on his cheek, coaxing him to look at her.

"Your parents probably wake up every single day wondering where you are and if you're safe. All you have to do is say it's you and once they believe it, nothing else will matter. I'm sure of it."

He huffed out a breath and his broad shoulders slumped. He looked more like a lost little boy than a man. Maybe that was what his parents needed right now. "I *am* anxious to see them. I'm just afraid of how they'll react."

She gave him a gentle push towards the house once more. "Go on. I'll be right here."

"You're lucky I love you."

"I'm lucky about a lot of things."

He shook his head, releasing a wry laugh, then turned all seriousness once more as he rapped on the door.

The face that answered the knock could have been Enitan's double. He was a little stouter and had fine lines and streaks of white in his black hair, but Nia was certain this was Enitan's father.

"Can I help you?" the man asked.

Enitan opened his mouth, but in that same instant a shock of realization came over the man at the door.

"Enitan? My boy, is it really you?"

Enitan's head bobbed quickly in reply and his father's eyes grew round. Then, his face broke into a smile that was all teeth as he cupped Enitan's face in his hands.

"Abeni! Abeni, come quickly! Our son has returned!"

Sunshine filled Nia's heart as Enitan's father pulled his dumbfounded son into the house. Everything was going to be just fine.

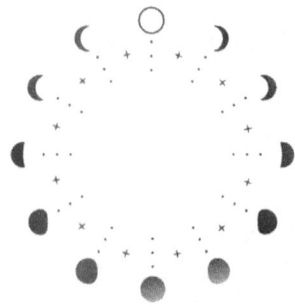

Chapter 34

Nia paused to catch her breath as Enitan did the same at her side. They had finally reached the summit of Mount Echoes, which towered high enough to give a splendid view of Ravenskeep.

The little village glowed in the light of dawn. From their vantage point on the overlook, Nia and Enitan had a perfect view of the shops and houses below. She shivered as a strong gust of wind whipped over her. But a windy day was precisely what she wanted.

She could imagine everyone below as the day stirred to life. Some of the farmers would have gotten started hours ago, and the Blacksmith, Roland, would be stoking the fires in his workshop. The seamstress, Hannah, who had sewn the very dress Nia wore would be pressing a new set of gowns for her shop window. The three little siblings, Lydia, Raul, and Emelia would be eyeing the bakery in hopes of snagging some of yesterday's sweets for a bargain...or for free if baker Chantel was feeling generous (which she often was). Their father would be along shortly after to shepherd them back home. The local artist, Sara, would stop by Magala's cart—it would always be Magala's in Nia's mind—to press for the latest details on Nia's engagement to Enitan. The little dog, Trinket, who had been adopted by the village would be out looking for a willing hand to scratch his head. On and on Nia's mind played through the faces of people and creatures who were now more cherished to her than the stone ever was.

Nia had taken every word from Magala's note to heart. Instead of slinking around and hiding under her cloak, she had gotten to know the people of Ravenskeep, and she loved them. She loved her village and everything in it. And they loved her back. Her heart warmed as she reflected on the kindness and fellowship they had shown these past several months.

She also had her friends from the castle. Antonia, Uma, and Perla sometimes visited, and they wrote often. She and Enitan traveled to them as often as they were able. Her friends now ran the castle along with the other servants as a boarding house for weary travelers, and they made sure Nia knew she was always welcome.

Nia no longer simply had four walls and a roof to shut herself away in while she rode out the storms of life, hoping they would pass her by entirely. Now she had a *true* home and people who would weather those storms with her when they came. She was made of something even stronger than the stone and the magic that formed it. Her life no longer revolved around the phases of the moon or the favors that fortune won her. Now her days were spent with people, full of purpose, and in love.

While things steadily grew to a more comfortable place without Neilos around to sow discord and catastrophe, there was still so much the people of Ravenskeep needed. So much they lacked. The fields were still a little too bare. The supplies a little too hard to come by. Nia wanted to give them everything.

Nia kept the stone with her sometimes when she wasn't with Enitan, but she didn't cling to it anymore, and she sensed the stone was ready to move on too. It had made its wishes known to her in gentle coaxing and whispers. It took time to understand, but now Nia knew exactly what it wanted.

"Are you ready?"

Nia flashed Enitan a brilliant smile as he drew her out of her thoughts. His expression was eager rather than impatient, as bright-eyed and enchanting as ever. Nia nodded. "I'm ready."

Enitan held the little wooden box towards her. She ran her fingers over it one last time, then placed her key inside the lock. Shimmering dust sat inside the box, pale blue. It was everything left of the stone after she and Enitan ground it into powder.

They each held a hand under the box and Nia cleared her throat. Speaking clearly, she proclaimed, "I Nia do bestow this stone of fortune onto the town of Ravenskeep, that it may serve its people all their days."

With that, she and Enitan shook the box's contents free, allowing the shimmering powder to catch in the wind. A tinkling sound met Nia's ears, and a group of wind pixies burst forth, further scattering the dust of the fortune stone into oblivion. In spite of Enitan's presence, Nia felt the essence of luck spreading, and she was certain she sensed joy from the stone as its magic broke free to fulfill a broader purpose. Eventually the town's luck would disperse and fade, but her hope was that this would be enough to get everyone back on their feet.

"They'll never know what you did for them," Enitan said, gazing at the town in the distance.

Nia sidled closer to him, hugging his arm and resting her cheek against him. "Good. I prefer it that way."

As she and Enitan worked their way back down the mountain, hands and hearts woven together, she felt truly lucky.

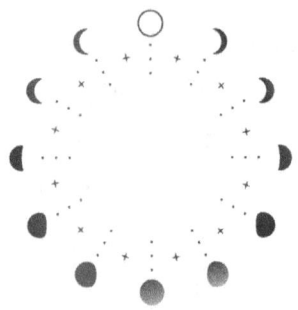

Chapter 35

The coat of the nightstripe gleamed in the light of the full moon as it crouched in the silverfern, almost as if it knew Nia would come. Her heartbeat sped. Why was she doing this? Even though her life had been infinitely more joyful since she and Enitan discarded the fortune stone, something in her had a point to prove. Not to Enitan. Not to the people of Ravenskeep. She needed to prove it to herself.

The nightstripe sprang forward, bolting toward Nia on rapid paws. She wanted to run, but then she caught sight of the tufts of fur on the creature's pointed ears. She held her ground and the animal collided with her.

Its tongue was rough on her skin, and she wiped her face with her sleeve as she shoved the nightstripe off of her. The creature was as docile as a kitten.

A smug smile curved her lips as she plucked a stalk of silverfern and teased the nightstripe, pulling the plant away from its massive, batting paws.

She didn't need to be lucky.

She just needed to be Nia.

Acknowledgements

After four books, you would think acknowledgments would get easier. There are too many people to thank for these pages!

First and foremost, thank you to my Heavenly Father who gave me this gift and allowed me to stay on this path. I could write a whole other novel on the blessings He has mercifully given.

I can't express enough gratitude to Quill & Flame for taking me under their wing and making it possible to put this book out into the world. Special thanks to AJ for believing in me and my story and being an epic source of knowledge, support, and kindness. Thank you to Brittney for keeping the wheels turning and my awesome editor Stephany for making sure *Miss Fortune* was polished up nice and shiny! Big thank you to Amanda for being one of the earliest readers and catching tricky snags. And thank you to all the other Q&F authors who have cheered me on from the beginning. My Q&F family has been incredible to work with and the support and love we all have for one another is something truly special.

Thank you to my husband and kids for sharing me. I know this crazy career I've chosen sometimes takes a lot, but you're all so excited and supportive and this would be meaningless without you. There's a little bit of you in all of my stories. Chris, I truly couldn't do this without you in my corner. Thank you for always talking through these stories with me and for helping me feel like I can do all the things. I love you!

Sara, Chantel, and Hannah: this book exists because the three of you refused to let me give up. Thank you for your non-stop cheerleading, reads and re-reads, and moral support. Friends like you come around once in a blue moon and I'm forever grateful to have you in my corner. Elise, thank you for being there to help keep me sane by making me smile, fangirling over Taylor Swift with me, being enraged on my behalf, and just being an incredible, inspirational human! Love you girls!

To my many writing friends, thank you for being the support and community I never knew I needed. Special shoutouts to Lisa Mangum, Dennis Gaunt, and Jessica Guernsey for being amazing humans and providing endless wisdom and encouragement. Maddy and Shannon, you guys rock and have buoyed me up through so many challenges. Love you!

Huge thank you to my beta readers! This story wouldn't be what it is without the extra insights you provided. Special thanks to Bodie for being one of my earliest readers and for loving the story so much. Mega, gigantic, colossal thanks to my awesome street team and the Ink Team for shouting about *Miss Fortune* from the rooftops on my behalf! You are incredible!

Thank you to Mom and Dad for continuing to boost me up and champion my books wherever you go. I'm very fortunate that you've nurtured my creative side. Thank you to the rest of my family as well for your continued excitement and for spreading the word. Thanks especially to my brother Zane for being a great listening ear and offering advice and encouragement in times where it was much needed. Thank you to my grandparents, both here and on the other side, for giving me a rich history of storytelling and curiosity.

I'd be remiss if I didn't give a shout out to the many young readers who have boosted me up over the years. It fills my bucket to see you loving my stories and reading them voraciously. In particular, thank you to Ingrid Oakley, Lexi Frederick, Eva Muhlenkamp and Sophie Flaherty for being some of my biggest fans!

Because I have to stop at some point, I'll close with a HUMONGOUS thank you to my readers. You amaze me every day and I thank you for sharing in the words I write and for being the best readers any author could hope for. To all of you who have reached out with messages, chatted with me on social media, shared my book with a friend, left a review, thank you. You are a blessing in my life.

About the Author

Ashley Bustamante has created stories from the moment she could scribble and staple sheets of paper together. She simply cannot recall a time when writing was not a force in her life. When not running through lines of dialogue in her mind, she enjoys taking photographs and spending time with her husband, three children, and any furry, feathered, or scaly creature she can find. She's happy to connect with readers at www.ashleybustamante.com.

IF YOU LIKED

CONSIDER CHECKING OUT MORE QUILL & FLAME PUBLISHING HOUSE TITLES

HEAT WITHOUT THE SCORCH

Quill & Flame
PUBLISHING HOUSE

www.quillandflame.com

www.ingramcontent.com/pod-product-compliance
Lightning Source LLC
LaVergne TN
LVHW012033070526
838202LV00056B/5477